I0654270

This Languid Earth

Paul McCormack

Ichabod Dozer Press

ISBN 978-0-9854620-7-9

for Charles Yellow Bird

Prologue

It would all someday be referred to as the "Waning Days of the Fourteenth Lesser Universal Narrative" if Nicola was to be believed, although even she admitted she couldn't be sure of exactly what was happening in those final days. Just as she said she and Hope were unaware of the reasons they came to be bridged between worlds, Lyle couldn't be sure exactly what or who Nicola or Hope really were. It didn't even distress him that Nicola and Hope lacked a physical, tangible form—some of Hope's stranger behaviors notwithstanding, of course.

Nicola had whispered to him on their first night together "This is all for you. There is nothing else." If that was true, if reality as he knew it was just a series of perceptions and ideas constructed for his benefit, then it wouldn't matter if he did tell anyone about them. And even if Nicola was a dream or a visual hallucination prompted by some subconscious desire, it still made for a happier thought than facing a world without her.

"Is it time?" Hope asked from the hallway.

Lyle had been daydreaming at the kitchen table and her voice gave him a bit of start. He looked over at her. She stood peeking around the door frame clutching at her dirty white dress nervously. Lyle smiled, "No, not yet. I'm sure Nicola knows better than I would, though. You should ask her.

"She's gone."

"She'll be back soon."

"No. She's *gone.*"

Lyle sat up in his chair and turned sideways to face her. She lowered her head to avoid his gaze. "What do you mean by that?" he asked.

Hope shook her head.

"Well, where would she be then?"

"She went back. She said that there was something more for her there."

"More? She said everything was gone."

Hope shrugged. "Maybe she's like me now. Maybe there was something she wanted to see."

Lyle's brow furrowed as he tried to sort out what Nicola being gone meant. "Did she say if she was coming back?"

Hope shook her head again.

"'No' as in she didn't say, or 'no' as in she's not coming back?"

2

Hope shrugged. "Words don't mean the same there as they do here."

She had to be coming back, Lyle thought to himself. Besides, it wouldn't have been the first time Hope misunderstood what was going on—she was only a child after all. But if Nicola had left then what was he supposed to do? She had promised him that she would be there to guide him through the coming events—that she was there to be with him. That had been the first thing she told him.

Part I: A Eulogy for Heaven

There was a nose hair that was torturing him. Lyle slunk down in his cubicle and tried to extricate it. The hair remained, tickling the outer ridge of his nostril but still not long enough to easily grasp. In retrospect it either was the strangest moment for an epiphany or the most natural one, depending on whether or not you believed the universe had a sense of humor.

He'd grasped just enough of the end of the hair to get a grip and gave a quick, hard tug. The hair slipped from his grasp but the sting made his eyes water and caused him to convulse in a series of sneezes. As he blinked his eyes clear he saw a woman standing by his cubicle, smiling. Lyle fumbled awkwardly trying to make it look as if he hadn't just had his fingers up his nose but only succeeded in knocking his pen onto the floor. He bent down quickly to retrieve it, but in the process stole a look at her.

She looked familiar, but he didn't know from where. She was average height with wavy auburn hair—not quite shoulder length. She was pretty, but not in a model kind of way. She wasn't thin, but wasn't heavy, either. Lyle's mother would've said she was a "real girl." Her eyes were a deep muddy brown and there were traces of freckles on her cheeks that complimented her crooked smile. Her skin was otherwise pale with more light freckles running down the top of her arms. She wore a plain navy blue dress that came down to her knees and a mustard yellow cardigan with sleeves that ran just below her elbows. It wasn't flashy but it was flattering in an understated way.

"Oh, um, hi?" he offered. He would've been more preoccupied with embarrassment but he was trying to stifle another sneeze.

The woman looked at him with a warmth that was simultaneously confusing and reassuring. There was a moment of silence before she seemed to realize she had been spoken to.

"…Hi."

Another moment of silence. Lyle had hoped for more—an explanation or something that would have jarred loose a rogue fragment of a memory or an impression of her. It was like a sneeze that wouldn't come, he thought, as he sneezed one last time.

"Um, can I help you?"

"Yes… but not yet."

Lyle's face must have contorted in a look that matched his confusion because she shyly covered her mouth to stifle a little giggle.

"I'm sorry. This must be awfully confusing for you. I'm Nicola—"

"Nicola," he said a split second after her.

She smiled widely. "It'll come. This is just the next step. You've already known me for years but it's just below the surface. But this is when you first begin to understand."

"Um."

She laughed. "You always get this look when you're confused by something. I always called it your 'Rufus' face."

Rufus had been Lyle's dog in college. He was a bright-eyed Brittany mix with a penchant for digging, a love for belly rubs and an impeccable knack for escaping from the backyard. When confused he'd cock his head nearly 45 degrees to the right, pause, and then tilt it 45 degrees to the left. His brow seemed to furl in a mix of befuddlement and wonder and he'd sit transfixed by whatever event or object he was witnessing. Rufus had been diagnosed with cancer six months after Lyle had graduated and he had to put him to sleep. Lyle had thought of the "Rufus face" to himself many times, but never had said the phrase aloud.

"How did I know about Rufus?" Nicola asked. "I was there. I knew Rufus. I still miss him, too, even if he did have the worst smelling farts when he slept in our bedroom."

"Wait, *our* bedroom?"

Nicola just smiled again. "I must go. You'll see me again when you're ready." She turned to leave but paused for a moment and looked back at him. "It was good seeing you again, Lyle. You'll never know how much seeing you makes me happy."

She turned and walked around the corner and down the hallway. Lyle waited a moment and then followed her, just to see what she'd do. He peeked around the corner and there was no one there. The restrooms were down the hall. Maybe she'd slipped in one of them, he thought, but he hadn't heard any of the doors close.

The elevator down the hall rumbled open and Orin, the night janitor, wheeled his cart out. "Just you up here?" he asked.

"Um, maybe. Did you see a girl come in?"

"No, but I was cleaning up on third floor. There are all sorts people coming in and out of here at all hours. Can't believe more stuff isn't stolen."

Lyle stood, waiting to hear if any sound came from the restrooms, but everything was quiet.

"You mind if I start cleaning up here, or should I come back later?"

"No, no, that's fine. I'm just about done, anyway."

*****

That night after he'd gotten off work and suffered through an obligatory workout session at the gym, Lyle settled in at home for the night. He flipped through a bunch of reruns and "edited for time and content" movies as he ate a dinner of pretzels he had left over from the weekend and drive-thru tacos.

The apartment was a small but comfortable one-bedroom unit. The front door led directly into the kitchen. The kitchen was separated from the living room by a breakfast bar. Running in line with the breakfast bar was a short hallway branching off to the bedroom on the left and the bathroom straight ahead.

The TV was situated near the hallway so it would be visible from both the kitchen and the living room. Lyle had an easy chair—the only piece of furniture he'd ever purchased new—facing it just a few feet from the breakfast bar. There were two large windows at the end of the living room with a couch angled slightly away from the wall so it also faced the TV more directly. Between the couch and the easy chair was a bookshelf with a collection of dusty books and less dusty movies and console games. A coffee table sat in front of the couch and served as a makeshift ottoman for the few times Lyle had old college friends by to hang out. The convenient thing about the room layout was that the easy chair was centrally located so the refrigerator was easily accessible (or as easily as it could be with the breakfast bar in the way) and it offered a nearly direct line to the bathroom. The sink and mirror were in his line of sight with the toilet and bathtub out of sight to the right.

The bedroom was a collection of strewn about sheets and piles of laundry—some dirty, some clean—with a few ironed sets of work clothes hanging in an otherwise empty closet. The bed was spartan, lacking even a headboard. There was a small nightstand between the bed and the closet that had an alarm clock, some pocket change, a cell phone charger and a book that Lyle hadn't opened in two years. The bedroom had a faint odor of feet and body odor which would've been off-putting to many, but it hadn't really mattered since Lyle had been the only to sleep in the room in the last six and a half years. There was no immediate threat of nighttime companionship either, much to his chagrin.

Lyle's life had been reduced to a series of interweaving routines: Wake up at seven. Check headlines and online messages. Masturbate to internet porn or memories of old girlfriends. Spend five minutes recovering and wishing he could go back to bed. Go to the bathroom, brush his teeth and shave—although shaving didn't happen every day. Hop into the shower—sometimes he'd masturbate in the shower to save on clean up time, but not often. Hurry and get dressed because he'd spent too much time earlier either watching porn or enjoying the shower and then rush off to work.

At work he'd settle in, get a cup of coffee, and check the scores from the night before. There was usually some sort of staff meeting a couple times a week. He'd have some reports to run and analysis to do. He'd leave a few minutes early for lunch which he'd eat alone. On returning he'd spend the next hour or two trying to stay awake. The last couple of hours would either devolve into browsing and online shopping or a furious stretch to finish a project that was due. The last half hour he'd usually end up talking to Pavel, a business development analyst, about sports or movies or whatever else.

The way home usually consisted of grabbing some drive thru food or a stop at the gym depending on the day. At the gym he'd go through his reps and feel miserable the entire time.

When she was around he'd attempt to flirt with Jeannine, a single mom who came in Tuesdays and Thursdays. She was a little on the heavy side, but had a nice face and a warm voice. They'd joke back and forth a little and then she'd excuse herself because she'd say she needed to keep her heart rate up, or that she needed to go pick up her two year-old from her mother's house. They would exchange goodbyes with a perfunctory asexual cordiality and then he'd spend the rest of his workout wondering why he couldn't have been a little funnier, a little more charming or a little braver.

Once at home he'd channel surf. Sometimes he'd play video games or watch a movie. On the days he'd seen Jeannine he'd fantasize about fucking her and finish with her whispering about how she liked feeling close to him. The other days it would be more TV and internet porn and then off to bed.

On that particular night, he finished off his taco and stretched in the chair. He laid back and closed his eyes and pictured Jeannine stripping off her sports bra, exposing herself playfully to him. He always pictured her with a different body from her breasts down since she was a bit heavier than he preferred. He vaguely wondered if that was insensitive but the thought drifted out of his mind as Jeannine, with her new waist, hips and legs, leaned back and encouraged him forward.

This was how it usually went. Sometimes there would be some variation, but Lyle had long ago given up the notion that he was sexually adventurous even in his fantasy life. His last girlfriend always had talked a big game about things she'd like to try, but in the end wasn't interested in much beyond getting it over with it seemed.

Lyle was trying to picture Jeannine's face, scrunched up in pleasure moaning little words of encouragement. Usually it was a couple more seconds and he'd be done, but this time Nicola's face flashed across his mind. He was puzzled at the strong emotional response he had at remembering her smiling at him earlier in the day. The familiarity was comforting. There was something very "nice" about it.

He realized that the physical sensation was starting to fade so he tried to focus doubly hard on Jeannine again. She was whispering how he felt so good on top of her and her body bounced beneath him. But she was a just a face. He tried stroking faster in hopes of mechanically making himself finish, but as he worked harder the image of Jeannine vanished altogether. Instead there was Nicola smiling and he felt strangely peaceful.

After a few more seconds of frantically trying to cum he gave up. His heart wasn't in it anymore. He was a little frustrated that he hadn't been able to finish but more confused at why Nicola had affected him so much. He was trying to place her. He was sure knew her from somewhere. Her statement about "their bedroom" didn't make any sense since he knew he would have remembered sleeping with her. She didn't seem like a creepy stalker-type, but Lyle admitted to himself that some of her comments were objectively pretty eerie.

Lyle lay spread out in the chair, flaccid both mentally and physically. With a sigh he began flipping through channels and bounced from one unenticing program to another for a half hour before just going to bed.

*****

Late at night there was a radio preacher. It was on the AM band and clearly from far away as it had background interference and would fade in and out sometimes. It was a signal firing off from some distant land and ricocheting off the ionosphere as Lyle's 7th grade Earth Studies teacher had explained. Lyle was never able to figure out where it came from precisely. There were times it sounded like it was coming from a different time with the melodramatic organ chords playing the background and the staticy, tinny sound of the broadcast as the preacher, Pastor Dave, warbled and proclaimed the gospel.

On the nights Lyle couldn't sleep he'd turn on his radio and search for it. He wasn't even sure how long the program ran. The few times Lyle didn't fall asleep he'd listen until the signal faded away, lost in a sea of static and country music. There were never any commercials, only an occasional interlude where the organist, who never spoke and was never mentioned by name, played a hymn. No one sang along with it, it just played, presumably as Pastor Dave took a brief break.

Lyle lay staring at the ceiling, trying to make sense of his encounter with Nicola earlier in the day as he listened to the radio crackle and Pastor Dave calling out to his invisible radio flock.

"Friends, Peter—the apostle of Jesus, the cornerstone of His church—has warned us that the Devil is a roaring lion seeking whom he may devour," Pastor Dave intoned solemnly and evenly. "The Prince of Power of the Air, the Ruler of This World, the Accuser—he is out there devouring, consuming, the souls of the lost. He hungers for the hearts of God's faithful and as the End Times approach—No, as the

End Times have arrived—he is here to persecute God's chosen ones and lead them on to destruction and damnation.

"For it is not angels, nor principalities that we face; it is not things present nor things to come; nor height nor depth nor any other created thing. No, my brothers and sisters, it is none of those things we face, for none of those things can separate us from the love of God. No, it is us; our very sinful natures that we must face. We have all been devoured. There is none who is righteous—not even one! All our acts are as of filthy rags. Do you understand what I'm telling you, brothers and sisters?"

Pastor Dave had a nasally voice and lacked a baritone rumble that would have given his words the weight of God himself. But what he lacked in natural gravitas he made up for with a carefully measured intensity. Lyle would find himself going from detached amusement to hanging on each word. Pastor Dave would slowly build in volume and fervor methodically bringing his voice to a frantic warble and then stopping dead. The silence would be deafening and then gently, softly, he would finish his thought. That soft coda could be either reassuring or deliver a crushing blow.

"I speak with people every day who tell me that 'I want to go to heaven! I want to spend everlasting life in my eternal reward!' and I ask them 'Why do you think you're going to heaven?' They start listing the good things they've done; they talk of the church services they've attended or how they've helped neighbors. Some talk about giving to charity or nice things they've done for strangers. They say 'Pastor Dave, I've lived a good life. I've been a *good* person.'

"Now, brothers and sisters, I am not ashamed of the Gospel of Christ for it is the power of God unto salvation, but every time I hear someone tell me things I get a knot in the pit of my stomach. God will render upon each man according to his deeds and to those who do not obey he brings anguish and tribulation and I am called to testify to the goodness of God and the vileness of our sin. I take them by the hand and I look them in the eye and say 'While we may not be friends after I finish, I will always love you the way Jesus commands.'"

There was a pause followed by a heavy sigh—nearly a sob—as if Pastor Dave were talking to someone right next to him.

"I squeeze their hand because the truth does not come to bring peace, but to bring a sword—to set son against father, daughter against mother, to set households against themselves and the weight of the words I have to deliver hang heavy on my heart. I say 'You want to go to heaven. You want to be welcomed by the Heavenly Host and led to still waters. You want Jesus to greet you and say "Well done, my faithful servant," and to spend eternity feeling fulfilled and rewarded for your good works. My friend, I need to tell you that if you believe that is heaven, then it doesn't exist.'

"No, that heaven has perished. It is dead and buried. It's okay to feel sad that it's gone because you believed in it so long, but today I'm presiding over its funeral. This is my eulogy for heaven—it was very comforting; it was a nice idea.

"Because that's what eulogies are for: we say all sorts of nice things about something gone that may or may not be entirely true. We do it to pay tribute to the hopes and dreams that are now gone and the ones who were left behind, orphaned and homeless. I'll be honest, at this point most people are confused or think I'm joking. 'How can a man of God say that heaven doesn't exist? How can a man who testifies to the goodness of Christ say that heaven is dead?' they ask me.

"'I'm not joking,' I tell them. 'Your heaven is a fairy tale land. It doesn't exist and, my brother or sister in Christ, you know there are only two places you can go and if your heaven doesn't exist then you know what that means. You are destined for the great lake of fire that burns with eternal torment. You will experience the second death with the faithless, the idolaters, the murderers and the liars.'

"Now they'll often respond angrily and say, 'Pastor Dave, how dare you say these things to me? I am a *good* person. Jesus died for my sins and heaven awaits me! You should be ashamed of yourself; you are in no position to judge me!'

"Now you might be saying the same thing to yourself. 'How could I dare to presume on God's behalf?' you might wonder. You might be saying, 'God is love and wants everyone to be with him in heaven,' and to them and to you I can only say the following:

"I don't condemn you to Hell. I love you and Jesus loves you, but even in love you are lost. There is no heaven because heaven to you is a place where are all your needs are met; it's a place where God serves you. No, out of love I tell you that this is no heaven but an empty, despicable, graven image of God and heaven that you have fashioned in your own image. You have constructed a house on the sand that will collapse mightily when beat down upon by the rain and wind.

"In fact, if you're looking to heaven as a reward you've already fallen to pride. I am commanded to break the pride of your power and rend your heaven into rags in the name of Jesus! There is *no heaven* for you. There is *no place* for you!"

Pastor Dave's voice was shrill and impassioned and then there was silence. Lyle lay staring at the ceiling, mouth dry with existential dread, hoping for a word of comfort. The silence drawing out the fear that there was nothing more to be said. Then, largely muffled by the radio interference there was a labored sigh. Pastor Dave cleared his throat quietly, and, voice breaking slightly said:

"There is no place for any of us anymore. There is only a place for God. Amen…"

Lyle wasn't sure if that was supposed to be reassuring or not. The organist began playing a hymn that Lyle didn't recognize. The words haunted him.

"There is no place for any of us anymore…"

It wouldn't have been so unsettling if hadn't felt true.

*****

Moses J. Reed held the chord until he heard Irvin say, "Aaaaaaaand we're clear." The sun was starting to rise and sky was a deep shade of amaranth with the skyline outside the window standing stark and black against it. "That was one of the good ones," Irvin announced. "That's one worth saving."

To be fair. Irvin said that most nights. It gave him the excuse to keep the tape and listen to it later to admire his handiwork.

He did the show as "a service for the Lord" but it was evident that he also gained no small amount of personal satisfaction from his marathon broadcasts.

Moses had met Irvin four years earlier at a smoky, dimly-lit honky-tonk that aspired to be good enough to be called a dive. It had been open mic night and Moses was playing regularly with a few musicians he'd met there. The other musicians had been horrible, but Moses didn't mind—he just enjoyed being able to play. At the end of their set the other band members high-fived and yee-hawed and then disappeared into the back where there was a poker game and some girls from "out of town"—which given how they'd said it, Moses thought was likely code for something more salacious. The cracked and beaten electric keyboard Moses had been playing was off, but he stayed behind, playing out melodies he heard in his head as the rest of the bar, which consisted of maybe 20 other patrons in total, continued the conversations they'd carried on through the set.

Moses smiled to himself, feeling a particularly soulful turn in the keys beneath his fingers. If the keyboard had been on, it wouldn't have been able to do justice to the mournful, blues-tinged melody he'd been weaving. He was almost sad to end it, but the next performer was starting to get his gear together and so Moses left the stage, his little orphan song left to fend for itself.

When he got to the bar the bartender looked at him, inviting an order. Moses ordered a Rolling Rock and sat on the bar stool, aimlessly reading the advertisements on the coasters.

"That was quite the song you played there," a voice interrupted his thoughts. Moses looked up and saw a potbellied man, slightly below average height, grinning with a face flushed red and glistening with sweat. He had thinning, sandy hair with the beginning of a comb-over trying to mask exposed scalp. He wore a white western shirt tucked into a pair of jeans that were probably a size smaller than they should have been. The clasp and tips of the bolo shone brightly in the dimly-lit bar. His clothing had a western twinge to them, but he wasn't wearing cowboy boots, didn't have a cowboy hat and was missing the gaudy belt buckle that most patrons seemed to be wearing. In context he almost looked normal.

"Thanks," Moses nodded quietly. "We've only been playing together a couple weeks."

"I wasn't talking about that. That sounded god-awful. No, that tune you were playing to yourself just now."

Moses looked at him quizzically—he was sure that the keyboard had been off. The other man chuckled.

"It was all over your face. I could hear it from the look you had," he winked. "Name's Irvin Westmeuller," he offered out a meaty hand. Moses shook it with a nod.

"You know, a lot of people would be shocked to know I was in a place like this," Irvin continued. "I have a reputation as a puritanical sort, but there's nothing like a nice cold brew and a dose of some good ol' country blues, am I right?"

Moses nodded, although he didn't have strong feelings about it either way.

"Listen, I don't mean to pry, but I can always spot a fellow traveler when I see one," Moses shot him a wary glance.

"Easy there, friend," grinned Irvin. "I'm not passing judgment. I've spent time on the open road myself. If anything those I met who called no place 'home' were some of the best family I've ever had. No, I think there's a certain camaraderie guys like us share that most people just wouldn't understand."

Irvin took a deliberate swig from his beer and nodded, as if in deep thought. "Can I ask you two things?"

"I s'pose."

"The first is easy, and the second has two parts. First, what's your name? I feel a little funny just calling you 'friend' or 'brother'."

"Moses."

"Ah, the baby in the water. Wonderful name. Lots of character in that name," Irvin beamed. "We'll see if that name's prescient. My second question, part one, do you know Jesus as your personal Lord and savior?"

Moses wasn't sure if his eyes rolled or not. Wherever he went, they always seemed to find him. "I don't ascribe to any one church or anything," he answered. "I believe God is everywhere and in everything and is a unifying force of love." That kind of answer usually meant people would leave him alone. If you said you were an atheist they'd argue; an agnostic they'd try to persuade you. But the new-age pseudo-Zen thing usually got a nod and an air of resignation.

"Well said, Moses. I mean I disagree with the pantheistic undertones, but God is love and looking to bring us all to his bosom," Irvin replied undeterred. "The second part of the question is: are you open-minded enough to help someone even if you don't agree with them 100%?"

Moses looked him over skeptically. He'd seen plenty of grifts start out similarly. "Depends, I suppose."

"Well, like I said earlier, I have this reputation. You ever heard of the 'Old Rugged Cross Midnight Revival with Pastor Dave'?"

Moses shook his head 'no'. Irvin frowned slightly, but quickly returned to his grin.

"Well, not really your demographic, I suppose. We're coast to coast. Literally an audience of millions out there every night that we reach out to, spreading the Word of God to the lost. We are beacon of light in a world of darkness and hopelessness. It's a labor of love, really, but we've been incredibly blessed."

"Hm," Moses nodded.

"Yes, we've reaped the bounty that the Lord's work yields. But there are always highs and valleys. Jim Prado, our longtime organist and dear, dear friend, recently and very suddenly went to his eternal reward."

Irvin's expression changed and he paused a moment. For the first time since he'd started talking it appeared that he wasn't selling something. Moses still sat facing forward, but was watching him much more keenly. For the first time since the conversation started Irvin actually seemed interesting.

Irvin cleared his throat and tried to start again, but his voice cracked ever so slightly as if his throat was incredibly dry or as if he'd swallowed wrong.

"I'm sorry. The Lord works in mysterious ways as they say. There should be no mourning for those who are now with Jesus, but he had been a brother to me since I came to this town—" he cleared his throat and half coughed as he tried to maintain his composure. "Folks like us who travel don't have families waiting for us in some distant city, but we build our families as we go. I often told him that if I ever need further evidence of God's providence I had to do no more than look to the man at my left who was with me night in and night out at the organ. I am lucky that the Lord allowed him to be part of my piece-meal earthly family as well as a member of my heavenly family…"

Irvin trailed off, still clearing his throat every few seconds. Neither man said anything. Moses felt a little awkward sitting next to a man who had just bared his soul to him with no provocation. Irvin sighed and then took a few large and quick swallows of his beer after which he let out an exaggerated "Ahhhhhhh," as if the drink was all he needed to be refreshed and jovial again.

"Anyway, what I was meaning to ask before I got sidetracked is this: We've got an opening for an organist. I saw you playing; you know what you're doing and the losers around here will never be worthy of your considerable abilities. More than that, you *feel* the music. You feel it the way ol' King Saul did when music was the only thing that could ease his torment. Us travelers may travel light but always carry heavy burdens, am I right?" Irvin raised his beer as a sign of solidarity. Moses nodded and tipped his beer Irvin's way.

"You're just the kind of guy we need. The hours are terrible and the pay is a joke, but you get the chance to play every night and let that beautiful, soulful sound roll across the country. If I have any sense about you, and I think I do, that's all the convincing you'll need."

Moses traced the outline of his coaster absent-mindedly with the bottom of his beer bottle. The idea was intriguing. The whole religious part didn't interest him that much, but the idea of being able to play for a nationwide audience was appealing and the thought of being a fly on the wall for a large, influential media outlet was very intriguing.

"Would I have to sing or have my name on anything?"

"Not if you didn't want to. For the singing part, I'd prefer you just play, anyway. You'll have some hymns from time to time, but for the rest you can just use hymns a basis for improvisation. I love that soul you've got—I'd love some of our old, dusty hymns to get an injection of some of that."

Moses swirled the remnants of his beer in the bottom of his bottle as he thought for a moment.

"If I don't like it?"

"Then I'll shake your hand and wish you nothing but the best. No reason for acrimony the way I see it. Either it makes that part of your mind click or it doesn't. No harm for trying and no foul if it doesn't pan out."

"I suppose I could take a look—"

"Ha!" Irvin laughed and clapped loudly. "I knew it! Trust me, you won't be sorry," he began scribbling something on a bar napkin. "This is the address. Be there by 9pm. I'll be able to give you a little tour and kinda walk you through what we do."

Moses looked at the address. It was in an industrial area if he had the area right. It seemed a little odd, but he didn't know much about radio or broadcasting.

Irvin slapped a ten dollar bill on the bar, "I gotta run, but I'll see you tonight," he gestured at the bartender, "His next one's on me," as he slid the bill across the bar. The bartender nodded disinterestedly as he wiped down the bar. For as much noise as he made, no one seemed to pay Irvin much mind, Moses thought.

That night Moses made his way to the address. The building was office space in a large old warehouse. The police sirens seemed to be calling out back and forth to each other like neighborhood dogs. The street was poorly lit and didn't have the safest feel about it. Moses had seen worse in his travels, but still if anyone asked for a nice area to bed down for a night, this wouldn't be it.

The lot was surrounded by rickety looking chain link fencing with barbed wire running along the top, complete with shredded garbage and grocery bags crackling in the evening breeze and loose and sagging lengths of wire throughout. A couple of old floodlights illuminated part of the parking lot. From the looks of it there were several other lights that were either broken or not even turned on. There was a large sliding fence leading to the park dock. To its side there was an old battered call box. It had been tagged with paint and stickers; the remnants of which still stained it or remained stuck on in shredded paper swaths.

He pressed the black button below the largely obscured speaker grill and waited. In the distance he heard tires squealing and what he hoped was a car backfiring. He pressed the button again, unsure of whether the call box was even functional. The box suddenly crackled and a tinny cry came from somewhere within it.

"Fuckin' knock it off, asshole!"

Moses was taken aback but answered tentatively, "Hello? I'm supposed to meet Irvin."

A minute passed with no response. He didn't really want to, but Moses thought he probably needed to hit the button again. He winced as pressed it again. The response came much faster this time, but there was a few second delay.

"You hit that fuckin' button again I'll be out with a baseball bat and I'm going to end you, you little skateboarding shits."

"Um, excuse me... Uh, is Irvin there?"

"...Who the fuck is this?"

"I'm Moses. Irvin told me to come by."

"...Hold on."

24

There was silence for a couple of minutes. Moses was starting to wonder if he should hit the button again when the door beneath the floodlights opened. Irvin walked out and waved enthusiastically as he propped the door open. "It's alright Karl. It's the guy I was telling you about." Something must have been said in reply because Irvin's expression changed to mock annoyance. "That's why only your dog likes you—and that's only 'cuz you feed him," Irvin laughed. After another moment the gate clicked and slid open. Irvin gestured for Moses to come in.

"Where'd you park?"

"I didn't drive."

Irvin looked at him dubiously for a second. "Brave man. C'mon in. Let me show you around."

They walked inside. The carpet was old and even though it was a dark red and black pattern it was evident that it was both heavily worn and stained throughout. The walls were covered with wood paneling that was scratched, worn and faded from decades of neglect as well as the odd hole punched in it here and there. The fluorescent light had a purplish hue and flickered anemically. The ceiling was low and the smell from the ballast reminded Moses of boxelder bugs and stale chewing tobacco. Overall, the building had a dingy, oily feel about it. There were "no smoking" placards at the front door and by the fire alarms, but the building had been smoked in for years and the ghosts of old Lucky Strikes and KOOLs (not to mention a few stogies thrown in for good measure) still haunted every inch of the place.

On the opposite wall in two foot high, red plastic letters were the station call letters. They had seen better days, like everything else about the place, but they at least seemed to indicate a happier era. At one time, decades before, the bold KBQJ letters were a sign of prestige. But since then there had been hippies, folk music, stadium rock, new wave, hair metal, new R&B and finally the age of corporate radio. Each wave had taken a toll on KBQJ. Originally a regional talk and country music station, each incarnation seemed to move them further away from their heyday—whether they'd switched formats or held steady leaving their competitors to adapt. Of course, that could be said about radio in general, Moses mused.

It was hard to say what kind of station it was now. It didn't seem overtly religious. The music playing over the speaker was kind of a folksy bluegrass sounding thing. Irvin led Moses down the hallway and around a corner where there was an office just to the right. A thin, greasy guy sporting a moustache that probably had seen its last gasp of popularity about the same time the station had, sat slouched over a desk, fiddling on a laptop.

"Karl, this is Moses. He's checking out the show. I'm trying to convince him to join our little band of roustabouts," Irvin proclaimed.

"Mm," Karl grunted in reply. "If he's going to be working get him a key. I don't need him using that fucking call box every night," he said never looking up from his laptop.

Irvin chuckled, unphased by Karl's crassness or apparent disinterest. "Always a charmer, aren't ya? C'mon, Moses, let me show you the rest of the place."

Irvin guided him down the hall, up a flight of stairs and through a metal door that opened up to a hallway with rooms on either side.

"They used to have four studios up here back in the day. Two on each side. Not much call for that anymore. They use the last two for storage nowadays," Irvin waved through the glass of the first room at a morose looking Hispanic man who appeared to be speaking solemnly into a microphone. He gave a half-wave back. There was a man in a smaller room adjacent to the door of the studio with his back towards the window.

"That's Tony—he does a talk show every Thursday night. Not sure what it's about—I don't speak a lick of Spanish. But he's a very nice guy. The engineer is Marlon. Marlon isn't a very nice guy. I don't like to speak ill of anyone, but don't use the breakroom fridge for your lunch. Or leave money out. Or tell him anything about anything you care about. Just trust me on that.

"Anyway, we're down here," Irvin pointed to the adjacent studio.

The second studio was a bit smaller and in much worse repair. The carpet had been ripped and then tacked back down with gaffer's tape. The wall was marked and scuffed. The microphone hung precariously on a swivel stand that was bonded together by unseen and mysterious forces that held it in one piece as an act of sheer will. Unlike the other studio there wasn't a separate room for an engineer, just an ancient mixing board at the desk with the microphone and a couple other consoles presumably having some radio-y function. In the corner were various boxes, an old electronic keyboard, an old computer monitor, a wobbly microphone stand and a broken folding chair.

"Home sweet home," Irvin beamed.

Moses didn't know what to make of it all. It certainly didn't seem like a beacon of light that reached millions each night. "So, who else is coming?"

Irvin just laughed, "That's the beauty of modern technology, my friend. There's no one else coming; it's just us."

"What about Dave?"

"Dave?" Irvin looked confused. "Oh, you mean *Pastor* Dave? I'm Pastor Dave."

Moses looked at him quizzically.

"It's all about presentation—that's the first thing they teach you. No one is going to tune into the 'Layperson Irvin Talks About God At Night Show'. You gotta dress it up. It's gotta be something kinda flashy that still evokes kind of that old-school flavor from the faith of their youth, you know? So I become Pastor Dave and the show becomes the 'Old Rugged Cross Midnight Revival'."

Irvin saw the skepticism in Moses' face and offered his reassurance. "This is the era of the internet. Honestly that's where most the audience is these days. The radio is good for reaching the old-timers, the night owls, truck drivers, night auditors—good workin' folk. Those are our people—you and me—we understand those people. Most days we are those people.

"I guess that's why I feel it's my calling. Jesus has spoken to me and brought me great comfort and at the same time challenged me. That challenge caused me to lose many nights of sleep and I spent them feeling alone, tossing and turning. I know he speaks to others much the same way and it just seems to me that maybe I'm supposed to tell them they're not alone and that the hard truths are very hard, but the burden is light."

Irvin paused for a moment and then laughed, shaking his head.

"You caught me sermonizing, didn't you? Sorry, it's kinda what I do. Anyway, I know it doesn't look like much, but this is a pretty big deal. I think you're in for a treat.

"Well, I suppose we better start getting set up. I usually go over my notes for preparation for an hour or so. You don't have to be here for that, obviously. Jim would usually show up somewhere from an hour to a half hour before and get set up, do some rehearsing, stuff like that. He used that old keyboard there—" Irvin pointed at a battered old Yamaha DX-7 on a stand. "There are a couple other ones over there. You can use any of them. I don't know which ones work or anything, but they're fair game."

Moses didn't say anything but looked at them. The Yamaha powered up and Moses noodled around on it. The best voices on it sounded like he should be playing "Axel F" on it, not church music. There was a Casio that didn't even power up. There was another Casio, but that was a mini keyboard. It felt like a toy and sounded silly to boot. Moses reluctantly messed around with the Yamaha a bit more. He could make it work, but it wouldn't be what he wanted. At the desk Irvin was lost in his own world, mouthing words from his notes, occasionally gesturing widely as if re-enacting what he thought it should look like to express his point.

Moses rummaged around absent-mindedly, killing time. After a few minutes he gestured to Irvin that he was leaving for a minute. He wandered down the hallway and found the restrooms behind a set of double doors to a landing. There were steps leading down to some other part of the building—storage area, most likely, and then there was an old Coke machine. It only took coins, no bill reader, and had a faux wood-grain panel on the front. Moses went into the bathroom to pee, even though he really didn't feel like he needed to.

The bathroom itself had the overwhelming scent of chemical air freshener—the scent that you could tell was supposed to smell "good" but really didn't and didn't resemble anything occurring in nature. There was a distinctly urine-y odor just beneath the artificial flowery haze, but it wasn't anything worse than most gas station bathrooms. At least the floors didn't have the suspiciously damp gleam that many scarier public restrooms did. He ambled up to a urinal with its obligatory pink urinal cake and coaxed out a half-hearted stream of piss.

He wasn't sure what he was going to do. Irvin seemed nice enough, but any thought that this experiment was going to play out well was quickly fading. The place was a dump and, aside from Irvin, it seemed unlikely that anybody, anywhere, was at all interested in what they were doing. Moses was unhappy with the equipment he had been given to work with and there seemed to be no upside to continuing. He felt like by showing up he at least had agreed to do the one night, but it was starting to feel like it was going to be a very, very long night.

Moses finished up and washed his hands. The bathroom used the powdery soap—he hadn't seen that anywhere in ages. The entire place seemed stuck in a time warp. Moses wondered how he had ended up here of all places. He could've chosen any number of destinations that were out-of-the-way but he somehow ended up there. Granted a lot of those decisions had been more reactionary than well thought out, but still, things did seem a bit unfair in the grander scale.

Moses bought a root beer from the Coke machine and headed back to the studio. Irvin was still lost in his notes, intensely murmuring and occasionally exploding with wild hand motions. Moses sat on a stool in the corner and sipped on his root beer, trying to will time to move faster. After a few more minutes of silence he went around the room one more time. There was more crap—old boxes of paperwork, a stack of old National Geographics (seriously, everywhere seemed to have a pile of those *somewhere*) some patch cables. In the corner propped up length-wise was a folding table. There was a desk on the near side of it so it wasn't until Moses pulled it back that he saw there was something behind it. Dusty, with a cracked case sat an old Wurlitzer electric piano. Moses picked it up gingerly. The legs had been removed and the sustain pedal was nowhere to be found, but it was still mostly intact.

He maneuvered carefully around the table and the desk and brought the piano over to the stand that the Yamaha sat on.

He probably was rougher than he meant to be in moving the Yamaha. Irvin even glanced over at Moses after he flipped it casually against the wall and it slammed louder than he had intended. He gingerly, almost reverently, placed the Wurly on the stand. It smelled of aged plastic and the cigarettes (tobacco and otherwise) of days past. He wiped the dust away with the palm of his hand, relishing the cool smoothness of the casing.

He plugged it in and, with breath held, turned the knob. There was a pop and the power light begrudgingly lit up. Moses ran his fingers up and down the keys before playing a chord. To his surprise it actually worked. One of the speakers was blown or the pot was incredibly dirty so it gave it as bass-y, crackling sound, but that actually made it sound better to him. He noodled through a few scales and an impromptu take on "What'd I Say".

He could feel himself grinning, almost stupidly, at the warmth of the sound. He started improvising over some soul progressions. He wished there was a way he could sneak it out and take it with him; it was everything he'd wanted in an instrument.

"Now that's the stuff," Irvin declared. Moses looked up at him. Irvin was grinning at him, nodding appreciatively. "Now, you're the musical guy and I don't want to mess with what you've got going on there—it sounds mighty fine—but could you make it a little more gospel-y? If you can combine what you've got there with more of a traditional sound, well, then you'd have lightning in a bottle."

Moses nodded and started in on "His Eye is on the Sparrow" running through it twice more or less straight before letting the tune wander a bit beneath his fingers. Irvin was beaming and nodding. "My friend, God never errs and he has shown once again that he knew what he was doing when our paths crossed. This is gonna be something special."

Moses didn't remember much more about that night. He'd had some missteps while playing, but Irvin didn't seem to notice or care about them. Irvin, for his part, was actually even more dynamic than Moses had thought. The Pastor Dave persona rose and crashed like ocean waves over the six hour broadcast. That was the other thing—it was incredibly long. At the end of the night, as the sun was cracking across the horizon, making the pollution glow like a dawn on Mars, Moses and Irvin both stumbled out of the studio and barely so much as spoke a goodbye. Moses' feet were aching, his eyes were dry and itchy and his brain seemed to be blaring a test tone like an old TV broadcast. For his part, Irvin's top button was undone and the bolo was long gone. The hair in his sideburns and the sides of his head were banded together, still damp from sweat. His eyes were distant and the flushing was finally starting to fade, but his cheeks, neck and the exposed parts of his chest were still red.

Later Irvin admitted that the adrenaline from having Moses on-board along with a particularly good sermon had caused him to peak too early, but even so it wasn't as if there was a morning where they both weren't drained from the night before.

"You need a ride?" Irvin offered.

"No, it's fine. I have it taken care of," Moses answered.

"You coming back tonight?"

"Yeah, I'll be here."

Irvin smiled tiredly, "I knew you were the right one."

Moses nodded and gave a half-wave. "See you tonight."

Irvin got into his rusted out Subaru hatchback and drove away without fanfare.

"So much for lying low," Moses mumbled to himself before returning home.

Part II: Letters to My Lost Love

There was a box in the attic of the house Lyle grew up in. It had been forgotten over the years and eventually was buried under a blanket of dust and fallen insulation.

Lyle had been an "accident" baby. His parents hadn't planned on having kids, especially when his father was 50 and his mother was 42. His father had died of a heart attack when he was a sophomore in high school. His mother had died nine days after his 25th birthday. Her death hadn't had near the impact that his father's death had. With his parents older than his peers he'd been forced to deal with the implications of age and mortality at a far younger age. While his mother's passing did seem sudden, she had been 67. His parents had lost friends and family members of a similar age in the years leading up to her death. It could all happen very suddenly and 65 seemed to be the point where it could go sideways in a hurry. By age 27 Lyle was on his own: No parents, no siblings, and the last few aging aunts and uncles had died. They had been so spread out and far away from where he'd grown up that he'd never really known them anyway.

After his mother died, Lyle had gathered a few knick-knacks and some old photo albums and let the rest go in an estate auction. The box, in its insulated cave, was missed, although it would have likely been thrown out in either case. All it held were some drawings that Lyle had made that had graced the refrigerator, some participation ribbons and the letters.

When Lyle was little had dreamed that he had a special friend. Sometimes she was young, sometimes she was old but it was always the same person. When he was in first grade he tried to explain her to his mother. He explained she came and they played together when she was young and when she was old she'd tell him stories about where she came from. He told his mother that when he woke he remembered all sorts of things he wanted to say and things he wanted to ask her about, but he'd forget before he saw her again. His mother nodded, half-listening as she did the dishes and watched the People's Court. "That's nice Lyle. If you have something you want to tell her, why don't you write her a letter? Then you can give it to her when you see her again."

It really wasn't the answer he was hoping to hear—he was hoping his mother would let him use the phone so he could call the operator and she could connect him, just like they did on television. But the letters were as good as he was going to do.

"Thank you for coming to play with me. I like it when you are a kid like me. You should come over and we can ride bikes and go to the Dairy Queen. Lyle."

The spelling was dicey, but that's what he'd meant to say. He gave the letter to his mother and she read it and smiled. "I'll make sure it goes out," she said. She folded it and put it in the drawer.

The older version came to him that night.

"Did you get my letter?"

"Did you send one? Was it the first one?"

Lyle nodded. She beamed happily, "Then yes, I've seen it. I've seen them all. I'm sorry I wasn't younger for you today. We'll ride bikes another time, okay?"

Lyle smiled. She then had him sit down with her and she told him about when she was a little girl that she had been very sick but the doctor's hadn't found a cure for her.

"What were you sick with?" Lyle asked.

"It has many names depending where you're at. Where you're from it has a scary name. The doctors don't have medicine for it yet where you're at."

Lyle gave her an uneasy look and she gave him a little hug. "Don't worry, you won't get it. You'll be fine. You don't have anything to be afraid of. Listen, every time you have a question, or are afraid of something you do like your mother said, you write me a letter, ok?"

Lyle nodded. She smiled at him warmly. "You're so young, but you're going to grow up and be amazing."

Lyle told her about what he'd done that day. He laid his head against her chest and she lightly tussled his hair.

He could never remember how the dreams ended. It was like he'd drift off to sleep in his own dream and start having regular dreams at some point. She would come and go, sometimes visiting him several times a week and then not again for months, at least as much as he could remember. Dreams would come and go, and while they felt different they often were as nebulous and patchwork as other dreams come morning.

But still the letters came. It eventually evolved into a journal of sorts with the last letter written the day after his father died.

*****

I wanted to go swimming today. Mom said we could yesterday but then she said it was too cold. I got real mad and I got sent to my room because Mom wouldn't keep her promise. She told me I had to write "I'm sorry, Mom" a hundred times. I am writing you a letter instead because I'm not sorry.

It's not too cold outside. I said I would be okay but she still said no. She's stupid.

Lyle (age 7)

*****

There was a dead bird in the grass at school. I touched it and it felt funny. There wasn't blood or guts. I picked it up. It was very light. It didn't really move except the head moved around. It smelled funny. It smelled like dad's toolshed does when it's hot outside, except it wasn't hot outside.

When I had it in my hands it looked like it could still fly away. I imagined it could but that it liked it when I held it so it stayed. Then recess ended and I had to go inside.

I wish I had something to hold like the bird. I asked mom if we could get a kitten and she said no. I asked her if she would have another baby and she made me go outside.

I hope you come and see me soon.

Lyle (age 8)

*****

We had the 4th of July tonight. Dad grilled hotdogs and hamburgers and there were people from all over who came by. Mom let me choose what we drank and we had grape Kool-Aid. We had chips and everything. Then Dad gave me some sparklers. I tried to write my name in the air with them. Then he lit some snakes in driveway. You light these little black circles on fire and they grow into these long black worms. They were kind of boring, but then he lit off some smoke bombs, too. There was one with green smoke and one that was blue and one that was red. I wish I could keep some and use them for hide and seek at school. They could come up and I could light it off and run and hide before they found me.

Then after we ate dad let me shoot off some bottle rockets. He showed me how to hold them right at the end and he'd light it and then it would fly out of my hand into the sky. He had regular ones and the ones that made the screaming noise when they took off. Mom came out and yelled at him for letting me hold the bottle rockets so he took them back. But after she left he let me shoot off the last three. He told me not to tell Mom.

It got real dark but Mom didn't make me go to bed. Dad called me out to the front yard. He had me sit in next to him in a lawn chair. Everyone else had gone home by then. There were fireflies glowing off and on and then big fireworks started going off. Some shot all colors everywhere and some were just white and came down like rain. There were a couple so big it was like lightning.

Then all of a sudden you saw all these different ones shooting up at the same time and it was kinda going off together. Dad laughed and clapped his hands. He said to me "Isn't that something, Champ? Isn't that something!"

That was the end of the fireworks and Mom came and made me go to bed. I'm not tired though. She said I still had to lie down and be quiet. She doesn't know I'm writing you a letter. I wish everyday was the 4th of July.

Lyle (age 10)

*****

That night he dreamed it all again: The hotdogs and the Kool-Aid, the fireflies, the smoke bombs and it all ended with the giant fireworks show. But this time she was with him.

She was young this time, wearing a bright orange dress with matching ribbons pulling her hair into pigtails just over and behind her ears. They played tag in the yard and his Dad got on his hands and knees and gave them "bronco rides" bouncing up and down until they fell off. They hid under the dining room table and pretended that no one could see them.

"This is how I remember it," she whispered to him as they peeked between chair legs at the disinterested adults mulling around the living room. "Just like this. This is how it was supposed to be."

His mother entered the room talking to someone in the kitchen, "I don't know, they're running around here somewhere. Go out and yell at Ernie. He said he was going to get some sparklers for the kids; maybe they're doing that."

They both giggled. There was a special delight at the cleverness of being unseen while Lyle secretly felt a thrill at the prospect of being caught.

"I don't know where those kids are," his mother barked irritably. "I'm sure they're around somewhere. They better not be messing around with those fireworks. I told Ernie that the last thing I need is one of them losing an eye or blowing off some fingers or something. But I just know he's going to be letting them do whatever they please. Sometimes I don't know which one acts younger between those two. You've got it easy—you've got girls…"

The two of them snickered from their hiding spot but his mother didn't seem to hear them. Once all the adults seemed contained to outside or other rooms the sense of playful danger was gone. They crept out from under the table and pretended to be sneaky a little while longer, but even their imaginations couldn't change the fact it was obvious that they weren't being crafty, the adults just didn't care.

"I've got something to show you," she whispered to Lyle.

"What?"

She grinned and ran out the front door. Lyle followed her. She ran across the street into Mrs. Delmar's yard and then around the side. There was a small wooded area behind the house that extended to a coulee that ran along the frontage road alongside the railroad tracks. He lost sight of her in the trees. He weaved through the brush and blundered through the long grass, kicking aside the empty beer cans that the older kids left behind when they snuck out there at night to drink and smoke.

There was a large tree at the edge of the embankment, its roots spilled out, gnarled and exposed into the coulee below. The tree had grown at an angle with a part where he could just step up without having to climb. He hopped up on it to try and get a little better view, but she was nowhere to be found. Her bright orange dress should've been easy to see, even in the shaded wooded area.

"Hello?" he called out. He didn't see anything and other than a light gust of wind causing the leaves to quietly applaud there was no sound. "HELLOOOOO?"

Then he heard a snicker. He turned and saw nothing. He looked up the tree but there was nothing there, either. "Can't you see me?" he heard her tease.

"Where are you?"

There was a rustle and then she sprung up from between the roots of the tree. Even as she came climbing out he could barely see the hole. It almost looked as if she was crawling up through the ground.

"It's ok, it's hidden," she said.

"Could we build a secret fort there? I could get some stuff from home and we could make a spot."

She smiled and shook her head. "No, even if you could see it, it wouldn't be a good idea. Besides, it wouldn't even be a secret."

Lyle was puzzled. She sat down next to him on the tree, pulling a leaf that had been growing from a little sprout on its side. "We're not alone here. You haven't been alone for a long time, actually. I didn't notice until just recently, though. Haven't you seen her?"

Lyle looked down at her and she glanced up at him with a matter-of-fact expression, as if everything she was saying made sense.

"I think she's fine. She's not scary or anything. You never told me about her, though, so I didn't know."

"I don't know what you're talking about. Who is here?"

She smiled as she delicately tore the blade away from the veins in the leaf leaving a little green leaf skeleton. "Just look. Look so hard that you're not seeing anything and then let your eyes blur."

"Where?"

"Anywhere. She's everywhere here at different times."

Lyle stared hard across the coulee at a tree.

"Don't stare at something, stare at the space between things," she said. "If you stare hard at a tree, all you'll see is a tree," she laughed.

Lyle stared at the space between the tree and the one next to it. His eyes itched and burned and he finally blinked.

"This is dumb. There's nothing there."

"Just give it a second. It's there."

He tried again, but saw nothing.

"You're not looking hard enough."

Lyle snorted, starting to think she was just playing a trick on him. His forehead started to ache from squinting so hard.

"Now you're looking too hard—let your eyes blur."

"This is stupid. There's nothing there," he grumbled. He blinked his eyes and felt his forehead relax as he gave up.

And then there she was.

Just out of the corner of his eye he saw a girl, maybe a little younger than he was, in a dirty white dress, her hair wild and curly held back by a loosely tied ponytail. Her face was streaked with dirt and she looked ashen. Lyle turned his head to look at her straight on and she didn't move. It wasn't his imagination or something just out of the corner of his eye.

"She's been staring at you the whole time," the girl told him. "I think she can see me, but she doesn't care. It's a little rude if you ask me."

"But... who is she?"

"How should I know? She's been following you around, not me. She hasn't said anything, either. She just kind of comes and goes."

Lyle's mouth was dry and he was afraid to blink because he didn't know if she'd still be there.

"She won't," the girl answered his unspoken question. "It's ok. I think you'll see her again. I thought you'd like to know, anyway. We should get back. It's getting dark."

Lyle blinked and the girl in white was gone. His friend in orange hopped up nonchalantly. "Let's go, I want to do the sparklers now."

She headed back out of the woods towards the back of Mrs. Delmar's house. Lyle stayed a moment, trying to see the girl again but she was gone.

The rest of the day went as it had the first time, only with her there. They played with sparklers drawing pictures in the air. She ran and danced in the colored smoke of the smoke bombs. That night they sat side by side in the lawn chair as the fireworks lit up the sky. She squeezed his hand and whispered, "This is how it was supposed to be. Remember that. There's supposed to be so much more."

*****

I got in a fight at school today. Chris D and Chris L were throwing little bits of paper at me and I told them to stop it. They pretended like they weren't but I saw them. Then Mrs. Martinez caught them and made them stop. But at recess they said I told on them and that I was a crybaby. Then Chris D pushed me and I pushed him back and he fell over. Chris L started yelling that I was beating up Chris D but I hadn't done anything. Then Chris D got back up and tried to tackle me but I grabbed him and fell on top of him. He put his hands up in my face so I hit him and I hit him again until he took his hands away and then I saw his nose all bloody and his lip, too, and he was crying.

Mr. Sanders pull me off of him and made us go to the principal's office. Both Chris L and Chris D said I started it and that they hadn't done anything. I told him what really happened and he didn't believe me, but he still sent both me and Chris D home. I could hear Chris L in the hallway talking about the fight to the other kids and telling them how I cried, even though it wasn't me. The principal told us we had to wait on the bench in the hallway until our parents came to pick us up. The nurse took Chris D back to get some ice for his nose, so it was just me by myself.

Other teachers walked by and looked me like I'd done something bad. I looked at the floor the entire time. When the kindergartners came by for milk time they all stared at me. I felt so bad because I didn't do anything but everyone thought I was bad.

Dad got there and talked to the principal in his office. Then he came out and looked mad. He never yelled, he just said, "Let's go," and took me out to the truck. He didn't say anything the whole way back. We got home and Mom started to yell at me, but Dad told me to go to my room. I heard them talking, Mom was mad, but Dad's voice was really soft. I don't know what they were saying.

Then I saw Dad leave to go back to work in the truck. Mom didn't say anything. It sounds like she's vacuuming now.

I cried a little in my room. Not because I got hurt, my face hurts some, but that didn't make me cry. Everyone is mad me and I didn't do anything. I didn't hurt anyone on purpose but everyone thinks I did because of stupid Chris L.

I wish you were here. You could tell Mom and Dad what really happened. They'd listen to you.

Lyle (age 11)

*****

Today sucked. I was going to the park and play basketball. There were some other kids who had been going there a lot and they let me join in. There were even some older kids with them and they said I could play with them whenever. I played some Wednesday after school and they said Saturday they were going to get a few more kids together and have a five on five game. I even woke up a little early today so I could pick what team I was going to be on.

There's this guy JJ, he's one of the older kids and he said I should come and hang out with him. He's one of the guys everyone likes. I heard he made out with Stacy Martin and got to touch her boob. JJ was the one who asked me to come down. He said after the game I could go along with him and the guys. All the guys who hang out with him have girlfriends and get invited to parties and stuff. It would've been so cool but then I get to the kitchen and Mom and Dad are both there.

They were whispering and acting kinda weird when I got there but I didn't think anything of it. I grabbed a pop tart and was about to leave when Mom asked where I was going. I told her I was going to play ball and she told me to wait a minute and then gave Dad this look. Dad got this look on his face like he didn't want to be there. He said to me, "Well, just hold up for a minute, bud. We're gonna go fishing today."

I hate fishing. It's stupid. And boring. And Dad hardly ever goes fishing, either. I told him that I promised the guys I'd be there and that they were counting on me. He said when we were done he'd run me by the park to see if they were still there. I said it wasn't fair and that I didn't want to go fishing and then Mom yelled at me and said I had to go and that I should be glad I got to spend time with Dad.

I was so mad, I felt my face burn and my hands were shaking. Mom told me to go in the yard and wait until I learned how to be "respectful".

I went to the deck and sat in one of the chairs. I thought about just going to play ball and leaving, but that probably would've just made things worse. I was waiting for an hour at least. I don't know what took Dad so long to get his stupid fishing stuff together. He finally came out back and told me to hurry up, we were going.

I was still mad and didn't say anything to him the whole trip. The lake is, like, an hour away. Dad didn't say anything either, he just had the radio on listening to some crappy country music.

We finally get there and I'm thinking that if we hurry we can get back just before lunch and the guys might still be there. Dad grabs the rods and tells me I have to grab the tackle box and then he tells me to follow him. There were a few people around, some already fishing along the dock but Dad starts heading down a trail going the other way around the lake.

He kept walking and walking and walking and once I couldn't see the car anymore I just knew there was no way we'd make it back in time. I don't know how long we walked, seemed like an hour. We were walking along some sand dunes along the shore and he finally said "This'll do," and set down our stuff.

He got the rods set up with jigs and had me bait the hooks with nightcrawlers. We cast the lines out and slowly drew them back in. And then did it again. And again.

I never catch anything so it's just retarded that I had to go. Dad caught a couple of fish. He threw them both back, too. If we weren't even going to keep anything I don't know why we even bothered.

Finally he asks me how school's going. I told him it was fine. I mean, school sucks, but I didn't want to talk about it or anything.

Then a couple seconds later he asks if there are any girls I like. He's never asked me about girls before and it's weird talking about it—especially with him or Mom. I mean, I think about girls and stuff. I think about doing stuff with Stephanie Jensen. You know, that thing that guys do. I mean, I know how it all works and stuff kinda. JJ told about how he did it with some girl at his cousin's place last summer. And I've seen movies and stuff on cable.

"Well, we need to talk about girls," Dad says. I couldn't even think of anything to say.

"We—your mother and I—well, there's some things that you probably need to know about… things."

I wanted to die. I remember just casting my line out again and watching the bobber hopping that if I stared hard enough at it that I wouldn't hear anything more.

"You're getting to an age where there are certain changes going on. You know what I mean?"

I didn't want to think about it, but I said "Yeah," and hoped that would be enough. He didn't say anything for a minute and I thought maybe it had worked but then he went on again, "So you've noticed stuff about your penis then?"

I have never been so embarrassed in my life. And he didn't stop.

"Cuz it's going to get bigger. Not sure how big. I mean, between you and me, you don't have much to inherit from me in that regard. I mean, it does the job and all. Your mother always said it was okay, but you probably won't be breaking any records. You get me?"

My face felt so hot that I couldn't even focus my eyes. I think I just said "yeah" or something.

"So you'll start growing hair down there. That and your testicles—you know what those are: testicles? Your balls? Testicles is the proper name for them. Anyway, they'll start to grow and will drop eventually too. They haven't dropped already have they?"

I shook my head no because I couldn't speak.

"Didn't think so. When all this is going on you'll see other stuff happening. That's when guys hit their growth spurts and start to grow some whiskers. And your voice'll change. That's pretty miserable. I mean it doesn't hurt, but you sound stupid for a year just talking and then squeaking out of nowhere like a wayward clarinet.

"Now girls, they're going through their own thing. I'm sure you've noticed some girls have been developing—breasts and curves and stuff like that. Maybe you didn't notice. You don't really notice until you start doing your thing and then you can't stop noticing… Let me start this over.

"You know what a 'biological imperative' is? It's what something does because it's just wired to do it. Like salmon. You remember that nature show where the salmon were swimming upstream and getting eaten by bears and all that? You remember how the got to where they were spawned they did their thing and died afterwards? It's kinda like that for people, except we're not lucky enough to die afterwards; we just want to keep doing it.

"So you're gonna want to do the same thing the salmon do—procreate, you know what that means? Have babies? Except guys don't really want to have babies. We're just wired to make babies. Your mom would be better at explaining that kind of thing.

"So, making babies. You know how that works?"

This was the worst day, ever.

"Well, your mom will kill me if I don't tell you anyway. Just buckle in and hang on. Trust me, this isn't going to be any fun for either of us.

"You have a penis and girls have a vagina—you know that already. Well, when a man sees a girl he likes certain biological stuff can happen. His penis can get very stiff and erect. You've probably already seen that to some extent, right?"

I wished I could bury myself in sand in the shore and wait about a hundred years until I was dug up and there would be jetpacks and laser guns and maybe I wouldn't ever remember hearing Dad talking about erect penises.

"Well, that's where you're getting started. Now girls, different stuff happens with them. You know kinda what the vagina is, right? I mean it's kind of a hole. There's more than that, but we're just hitting the basics for now. Well when she sees a guy she likes her vagina gets ready, too. It, uh, well, it starts to lubricate itself. It sounds gross. I don't know, maybe it is gross. It's all gross on some level I guess—"

"OH MY GOD!" this yell comes from the other side of the sand dune. This guy stuck his head up over the dune. He was older; not old like Dad, but older. He had on sunglasses and a boonie hat. He wasn't wearing a shirt and was a deep tan. He had sandy, curly hair and a moustache that was the same.

"FOR CHRISSAKES, *I* DON'T EVEN WANT TO HAVE SEX ANYMORE!" he yelled at us. I didn't think it could get worse and then it did.

"Mind your own business, buddy!" Dad yelled back.

"Seriously, man, you're scarring that kid. You're gonna to have a fuckin' eunuch on your hands after this. Ugh!" The last exclamation was of pure revulsion. He stood up and grabbed his towel and took off down the trail.

"Yeah, just keep moving, you nosy sonuvabitch," Dad yelled.

The guy didn't say anything but flipped us off over his shoulder as he disappeared out of sight. Dad face was bright red and he cast and retrieved three or four times in quick succession, this look on his face like he'd just farted in an elevator and everyone heard it.

After a few minutes I couldn't take it anymore. I asked "Can we go home now?"

Dad didn't say anything for a few seconds before he cast one more time and said, "Yeah, might as well. You got the idea, right?"

I nodded. Then he said, "And if your mom asks, we talked about the clitoris, okay?"

I nodded again. He looked over at me "Do you know what a clitoris is?"

I shook my head no and he sighed. "Ask one of your friends. I'm sure one of them will tell you."

We didn't say anything more for the rest of the trip. Even Dad got tired of country music so he changed it to news, which was even more boring. We finally got back into town and Dad drove by the park. The guys were gone.

"You want me to stop?" Dad asked.

I told him no. This was the suckiest day ever. What made it worse was when we got home, Mom said JJ had actually come by to see if I was coming down. I was so mad.

Now I'm in my room and you told me if I ever got so mad I couldn't take anymore I should tell you about it. You said it would help me feel better. I don't really feel better about it. I just feel tired.

...I don't know. This is probably stupid, but when Dad was talking about having feelings about girls and stuff I thought about Steph, but I also thought about you. I know it's stupid because you're just in dreams and stuff, but when I think about you I kinda get those feelings. I mean, not just the reactions and stuff Dad talked about, but just wishing I could spend time with you. I mean I've never had a girlfriend or anything, but if they acted like you, I'd really like one.

Lyle (age 14)

They came from all over, but they always came. Every 38 days a new one would arrive scrawled in Moses' distinctive handwriting on bits of stationary, old envelopes, notebook paper—whatever was close at the moment. Over the course of thirty-odd years it made for quite a collection. Most varied from banal travelogue to diary-like accounting of people and events to confessions and apologies, usually in that order. A few had been singled out and were kept in a folder at the bottom of a drawer, little sections highlighted or underlined with notes scrawled in the margins...

D,

It's been a long time, I know. I think about you every day. Every day I think about all the things I'm sorry for. I think of all the things I'd apologize for—even the things that weren't my fault, because in the end everything that happened to us was my fault.

I haven't heard any word from home in quite a while. I know it's risky for them so they write when they can. I should be grateful that they write at all. Sometimes I wish they wouldn't —which I know sounds contrary to what I just said. It's just the hope that maybe someday I can come back that seems like a fantasy. I mean, it can't be how it was. Too much has changed. I've changed and the you I remember was so long ago. You can't still be that same person. You might be better, but that's a part of my memory. My memory is where I live now.

This place I'm at now, it's not so bad. I've been a lot worse places. It's nothing special, I mean it's not anywhere anyone would come visit, but it's cheap and under the radar. That's what my life has come to, I guess. Just enough to get by, but nothing that would catch anyone's attention. That's definitely not the same me as you remember—I had such big dreams back then. I was going to see everything; do everything. Now I just wish I could spend a quiet day at home and just see everyone. And not even in that "happy reunion" kind of way, but just watching everyone be themselves. Seeing everyone on their best behavior would just be strange to me. It would seem so disingenuous. Does that sound odd? Maybe it's selfish of me, but I miss the chaos and tension. If that's gone, I don't know if I'd even know what home would be like.

B told me that things were happening that might mean I might be able to come back. He said that at least I might be able to have contact with you and the family. If that's true, then, if nothing else, I could stop all this creeping around and hiding away. It's not a perfect scenario but it's better than how things are now.

You know how I hate writing letters. I never know what all to say or if I've said what I think I've said. You're always in my thoughts. Until the time we can be together again, I remain yours.

-M

(February, 1978. Dearborn, Michigan)

*****

My dearest D,

I'm on the move again. I've hunkered down in some pretty nasty places, but I couldn't take it here anymore. Now I know why B told me to move to East St Louis to begin with—if anyone had found me, they probably would have let me stay there as punishment. There were rats everywhere. There was raw sewage or chemicals (or both!) in standing pools in the backyard.

This is a strange place. There's so much disparity between the wealthy and the poor here. Not that I haven't seen that kind of thing before, but I have to admit that back home I was sheltered from much of this—although I have a hard time believing things were this bad.

There was a little boy who lived down the hall from me in my old apartment building. He had the biggest brown eyes and a big wide smile. He'd lived there with his mother all his life. His mother said he wasn't "quite right" which I guess was mainly her way of saying he was slow. He'd have seizures and collapse in the hallway. It was from all the chemicals. I don't know if it was from when his mother was pregnant or from all the shit that was around. The tap water smells. I'd taken to mainly drinking beer in hopes of limiting my exposure. But Myron—that was his name—he had to drink the water.

I came back one night last week from gigging at a club and she was there, in the hallway, Myron in her arms. She was rocking him back and forth quietly singing to him. His eyes were rolled back in his head and he was all rigid. She didn't act like she knew I was there. She just brushed his forehead and cleaned the vomit from the corner of his mouth. She was singing this song that I used to always hear on the radio, "You Keep Me Hangin' On."

I used to like that song but now every time I hear it all I see is her rocking Myron in that hallway with cockroaches scurrying around across the floor and the smell of rotting garbage and shit wafting through the broken fire escape window.

The words haunt me. I don't think she meant the words; I think she was just singing something she liked or maybe something he liked in order to soothe him. I went into my room but I could still hear her raspy whisper singing through the walls. Hearing the chorus gives me a sick, empty feeling in my stomach even now.

I know B will be upset that I left but I couldn't take it anymore. I sent him a message the usual way, but it's hard to tell what he actually gets. I sent another one just to be safe. I packed my rucksack with the few things I could carry and went down and bought a bus ticket west. I had a bit of money saved up but I took most of it and put it in an envelope and slid it under Myron's mother's door. I have a modest stipend to live on thanks to my father so I knew I'd be ok. She needed it more than I did, anyway.

This is such a unsettling place. I've never been to a place to vast and beautiful in one minute and the next so full of misery and filth. B chose this place well. It's hard to pick out something that doesn't fit here because from moment to moment what's normal seems to change.

I'm writing you from a bus. There's a big Seminole guy in the seat next to me, snoring loudly. His name is Norm. He's on his way to live with his sister in Oklahoma City. I'm not sure where I'm going, but I have a knack of catching on. Maybe some time with Norm and his people would be a nice diversion. From what he says no one much cares about what goes on where he's going. At least B would approve of that.

Do you remember our first night together? I watched you sleeping next to me. I imagined how it would be to wake up to that every day for the rest of my life. That was the first time with anyone that that idea didn't scare me. I'm sorry for everything that's happened. I want you to know that you're still the one who I want to wake up next to. Back then I was willing to commit in spite of the fact I thought it meant I'd be limited or restrained. I was so stupid then.

I want to be with you now because I realize that when I was with you I was at my best. You were the best part of me. It's the hope that we might be able to be together again that keeps me going here. I guess I miss home and realized that home isn't all the things I had, all the so-called "friends" or any of it. You were home.

They say you can't go home again. I hope they're wrong.

I live in hope to see you again.

-M

(August, 1986, outside of St Louis, Missouri)

*****

It took a while before I was able to contact B again. I'm sure it feels like you haven't heard from me in a long time. That's my fault—I should start this over.

Oklahoma was nice. Hotter than I would have liked, but Norm and his kin were good to me. I didn't really spend much time with Norm after the first couple months. He had a cousin named Alton that I hit it off with. He worked construction most of the year. He had a place his aunt left him when she died—nothing special, just a little two bedroom house. It was probably smaller than our pool house back home, but I've learned to appreciate having a space of my own, regardless of size.

Hard to believe we shared that place nearly ten years. I ended up being the "clean one"—I can imagine you laughing at that. I did the dishes and the vacuuming and such. Alton did most of the cooking and fixing of stuff that came up. We had a nice arrangement, really. He'd be up and out early when he worked and I'd do my thing, then I'd head out to the club or to practice, depending on whether I was playing with a band at the moment so we might both be around at dinner but that was usually about it.

There were times where we'd just hang out and watch TV in the evening if neither of us was busy. I really hadn't had many "friends" since I got here. B always discouraged it since he thought it could lead to "lapses" on my part or awkward questions. Maybe he was right, but Alton never really seemed to be too interested in where I came from as long as I paid my part of the bills on time. In fact, neither of really asked each other about our pasts. He knew me through Norm and that was good enough. I suppose it was the same for me. The other stuff didn't really matter—we weren't really concerned about stuff that wasn't immediate. He did his thing; I did mine and it worked.

I was playing with a bunch of guys here. They were good, real good. I played a bunch of different things, but settled into the keyboard/piano. Playing with them made me a lot better at what I was doing. You'd be surprised, I think. You always said you thought I was a good musician, but I knew better. I always liked that about you—you liked what I did just because I did it. But truthfully, to be really good I needed more discipline.

I guess all the free time and having to lie low helped teach me the discipline. As I get older I suppose it's become less about what I've done and more about what I've cared to get better at. I worry sometimes that you'll be disappointed that I'm not the young, hot-headed boy you remember. I fear that instead of someone you were excited by as I jumped from thing to thing, party to party, endeavor to endeavor, you'll find an old, dull, uninspired barfly with too many miles, too many memories and not enough of what you loved to make the rest of it seem worthwhile.

I guess I don't think I've made the most of my time. I could've made myself even better for you, but I think I haven't completely let you down, either. I've learned how to be responsible and independent in ways that I don't think I would have if I'd stayed living the life of privilege that I had when I was younger. I've learned a kindness and respect for others that I didn't have when you knew me. Remember when we spent the summer at my grandmother's summer home and how I treated the groundskeeper? Or the cleaning lady? Or the cook? I was horrible to all of them—you got so angry with me you threatened to leave, remember? I resented you for a long time for that. I think you could tell I stopped yelling at them because I thought you were watching me. I remember the contempt I had for all of them—like they were beneath me. If I could go back I would punch myself in the dick for that. I was so stupid and arrogant back then.

I wish I could have had some of the perspective then that I do now. I can't even remember the housekeeper's name and she was such a sweet person. I remember hearing her talk about her family and where she came from and how she'd come to work for my grandmother and wishing that she'd just shut up. Now I wish I'd listened to those stories. I wish I knew more about the people who were around me. There were so many stories; so much wisdom just there for the asking, but I thought I knew better because I was born with wealth and people respected my name. I acted as if I'd earned that respect instead of just riding its coattails into privilege and status.

I guess learning humility the hard way hasn't been an easy task. Hopefully you've seen some of that through my letters. There's been so much to tell, but I have to stick to the basics because B says it's hard to get things to you. I have boxes full of notes and journals full of letters I've written to you. I dream that someday I'll be able to give them to you so you can see how I became the way I am. Maybe I hope that if you read them you'll be able to recognize the person I am at the end instead of just seeing a stranger. That's my hope, anyway.

Look at me, I got going and lost what I was doing. The group I was playing with started getting noticed. They actually started getting some proper session work and I knew I had to quit. B can be overly cautious at times, but even I knew going any further with it would've been a bad idea. I managed to get myself kicked out or fired—not sure which fit best. I thought it would be better for them that way—they really were a great bunch of guys, but I didn't want them to be calling later if something came up. It was the best way to have a clean break. No muss, no fuss.

They found another piano player and did great. I even heard them on the radio a while back. It was some generic country starlet doing the singing but it was the guys who were playing behind her. I was proud of them. Maybe even a little jealous. But in the end, being a professional musician and getting to hobnob with famous performers didn't even hold a candle to the prospect of getting back to you.

Anyway, after I left the band stuff seemed to stall out. I still played around some, but nothing regular. Other groups approached me, but I thought it would be best to just keep an extra low profile for a while. After all that though, it just wasn't the same. It really felt like I was just going through the motions. It's not like me and Alton ever fought or didn't get along, but we were more apathetic about each other as time went on. I guess I'd been settled so long that I wondered if I ever could get the itch, but I got it hard.

It felt like it even happened overnight, but I went through my stuff and figured what I needed to take with me and what I could throw or give away. I paid Alton for a couple month's worth of bills (even though he didn't ask) and told him I was moving on. He seemed a little surprised, I suppose but didn't argue. He helped me get my stuff together and then took me out for a drink. I kind of thought it might be a wild night but it was really quiet. Just a quiet little place and we talked a little. He asked where I was going and I told him somewhere further west. We talked a little about people we knew and what he was thinking of doing with me leaving. "I dunno, maybe get a girl and have her move in," he deadpanned.

In the end it was an appropriate way for things to end, I think.

I drifted around for a while but finally ended up here. It's kind of a cool neighborhood called Silver Lake. Not too clean, not too dirty. I got a little place and have gotten settled. Maybe things are going in my favor finally. It wasn't a month after I moved away that some crazy fucker blew up a federal building in Oklahoma City. I didn't live directly in Oklahoma City, but there were enough investigators poking around for suspects that I'm glad I wasn't around just in case they ran across me. That sounds terrible. Lots of people died in that, but there wasn't anything I could do about it. I guess it's natural to feel relief when you weren't affected horribly by something like that.

B's said that things are settling down there. It's starting to sound more like I might be able to just come back. Maybe that's what I wanted to hear, though. I asked him about you but he didn't say much. I guess I hope that means everything is just normal and you're ok. If B is right maybe I'll be able to ask you myself soon. Until then, I remain always faithfully yours,

-M
(January, 1996, Los Angeles, California)

*****

B told me everything. He told me how you've been reporting my whereabouts to the authorities—or at least as near as you can. B at least was crafty enough to leave out some details. He's always looked out for me, even when I was too foolish to make it easy for him.

I don't know if you were forced into helping them or not. It doesn't matter anyway. I think I've found something that can take it all back. If I'm right none of this even has to happen.

Don't be afraid. Everything they told us was a lie. I'll make it right and then we can live the life we were meant to. Everything will be the way it was always supposed to be.

-M
(August 21, 2008, Topeka, Kansas)

*****

Her fingers ran through his hair slowly.

"You're getting too old for this," she whispered.

Lyle stretched out against her. He readjusted his head so he was lying against her breasts. She felt so warm.

"How am I too old?"

A flash of discomfort crossed her face. "You're changing. There are things that are about to happen—"

"Are you giving me 'the talk'? Didn't you think my dad scarred me enough with that already?"

"No, well, that's part of it, but there's more."

Lyle sat up to face her.

"What more is there?"

"It doesn't matter. You'll know soon enough. But beside that, I can't control things here anymore."

Lyle moved his hand to her arm and pulled her a closer to him. "What do you mean, 'control things'? Nothing happens here that you don't want to happen."

Lyle ran his hand up to her shoulder and down the front of her chest, tracing the curve of her breast. Their eyes met. She didn't look angry or upset. He had never seen that look from her before.

"Problem is that maybe there are things we both want to happen, but shouldn't," she closed her eyes as he slipped his hand inside her shirt. "When you were younger I didn't have to worry about this. I could show you what I wanted you to see and you'd follow."

Lyle leaned in and kissed her neck. "And now?"

She arched her back and pulled his head to her chest. "And now… now is when we can't go back again."

"I don't even know your name, you know that?" he mumbled as he kept kissing down her chest. He fumbled around the edge of the fabric of her blouse and bra. After a few seconds of pawing she gently pushed him back with a kiss to his forehead. She kept his gaze locked with hers as she unbuttoned and deftly removed and folded it. She slipped her bra off, exposing her breasts to Lyle. Her look was somewhere between uneasy self-consciousness and a singular directness. She moved to him, guiding his hand to her breast, her erect nipple teasing at the juncture of his thumb and forefinger. She placed his other hand on her shoulder, which initially seemed odd to him. But she scooted closer to him and deftly unbuttoned his pants, with his hands out of the way she was able to guide the action.

He felt his body react. He'd thought of her like this, but nothing had ever happened. He'd had sex dreams before but this one was so much more realistic—as far as he knew at least. He'd only kissed a girl twice up until then, and other than what he'd seen on late night cable and the odd porno clip he didn't *really* know what he was doing. He let out an audible groan as she grasped him.

"Remember this. If there's anything you should remember it's that this is what I want to do. You're the one I want to do it with. If things were the way they were supposed to be, we would have already been together like this, but I wouldn't be old like I am now. It would have been in the back of your dad's car and it would have been awkward and uncomfortable and over too soon and I would always remember it as one of the greatest moments of my life. But here, this will have to do. I'm sorry. I'm sorry that you'll just have to remember this, but hang on to it. I will come back to you when the time is right. Do you understand?"

Lyle's vision blurred at the sound of her voice and the sensation of her firm grasp on him. She placed her hand on his cheek to bring his attention back. "Are you with me?"

Lyle blinked a couple times and was aware she was addressing him. He nodded. "Do you understand what I said?" Another nod. She had a look of mild disappointment but gave a little smile. "That will have to do." She gently pushed him back and kissed him softly. "Call me Nicola," she whispered as she lowered her head and took him into her mouth.

*****

They pulled me out of 4th hour composition. I didn't know what was going on. I didn't think I'd done anything wrong, but you never can know for sure. They told me to report to the principal's office. The secretary gave me a weird, wide-eyed look when I came in. She called the office. She was whispering down the phone. Sounded like she said something like "He's here," and then something else I couldn't make out. She didn't even have a chance to say anything when the principal's door swung open and Mr. Lazlo came out. He usually has one of those fake smiles all the time and says stuff like "Hey there champ," or "How you doing, man?" like he's trying to fit in with the kids.

When he opened the door he had a fake-looking somber face. "Come on in, son," he tells me. As I walked in Mrs. Sanchez, the guidance counselor was sitting in the corner. I had no idea what was going on, but I hadn't even heard of anything like that happening before.

"You should take a seat," Mr. Lazlo said with a fake-sounding somber voice. He half sat on his desk a couple feet from me, crossed his arm and looked extra fake-somber. Mrs. Sanchez leaned forward in her chair putting her hand on my knee.

"Lyle, I have some hard news for you." She looked up at Mr. Lazlo and Mr. Lazlo nodded back with extra fake-somber approval. "Your father, well, he had a heart attack—a big one."

I must have sounded so stupid because the first thing I said was, "So am I supposed to walk home today, then?"

Mrs. Sanchez's eyes got all teary and then I realized it was something much worse. "I'm sorry, Lyle. Your father passed away."

"Passed away"? That's just a stupid phrase. He didn't blow off in the wind or something. He was a cold pile of meat waiting to go to the funeral home. "Passed away" makes it sound like he's gone. He's not gone. He's everywhere like a picture negative: there's this space that's all backwards and wrong that's shaped exactly like him.

"You need to be strong for your mother, son," Mr. Lazlo said as if that meant something or made a difference.

"Mrs. Oronofski is coming to pick you up. She'll take you to the hospital to be with your mother," Mrs. Sanchez said. Mrs. Oronofski is the old lady next door. Mom doesn't even like her. She always says that she's gossipy and horrible but that's who they sent to get me.

And then it all hit me at once and I couldn't stop crying. I didn't want to cry, but it just poured out. It didn't make me feel better, but I just couldn't stop.

"You have someone you'd like to get your things? A girlfriend or someone?" Mr. Lazlo asked. I could barely see but Mrs. Sanchez gestured or mouthed something to him and he said, "Nevermind, I'll get your things." He rocked disinterestedly for another few seconds while I was bawling like a baby and then looked like he just couldn't take looking fake sad anymore. "You two can have my office as long as you need. I'll grab your things out of your locker and leave them at the secretary's desk, ok? We're all very sorry about your loss, champ. You take the time you need and we'll talk about getting caught up when you get back."

He left and then it was just me and Mrs. Sanchez. She didn't say anything, but kept her hand on my shoulder and rubbed it. I could tell she was crying a little too which only made me feel worse.

I don't know how long we were in there. Felt like forever but then there was a little knock at the door and the secretary was holding out my jacket and backpack. "His ride is here," she whispered to Mrs. Sanchez.

Mrs. Oronofski was by the secretary's desk. "Oh you poor dear," she said in this loud, overly sobby voice. She grabbed me and gave me a big hug and tried to pull my head to her shoulder. She smelled like old lady perfume and pee.

She drove me to the hospital to pick up mom. She had the religious radio station on and turned way up. I knew she was doing it to show off. It wasn't even the religious music that sounded like bad Top 40 music, but it was hymns and shit. She even started singing along. "So I'll cherish the old rugged cross 'til my trophies at last I lay down. I will cling to the old rugged cross and exchange it some day for a crown."

It was barely singing. It was a half yell/half warble. It was a yarble. It's the sound I imagine a dying manatee might make.

She pulled up to the front of the hospital. I started to get out and she grabbed my arm and said, "Your mother will be out in a minute. No need for you to get out."

I felt offended. I should have been there. I should have been there before it was just to see a body but at the very least Mrs. Fucking Oronofski shouldn't be the one to tell me I can't go in. I thought about just going in. She wouldn't have been able to stop me but instead I just sat there with this sick, twisting feeling in my stomach.

"Here she comes, you get in the back now," she barked at me. And that was it; I got out and into the back. Mom didn't even say anything to me. Then again she didn't really have the opportunity because as soon as she was in earshot Mrs. Oronofski she started crying and saying "You poor dear," over and over again. The entire ride home she wouldn't shut up, talking about how Dad's with Jesus now and how there's always a purpose behind things and shit like that.

We got home and I got out of the car before she'd even turned off the ignition. The door was locked so I had to wait while Mom finished listening to Mrs. Oronofski. She finally came to the door with Mrs. Oronofski still calling out to her, "You let me know if there's anything you need, dear. You call me anytime. I'm right next door."

Mom unlocked the door without acknowledging her and we both tried to fit through the door at the same time—like we were both trying to hide. I know that's how it felt for me—I just wanted to be invisible so the Mr. Lazlo's and Mrs. Oronofski's of the world couldn't bother me.

The phone was ringing when walked in. Normally someone would've rushed to answer it, but we both just stood there listening to it, but not hearing it. I took my jacket off and dropped it and my backpack by the entry closet and took a step down the hall when Mom grabbed me. She hugged me, but not like she'd ever hugged me before. It was like she was hugging me like I was an adult, not her kid. At that moment I felt more alone than I ever had before in my life. It felt like the idea that Mom and Dad would be there to help make sense of everything or just be present was gone. She didn't feel like Mom anymore. She was a stranger. We were a couple of strangers who had to share a house and we didn't even know if we liked each other. We just knew that someone was missing.

She looked at me for a second. Her eyes were all red and swollen with tears. Then she let go and walked into the kitchen. On the way down the hallway she took the phone off the hook without answering it. I could hear a distant chirping of a confused caller saying "Hello? Hello?" She sat at the kitchen table, her arms crossed across the surface, and buried her head in them like she was trying to rest. I watched her for a minute. She was breathing deeply but quietly. She wasn't crying, or at least she wasn't sobbing. She just sat there silently, head resting on the table. I heard the abandoned caller hang up and a busy signal sounded.

I went to my room and laid on the bed for a while. I may have dozed off a little but I don't think so. Now I'm writing you.

I don't know why I keep dreaming about you. It's always you, since I was a little kid. You don't even exist—I mean you *can't* exist. After years of dreaming about you last night you

72

come to me for the first time in forever and you give me a blowjob. But you also say everything's going to change and I won't see you anymore. Did I know this was going to happen? Was I supposed to do something? That's the worst part—I should've known.

I don't even know why I'm writing this. I just hope that was the last time I'll ever dream of you because if you are real, then you let this happen and I'll never forgive you. And if you're not, then it's my fault and that's even worse.

I'm such an idiot writing to an imaginary girl. Such a fucking idiot.

(Lyle, age 16, March 4th, 1997)

*****

It had been another drive-thru dinner night. The double cheeseburger and fries were sitting in the bottom of Lyle's gut like ten pound weight. He'd gone through his ritual channel surfing and had moved on to his pre-bedtime masturbation session.

His mind had been wandering. No particular fantasy or piece of television eye candy had really stood out. He lost himself in thought while absent mindedly continuing to stimulate himself. He let his mind wander over the usual images and thoughts: Jeannine, the girl from the body wash commercial and Margot Kidder ("Amityville Horror"-era) but nothing caught his interest.

The dream he had the night before his father died sprung into his mind. He wasn't sure why, but he started thinking about it. At first it was just a curiosity but the longer he thought about it the more details came back to him and the more he got into it. He remembered her reddish hair in his fingers, the smoothness of her skin, the feel of her breath against his stomach. But her face, he couldn't quite remember her face. And then he saw it.

Nicola.

It had to have been a coincidence—a recent memory being superimposed over an old one. It didn't matter because it was doing the trick and he could feel his body responding quickly and intensely to the thought. The more he thought of it, the more it seemed like it had to be Nicola and the more he envisioned it being her, the more he wanted it to have been her.

His impending orgasm was building and his head was exploding with memories from his childhood dreams now with a familiar face. He was going to cum at any second. He repositioned himself on the easy chair and as he shifted he opened his eyes for a second.

"Oh shit!"

Down the hallway, in the dark bathroom there was a small girl staring at him from the mirror. It startled him. He wasn't sure what could be reflecting. He squinted trying to make out something more specific—it had to be a towel or something benign that he hadn't noticed before. The harder he looked he saw that it was the outline of a girl, but to reflect directly back at him, it would've been somewhere in front of him. It was some sort of optical illusion or trick of the light.

And then in an instant she was standing in the hallway about ten feet from him—grey and with a dirt-stained face that accompanied her torn and dirty dress. She whispered "It's cold."

Lyle screamed like a girl.

Part III: Hope's Ghost

If you were to look carefully through a copy of the Sun from August 20th, 1885 there was a very short article about a missing girl from Bethel Township. It said she had gone missing on the 9th of that month without a trace and locals had been searching the area. Vagrants or miscreants were being rounded up and questioned, but as of writing, no information on the girls' whereabouts had been obtained.

The fact of the matter was, and even is today, that there are people who just vanish. On August 9th, 1885, Hope Fruehauf, age 6, disappeared from her family's farmstead. Her family searched everywhere. Neighbors and friends formed search parties; tracking dogs were brought in but all their work was for naught.

Her mother always believed she would come back someday. Even in her last years would tell her great-grandchildren about their great-aunt Hope and how she would come and surprise them all someday soon by appearing with tales of adventure and a beautiful family of her own. She said how that would be the happiest day of her life: to see her family together again.

That day never came and she died of pneumonia in 1938.

Hope's disappearance wasn't the first day of a great adventure as her mother had hoped, but it also wasn't a horrible, grisly end at the hands of a stranger or animal. Her mother clung to the former out of fear of the latter. The truth was much simpler and, had anyone known, would have prompted a sense of melancholy in those who had heard.

Hope was the third of what was then five children. She hadn't been given much responsibility with the youngest two but she had been old enough to play on her own without the supervision of one of her older brothers.

The day had been unremarkable at the outset. Hope ventured out to her secret special spot after breakfast. She ran through the rows of corn, listening to the leaves rattle and crackle like the crashing of a distant waterfall as she weaved between them. The corn ended abruptly into a narrow strip of long grass. She pushed through it to the shade of the trees beyond. The woods surrounded a coulee and a narrow creek that had almost dried up.

Trees lined the upper ridge of the coulee. An old, rotted trunk had fallen and an old abandoned badger's den was nestled behind it. Over the years other animals had used it and, through weather and time, the opening was the perfect size for Hope to crawl inside. She'd dug it out and it extended back nearly five feet from the entrance.

She played up and down the coulee, climbing on the trees and following animal tracks down by the stream as far as she could. As the day wore on, it became increasingly hot and muggy and she sought refuge in her hideaway. She found a stick and spent some time burrowing in the back of the cave.

When she tired of that she played house, complete with some wild rhubarb leaves for plates, grass for food and sticks for utensils.

"Hope. You down here?" came a call from outside. She peered out from her hole and saw her oldest brother, Isaiah, walking along the creek. "Hope, you better get back up home. Ma says she wants you up there right away," he yelled.

Hope watched him, silently loving that he had no idea that she was there. Isaiah wasn't even looking to see her, he was just repeating the message he'd been given. "You'll get a whipping if you don't hurry up," he called as he swung a stick at the tall grass. After a few minutes he headed back towards the house. Went he got to the top of the ridge he paused and shrugged to someone further off. "She's not down here… I don't know. Did you check the barn? She goes there sometimes…" and then he was gone.

She liked having a secret. It was her quiet place where there were no big brothers, no younger siblings, no parents to tell her what to do. She could just hide away and keep all her moments to herself there. After she was sure Isaiah was gone she played a little longer but grew tired. She made her way to the back of the den. It was a snug fit but she was able to curl up and rest.

She awoke to a rumble of thunder. She crawled out of the burrow and saw that everything had become an ominous smoky brownish-grey. The air was getting heavier and the breeze had picked up, but instead of being warm or cool, it was both—the wind would blow warm and then abruptly slap cool across her face and arms. She didn't know how long she'd slept, but it was still afternoon—the light, such as it was, was dark because of the clouds but the sun wasn't setting. There was a brilliant flash and immediately a massive crack. She'd never seen or heard lightning and thunder that close. Without so much as a slight sprinkle as a warning suddenly the rain came down in a torrent.

Hope wanted to be brave and not be afraid of the wind and the thunder. Isaiah would tease her when she'd try and snuggle closer to one of them at night during a storm. She retreated back into her hole as the rain pounded down and the wind whipped the trees so hard they crackled and snapped like kindling in the fireplace. The walls of the den were getting wet; she thought that was a little odd. She wondered how much longer it would keep raining. She was sure she'd be in trouble now, especially since her dress was getting muddy. From the back of cave she could see just above the fallen tree. It looked as if might actually be subsiding a—

Weight, darkness and a struggle for air were the last things Hope would remember before the Windy Place.

The cave had collapsed. For all those years and all those hopes and dreams that her mother had, Hope had never left the farm. A large white ash tree sprouted over her final resting place. It was as if the earth offered it as a makeshift marker to remember that she had once been there—running through the fields and dancing beneath the trees in the coulee.

Now she was in the Windy Place. That's what she called it, at least. She was there. She remembered trying to claw through the darkness and then she was there. It wasn't like waking up, or that she fell asleep first, she went from one place to the other in an instant.

It was the coulee she'd been playing in before, but now everything was gray—the sky, the ground, most of the objects. If she could see any colors in the objects it was just a hint, a suggestion of a color. Everything appeared to be draped in a heavy fog, but if she looked at anything closely they would change from moment to moment. They were usually subtle changes: cracks would appear or disappear; things would grow or shrink a little as she looked at them. It reminded her of the thickest fog she'd ever seen where only vague shapes would be recognizable with 20 feet or so and even standing next to them they seemed nebulous and out of focus. And there was the sound—a constant, dull roaring like a gale was blowing somewhere in the distance. Hope only felt the slightest of breezes for the most part, but it sounded like at any second the wind could whip up everything around her and blow it away.

She was standing by a large white ash tree above the spot where her hiding place had been. The tree was the one thing that seemed solid and unchanging. The roaring wind actually became softer the closer she came to the tree and once she touched it, there was no noise at all. The tree itself felt slightly warm. It was the only sensation she had. She could feel a slight breeze but it was neither cool nor warm.

Time didn't seem to matter there. She'd see shadows in the distance: some she recognized, some she didn't, some looked like they were in the past and others appeared to be somewhere in the future. There didn't seem to be any rhyme or reason to which ones she saw, they just seemed to tumble out from the gray haze and disappear back into it.

She wandered into the gray expanse. Ghostly images rose and fell but nothing near her. Then she saw the form of a house appear before her. She walked towards it and as she got closer the sound of wind got louder and louder. As she came within ten feet of the house, the light breeze she'd felt began to pick up. She walked closer and with each step the noise became louder and the more the wind's intensity grew. Within three feet Hope's hair was whipping around her face and her dress was flapping around wildly. The wind didn't seem to be coming from any specific place, but enveloped her like a whirlwind.

She was close enough that she was able to look through the windows. Inside there were different shadows moving back and forth but they were flashes of activity and didn't seem to be any specific thing or person. The wind got the better of her and she stumbled backwards and the wind subsided in proportion to the distance she'd fallen from the house. She remembered how the wind scared her, but she wasn't afraid anymore, just curious. She moved towards the house again and the wind swirled around her violently. It was hard to see with her hair being twisted around her head and face. She squinted to keep the wind out of her eyes but the closer she got the stronger the wind became. Her eyes were nearly closed and she reached forward towards the house and then —

She could feel the wood under her hand. It was solid, but didn't feel warm like the tree had. There was still some grey around but there was a natural light that hadn't been there before. Everything was silent; there were no shadows darting about, no blustering wind. It was just her and the house.

She walked along the outside of the house until she came to the front door. The door sat ajar and she slipped inside. She touched the wall and suddenly could see everything—when the house was built, people buzzing around, a small fire in the kitchen, the inside being gutted and remodeled and torn down. It wasn't linear, though, she could see them all at once and in no particular order. She reached out and touched a scene during the remodeling and suddenly she was there. It was a specific time and she was in that moment. She looked around the house. It was daytime and the sun was shining. She could hear birds outside and could see other houses along a street outside the window. She wasn't sure where the house was. It didn't seem to be the same area by the tree, but she couldn't tell for certain.

From the kitchen she heard a voice and some music. She walked towards the sound and there was a small black box with a metallic knob on its side sitting on the kitchen counter. The voice and music were coming from inside the box. As she approached it, the sound started getting fuzzier and crackled and popped. She touched it and, just like the house, was able to see everything about it. She could see it being assembled by people far away, purchased from a store, being taken by a family on trips and breaking and being thrown away and sitting in a giant pile of trash that had been buried. Again, she saw all these things at once but was able to piece together an order of sorts.

She focused on a day at the beach and suddenly she was there, right behind a girl who looked to be a few years older than her. She was wearing less than bloomers as she laughed and ran. Hope didn't feel shocked by her manner of dress—since she'd entered the Windy Place she realized things were what they were. There were things that were sad and things that were happy but there was nothing to be angry about.

Nevertheless, it was still very alien. She followed and observed the girl for a while and learned about the radio, cars, television and telephones. She never got to directly interact with those objects—she wasn't able to choose what to watch or listen to, call anyone or decide where to go. In that regard, while the technology seemed nearly magical, it didn't seem like any more than incidental to the people using it. She felt no particular connection to it and it all seemed fanciful. She was an observer and the particulars didn't seem to matter all that much.

She jumped from object to object, person to person. She saw months and years and travelled from coast to coast time and again. There were times where she couldn't tell exactly where or when she was. When it became too much or she just became disinterested she'd release the object and let it move away. The color and activity followed them like they were a lantern in the darkness and when released they'd drift off and the sound of wind and the color grey would slowly envelop her. The objects and people around her would fade and slowly familiar shapes and outlines would appear and the great white ash would appear as a dark shadow in the distance.

She called the shadows and phantoms, "Memories". It felt to her as if when she came in contact with them she was seeing someone else's memories. They didn't seem like ghosts since she couldn't interact with them, and they weren't scary at all like the ghosts her brothers told her about when it was storming at night and she couldn't sleep.

She curled up in a cleft in the roots of the tree, enjoying the sensation of warmth and the stillness. There was no sleep in the Windy Place, but she could feel her focus and sense of place drifting away. It wasn't sleeping so much as ceding the will to be aware. She felt the sensation in her skin slowly expand and spread across the tree. She could feel it creeping out, running into rivulets and hardening into the bark. She wasn't being consumed or eaten—it wasn't painful. Instead she was melding with the warmth and quiet. She could feel it spreading across her back and over her shoulders. Tree bark always seemed so barren and dry when she'd looked at it, but as she felt it overtake her it actually tickled a little as it split and dried in a protective husk. The further inward she was pulled the warmer it felt. It wasn't hot or stuffy like the summers she remembered back on the farm. It reminded her of the quilt her grandmother had made her on cold winter nights—it was just right and felt familiar. It was like home.

She was almost gone, her face barely jutting out from the trunk, covered in bark. Her arms and torso had melded into the trunk on the tree and her legs stretched out and started to take to the ground like roots.

A rumble of distant thunder interrupted the silence. Hope opened her eyes and in the distance, through the shapeless grey mist she saw a glowing orange ball. In her time in the Windy Place there hadn't been a direct source of light from anywhere, it just came from everywhere dimly. There was no color anywhere, either, just shapes, until she got very near an object, which made the glowing orb seem all the more out of place. There was another loud grumble far off and the leaves of the ash rustled as if a sudden breeze had whipped through the branches.

It was foreign. The Windy Place behaved a certain way and the glowing ball was not from there. Hope stood, the bark cracking and falling from her body. She headed towards the ball, leaving the warmth and safety of the tree behind her. She was curious about what it was; it was clear to her that it shouldn't be there and it felt as if there would be consequences if it remained.

The ball weaved and danced, blinking out and then reappearing a short distance away. As she approached it there was the smell of lightning on the wind. Unlike most of the objects it moved independently, sometimes nearer, sometimes further away and it didn't have a clear heading. The Memories would rise and fade in a linear way and didn't seem to interact with each other. They'd pass through each other as if the other didn't exist. But as she closed in on the ball it seemed to cause ripples and distortions with the things it came in contact with. When she'd reach out to the tattered remnants of the Memories, they'd pass through her fingers without so much as breeze.

Hope hadn't felt fear or anxiety since she arrived in the Windy Place, but the orange light gave her a tight, sick feeling in her stomach. She didn't know why she reacted to it other than it seemed out of place, unnatural. She couldn't tell if the Memories it breezed through were being destroyed or just interrupted. It just made her feel uneasy. She moved towards it deliberately, doing her best to swallow the ill-at-ease feeling to discover what was going on.

The light grew in intensity as she got closer as did the wind and the smell of electricity. She held her hands in front of her face, trying to peek through her fingers in order to see. It became almost blinding but just as she was about to touch it, she saw something. There was a dark globular form that the ball seemed tethered to. That was what the ball was following, it wasn't the light itself moving about aimlessly. The light seemed to have tendril-like appendages that snaked out from it and were wrapped around the dark form, keeping it close. She reached out and heard a crackling like thunder, the wind and the light making it impossible to see. She felt it graze her fingertips and…

She was in a bedroom. It was nighttime and there was hardly a sound. In the bed was a little boy—maybe three or four years old—asleep. She didn't know where she was. It seemed like the future but she couldn't tell if it was further than the girl and the radio. Nothing seemed strange at first, but then she saw a glow of light on the boy's forehead. She looked out the window there was no moon and no other lights. What appeared to be a stray moonbeam actually didn't seem to have an actual source. She stared at it and then suddenly a small, translucent orange-ish blob rose from the spot on his forehead. Hope took a step back into the corner of the room. The blob hovered over his head for a moment and then moved to the top of his head and came to rest on the pillow.

Hope didn't like the feeling she was getting about the whole situation and she tried to release the ball and return to the ash. She felt a searing pain in her hand and there was a violent flash of light and then she was at a tree. But it wasn't *her* tree. There was a coulee, but it wasn't as deep and there was a train track and a road running alongside it. There were more trees around than from the area she was accustomed to. Nothing was gray. It wasn't the Windy Place; she'd just appeared to another place in the regular world. She tried to will herself away from the orange ball again, and again there was a burning pain in her hand, blinding light, the whirlwind and the smell of burning air and she found herself next to the same tree, but now it was during the day. She couldn't tell if hours, days or years had passed.

When she touched objects, there was no wind and she couldn't see their histories. She could interact with objects in a limited way now—there was a leaf twirling toward the ground from the high branches of a tree and when she reached for it, it bounced as if buffeted by a small gust of wind. She focused all of her energy and concentration on a twig on the ground and was able to lift it a couple inches off the ground on one end.

For the first time since she'd found herself in the Windy Place, Hope felt very lonely. Emotion felt so alien to her. In the Windy Place there was no sadness or regret, but here there was so much uncertainty. It was stirring up so much inside her and she couldn't understand it. She didn't know where she was or why she was there. She didn't know where to find the orange light, or if she should try and find it. Her tree was nowhere to be found and there was no other place she felt like she belonged. She wanted to go to her mother and father and her siblings. She wanted to go to the Windy Place. She wanted to be with her tree. The feeling in her stomach intensified and twisted and settled. She remembered what feeling scared felt like. She curled up at the base of the tree and tried to wish her way back to the Windy Place.

Other than trying to return home, the only way now to pass time was just to wait. She learned early on that trying to separate herself from the orange ball like she did with normal objects would bump her ahead in time, but never a set amount. Sometimes it would be months, but normally it would be a day or two. She was forced to exist alongside the regular world, but was unable to meaningfully interact with it. Most days she chose to sit at the tree and wait for the hours to pass.

She wasn't able to stay detached for long. There was so much coming and going in the world, even sitting by her tree. The noise was incessant and gnawed at her until she couldn't take it any more—she had to get up and explore. She'd watch the trains come and go. She wandered the streets a little but the further away she got from the tree the more tired she became to the point where she'd collapse and have to slowly crawl back, or go through the pain of releasing and returning to the tree.

Through the woods, across a short field were some houses. She'd wandered by them a number of times. There was nothing particularly interesting about them—families bustling to and from jobs and schools. There were some housewives, retirees, shut-ins and the odd malingerer. One of the shut-ins was an old lady named Meredith. Her husband, Merle, had died several years before and she was alone. She had three children, all boys. They'd call regularly but they didn't visit often. Her friends would call her "Bitty" although Hope never learned why. When Hope wasn't at her tree she'd often stay near her.

In the evenings, Bitty would often sit at the dining room table with large photo albums and page through them. "There go Merle and Bitty," she'd say to herself sometimes when one of the pictures reminded her of a particularly happy memory.

Bitty didn't do much for social activities. She had some ladies over once a month for coffee. She'd go out to the shops once a week and would tend to her flowers as best she could.

Aside from that she'd read paperbacks she bought at garage sales and would write letters. People didn't write letters enough anymore, she'd say to Hope. There were so many things you could do to show what you were thinking—if you just sent a card it could be a nice little pick-me-up. If it was a smaller envelope on stationary it could feel more personal and intimate. If you added a touch of perfume it could almost feel like you were there when they read it, she'd say.

Bitty spoke to Hope, but she didn't really know about Hope. Bitty would talk to "her spirits." She believed spirits and angels and whatnot were around her all the time so she spoke to them. Hope didn't see anyone else besides herself and Bitty there, but Bitty still talked as if there were always a few people around. It wasn't exactly personal, but a part of Hope liked feeling acknowledged, even if it was just dumb luck.

The one spirit that Bitty believed wasn't there was Merle. Before she'd go to sleep she'd always whisper, "My spirits and my angels, you fly away to Merle and you tell him Bitty misses him. You tell him I'll be there soon and that I love him."

Hope spent a few years watching Bitty, listening to her prayers and her one-sided conversations and started to feel like she really was watching over her. Over time Bitty became more absent-minded. She'd have something cooking and then go to the other room and forget about it. The first couple times it happened the food would start to burn and an alarm would go off and Bitty would come back to the kitchen, fussing and muttering. But eventually it was if she wasn't even able to hear the alarm. The first time it had happened, Hope had learned how to manipulate things a little and had managed to turn off the stove. That night when Bitty thanked her spirits and angels before she went to bed, Hope felt a twinge of pride.

Hope watched over Bitty as best she could. Most days things were fine; Bitty would go through her photo albums and would write a letter or two. She'd take a walk around the block in the afternoon and then make herself a small dinner —usually some soup and a piece of buttered toast. Sometimes she would watch the news on the television, but more often it would remain off—Bitty complained when she did turn it on calling it a "noise maker for simpletons."

Things progressively got worse with her. She'd forget what she was doing. There were days she believed one of her boys was coming to visit and she'd wait in her easy chair peering out of the window. The thing that concerned Hope was when she'd get lost on her walks. One evening Bitty ended up sitting on a park bench, confused about where she was. The park was only three blocks away from her home but she couldn't seem to remember how to get there. Fortunately one of her neighbors came by walking her dog. She chatted a while with Bitty and then offered to walk with Bitty back home. It didn't seem like she had been aware that Bitty had been lost. If she had her suspicions, she didn't make any mention of it.

Out and about there really was very little Hope could do to help Bitty. That day sitting on the park bench next to Bitty Hope remembered the feeling she had her first day in the regular world when she'd realized she couldn't get back to her tree.

What came next was probably inevitable; Bitty woke up in the middle of the night and began rummaging around the bathroom. She didn't just get up to use the toilet like normal. Instead she started laying clothes out and mumbling to herself. She put on her slippers and her silky white robe and headed out the front door. Hope was worried from the start —Bitty had been talking about Merle and that someone should've been there already. When Bitty had reached for the front door Hope had tried with all her might to jam the latch, but with little more than a jiggle Bitty easily turned the handle and left the house. The effort exhausted Hope who did her best to keep up with Bitty. Even though Bitty moved slowly with a stiff-legged shuffle, Hope struggled to match her pace.

The night didn't appear cold—it looked like it might be like one of the hot and muggy nights she remembered from the farm. She'd lie awake next to her brothers in their bed and pray a rain would sweep through to take the sticky out of the air, even though the thunder and lightning scared her.

The mosquitoes appeared like a fuzzy halo around Bitty's head in the glow of the street lights. Hope did her best to swat at them but there were so many. Hope wasn't sure what else could go wrong but then the underground sprinklers came on. Bitty didn't try even try and avoid them but walked through the spray that encroached on the sidewalk. Her robe and nightdress began to cling to her legs. Bitty wrapped her robe around her a little tighter in an attempt to stay warm, but it wasn't working. Hope followed helplessly as Bitty kept shuffling on, now shivering. Hope couldn't see anyone around and there was nothing she could think of to do to either stop Bitty or get help.

They had made their way back to the park, but Bitty headed off the sidewalk and into the grass. Bitty was hit by more water as more sprinklers came alive. Her hair hung down in strands like icicles matted to the side of her head and face. She never said a word; the closest she came was a soft whimper when she was hit dead-on by a stream of water unexpectedly. She was moved forward with a determination that made Hope wonder if she was aware of what she was doing.

Bitty came over a gentle rise that tapered off to a large retention pond. She walked to the water, huddled over and shivering and sat down, the toes of her slippers teasing the water's edge. Hope sat down next to her and together they looked across the water. In the darkness the surface of the water looked like black silk lightly rippling with the breeze.

Hope sat cross-legged next to Bitty and looked up at the sky. The longer she was away from her tree, the more she missed it but the less she felt like she remembered it. Since she left the Windy Place she began to have feelings start to stir inside her. She had a deep longing for the peace she felt at the tree, but part of her had become attached to Bitty. While she wanted to return to the Windy Place, she had become invested in one little part of the active world. Her first thought was always to getting back to her tree, but in the back of her mind she had to admit she was enjoying some of her time in the regular world. When she was being honest with herself, part of her felt fulfilled by caring and being more involved in the world. Her father used to say, "You can't choose what you care about." Her mother would give him a disapproving look and would say, "If you don't choose then you don't really care." He would laugh and say something like "Well I wouldn't choose to care about anything more than you, anyway."

She couldn't help the fact that the active world wasn't where she belonged. If she felt sympathy or allegiance to the active world it would have been a betrayal to the one, unequivocal truth of her new existence—that her tree was where she was meant to be. But even so, she cared about Bitty and she didn't want anything bad to happen to her.

Bitty had curled up on her side, trembling and whimpering softly before breaking down into uneasy and ragged breaths. Hope ran her hand across Bitty's forehead. She realized that it had become easier for her to touch real objects. Before she had to focus all her energy on a specific point, but the emotions churning inside her seemed to make it easier to hone her focus. She could feel the pressure of her hand against Bitty's hair. It was just a few weak strokes in an attempt to comfort her, but Bitty's expression loosened slightly and her breath came a little easier.

Hope sat with her as the sun came up. It was still early, but the pink in the sky had mostly gone. In the distance she saw a runner with a dog jogging around the pond. Hope stood abruptly to see if they were going to see Bitty. At her sudden movement the dog started barking frantically. Hope moved towards it and it began to pull at its lead. The runner, a short, stringy man with a weathered face and a shock of white hair was trying to rein in the dog and was hissing, "Settle down, girl. Ruby, you heel right now… Goddammit, Ruby!"

The dog pulled him across the grass towards Hope. The man saw Bitty lying by the water and exclaimed, "Oh my God!" and let go of the leash. The dog ran forward to Hope and then stopped about three feet in front of her. They looked at each other. Hope wasn't used to being seen or acknowledged by anything and Ruby wasn't used to seeing ghosts.

Ruby leaned forward, sniffing cautiously. Hope crouched down to the dog's level and extended her hand. Ruby sniffed at it and tried to lick her, but got only air. The dog was confused, but no longer agitated. She sat, panting with a look that resembled a wide smile. Hope was reminded of the dogs on the farm. She was never that interested in them—her brothers usually had the dogs with them, but it was something familiar and warm—two things that she hadn't had felt in a long time.

"Call an ambulance! Someone, call an ambulance!" the man was shouting. Ruby let out a drawn out yawn and flopped down on her stomach switching glances between her owner and Hope. It was too early and there wasn't anyone around to speak of in the park. The man grabbed Ruby's lead and pulled her begrudgingly along with him as he ran towards where he thought the nearest phone would be. Hope waved goodbye to Ruby as the two of them disappeared over the hill.

Hope returned to Bitty's side. She was still shivering. Hope sat next to her and Bitty opened her eyes slightly, squinting out the early morning sun that was shining into her face. "I always knew you were there," she whispered. Hope didn't react at first because she thought Bitty was mixed up again.

"You're so pretty, so young," Bitty rasped. "I'm glad you came closer so I could see you." Hope looked down at her and realized Bitty was looking right at her. Bitty smiled when Hope looked at her. "That's right, you can hear me," she said almost to herself.

"You were here all night, weren't you? I could tell. You're a very sweet little spirit. I thank you every night in my prayers," she smiled.

Hope turned towards her and sat cross-legged, still a little wary that Bitty wasn't seeing her.

"I felt you around, but I could tell you came out when you saw the dog. Thank you for letting me see you after all this time," she smiled. She wore a slightly pained expression and her breaths were coming in ragged little sighs. "I went and got myself in it this time, didn't I? I just lose track of myself sometimes. Merle would tease me so when we first got married. He'd say, 'Girl, if I didn't know better I'd say you didn't want to know where you were.' I used to get cross with him sometimes when he said that and he'd laugh at me and give me a hug—even when I didn't want one. He'd say, 'It's ok, as long as you know you still want me around, I don't care if you don't know where you are.' He was a good man. He was very kind to me. I miss him very much. Do you see him?"

Hope shook her head. Bitty smiled sadly. "No, I suppose that's asking a lot. But still, someone sent you and that means he's out there waiting for me somewhere. That's good enough. That's good enough."

An ambulance siren wailed in the distance. "Oh I hope that's not for me. I'd hate for them to make a fuss."

Ruby came sauntering over the slight hill, her owner flailing to an unseen watcher. "Over here! She's down by the water!" he was yelling.

Bitty sighed. "Well, I suppose I'll be getting to take a ride soon. Could you do something for me?"

Hope bit her lower lip nervously. Bitty smiled and closed her eyes, "What's your name, sweetie? I want to know who to thank for watching over me."

Before she'd even realized it, a sound escaped from her throat. She hadn't spoken or even thought to speak for lifetimes. She didn't even think that she had the ability to speak anymore, but it came out like a tree branch creaking in the wind.

"Hope... I'm Hope."

Bitty smiled. "Of course you are. Thank you my spirits, my angels and my little Hope. If you see Merle you tell him I miss him and I'll be there soon to see him."

The ambulance rumbled over the incline, lights flashing. Ruby was barking, tail wagging frantically as men jumped out of the vehicle. "You go on, now. I'll be fine," Bitty said.

"Can you hear me, ma'am?" the first man asked her. Bitty waved at him dismissively.

"Do you know where you are? Ma'am? Can you hear me?" the man was feeling her wrist. He had a small light he took out and flashed in her eyes while he was trying to get her to speak.

Another man walked up, "Is she responsive?"

96

"She was a second ago; I think she's asleep now. Looks like exposure, hypothermia, probably dehydration, too," the other replied before gently shaking Bitty. "Ma'am, can you tell me your name?"

A police officer came over the hill. The second man turned to him and gave him an update in a low voice, "Elderly lady, looks like she may have wandered off. Dementia or Alzheimer's or something. You probably want to check the local nursing homes to see if they've had anyone turn up missing."

"She going to be ok?"

"I think so. We need to get her loaded up, but she seems stable."

Hope waved goodbye to Bitty as she was secured into a gurney and lifted into the ambulance. Ruby sniffed at Hope's other hand and tried to lick her again to no avail. Bitty had told her to leave, but Hope was torn. She stood next to Ruby watching the men secure Bitty in the ambulance and then they closed the doors. A small crowd had started to gather. A boy and his father were towards the back, the boy was craning his neck to try and see what was going on.

"I can't see," he was complaining.

"Just hush, looks like everything's ok anyway," the father replied.

"Is she going to be alright?"

"I'm sure everything will be fine. We should go. Mom said she'd have breakfast ready by now anyway."

"I want to see the ambulance drive away," the boy protested.

"You seen one drive around, you seen 'em all."

"I haven't seen one before."

"Well, then you'll be even happier when you see one another time."

"Da-a-ad."

"Oh geeze," he sighed annoyed. "Let's go," he pulled the boy behind him as the boy pouted and drug his feet.

Hope was about to turn her attention back to Ruby when she saw something. In the back of the boy's head she saw something—an orange something. It was like the bullheads back home when they would break the surface of the water at dusk. You could barely see anything, but there would be a slight color and texture change and you knew they were there. It was the same, except this was a translucent orange thing quietly breaking the surface before diving inside the boy's head.

She followed the two from a distance, trying to stay out of sight. Even though Bitty had seen her, she didn't think she was visible to anyone else. She was concerned about the orange... *thing* knowing she was there and watching it.

She trailed the two, keeping her distance, trying to stay behind trees or in the shadows. She didn't see the orange creature again. A few blocks from the park they came to a white house with black shutters and walked into it through the open garage door.

Hope waited across the street behind a tree, watching intently. There was nothing unusual or out of place about the house. There wasn't anything that made it stand out in any way or otherwise indicate what was there. She'd been through the neighborhood dozens of times and never had a clue that what she'd been looking for had been so close the entire time.

A couple hours later the boy and a woman—his mother presumably—left in the car while the boy's father mowed the lawn. With the boy out of the house, Hope thought it might be safe to poke around inside. It was possible the orange thing was still there, but she thought it was probably more likely still with the boy.

She entered the house. It was still unremarkable. In the front hallway there were photos on the wall of the family together and few more of the boy at different ages. To the right there was a living/dining room area. There was a staircase on the left going to the second story. Beyond that was a bathroom and at the end of the hall was kitchen. She looked around the main floor. Off the kitchen there was a set of stairs leading to a basement as well as a door to the garage. Things appeared well-maintained but not particularly nice. In her trips in the Memories, Hope had seen all sorts of homes, from hovels to grand estates. This one was a nice but modest home overall, she thought.

She circled around through the kitchen back through the dining and living rooms back to the entry area and went up the stairs. The stairs led up to the back corner of the house.

The first room at the top of the stairs was another bathroom. There was a hallway running back towards the front of the house. At the end of the hall was a large bedroom. Hope decided to explore it first.

There was a large bed, made neatly with a pile of pillows stacked against the headboard. On the far side of the bed there was a chair with a small end table between it and the bed. That seemed to be the father's side since there was a blazer hanging from the side of it and a pair of dark slippers at the foot of the chair. The other side was directly facing the closet and had a pair of pink slippers. Across the room was a large chest of drawers with a mirror mounted in the middle of it. On the chest there were odds and ends—some handkerchiefs, a jewelry box, a wristwatch, some hastily written and folded notes on scratch paper. By the door there was a laundry hamper with a shirt sleeve limply hanging over the side from under the lid.

The next door was a small study-turned-knitting room. It didn't look as if it was used very often, and everything was covered up and stacked neatly in clear plastic tote boxes. There were some old pictures and some stacks of old magazines on the floor. There was a desk and a sewing table butted up next to each other. The desk had a lamp and a covered typewriter, neither of which appeared to have been touched in a long time. The sewing table had some fabric and thread scraps around it. It also hadn't been used lately, but definitely had seen more action than the desk.

Hope moved on to the next room, opting to walk through the wall instead of going through the hallway. She found herself in a closet; the ground had dirty clothes and toys hurriedly pushed inside, out of sight. They were boys' things. Hope moved through the closet door and stopped suddenly.

It had changed. There were different toys strewn about. It was bright with the late morning sun instead of the blue darkness of the middle of the night. There were different things on the wall. But the bed, the room, they were the same. It was the room she had first appeared in when she'd touched the orange ball in the Windy Place. She couldn't believe she'd found it—after so many years it seemed too incredible that it had been so close the entire time. She felt a wave of giddy relief wash over her—sensations that she had long thought were lost to her.

She shivered with nervous excitement and it was the closest thing she'd felt to an actual chill since her days at the farm. It was a feeling that was so close to being alive she could almost recall it. There was still a great divide between where she was now and how it felt to run through the fields at dusk towards the sound of her mother calling to her, but she could remember now what it felt like. It made her feel like she wanted to live that life again instead of the detached existence she'd been leading.

Hope was lost in the excitement of the moment and didn't hear the hollow thump of footsteps coming up the stairs. Hope turned in time to see the door fly open and the boy come flying in. Hope instinctively pulled back and found herself at the tree. It was dusk, but she couldn't be sure what day it was. But now she knew where the boy lived. She knew she'd have to go back, but she needed a plan.

She decided to take her time and watch. It was agonizing to be so close to what she'd been searching and hoping for, but she knew it was best to keep her distance. Hope decided to observe from outside the house to start with until she got a sense of their routine: what they did, where they went, what they liked, who they were.

She learned that the boy's name was Lyle. He was a little older than she was—or at least the last age she had been. He was a quiet boy. There didn't seem to be a lot of kids in the neighborhood so he spent a lot of time setting up intricate battles between his toys in his bedroom or noodling in the backyard by himself. He also spent a lot of time watching television. He would've probably been planted in front of it almost permanently, but his mother, Doreen, had little patience for the loud, flashy, manic programs that he liked to watch and she'd often ban him to the outdoors just so she could turn the television off.

His father was named Ernie. He seemed relatively old, but he still tried to make time to do things with Lyle. Unfortunately, the two of them didn't seem to have much in common. They were well-meaning strangers, it seemed to Hope. The father tried to understand the boy's introspective demeanor and oddly obsessive interest in Thundercats. The boy, in turn, was unable to comprehend the enjoyment his father found in fishing, playing catch and taking naps. They both spent time trying to enjoy the other's interests as best they could, but it was clear from their grimace—a singular feature which they uncannily had in common—that neither was making much headway in understanding the other. Hope liked watching them try, though. There was a certain earnestness in which they both attempted, and failed, to find a common tongue.

The mother seemed to agree with both of them—she couldn't understand what either of them liked. She often took an exasperated, impatient tone when talking with or about them. Hope thought she was rather unpleasant at first with her constant sarcastic comments and nitpicking. Even when Doreen was with her friends or talking on the phone she would call them "the boys" and would make comments about ideas they got into their fool heads, or that it was hard to tell which was more immature or that her first beau, Dave Dinkle, had his own underground sprinkler business and was driving a BMW and had a swimming pool in his backyard, and if she'd had her head on straight back then she could be living the life of luxury now. She seemed to be the polar opposite of Bitty.

At one point Hope got so fed up of Doreen's constant sniping she went back to Bitty's house, but everything was packed up or in piles throughout the house. One of the sons was there with his wife. Hope watched them, with pangs of sadness. There were lots of calls to the other brothers with questions like "You want mom's wedding dress?" or "Should we auction off the furniture or put into storage for now?" Bitty wasn't dead. She'd been put into a home, but it seemed certain that she wouldn't be coming home. Her boys were going through everything before they sold the house.

"Mom would want you to have it," the man said. "I know, but Bruce doesn't have a place for it and me and Sharon thought it would be better with you... No, it's fine. If there's anything you want, let us know. I don't think any of us want to squabble over any of this. We don't want it to be like you hear some families getting—all cutthroat about the estate and such. I think we're all on the same page... Absolutely, absolutely... No, she's fine. She's still kind of confused. It was better than the last time we were there when she was crying because she wanted to come home. When she's lucid she's ok, more or less… You know how she is; she fusses that we shouldn't have to take care of the house and everything on our own and that she should have taken care of who gets what already. I have to tell her, 'Mom, we're grown men. We can take care of this. You took care of us all those years, just let us do this and don't worry.'

"And then she goes and worries some more. Typical Mom." He laughed at an unheard reply. "She's settling in. The nurse says she's been fine. None of the bad stuff you hear about sometimes in these situations. I told her that you guys would be down end of next month and that Bruce said he'd be down to see her, too… I mean, it's tough to see the place go but we all knew it was coming and we're just thankful that she didn't get hurt and still recognizes us and all that. I mean, she's still in good health. That's huge, really… Right, right… Ok, sounds good. We just wanted to call and let you know that we're holding it for you and to give you a little status update… Alright, talk to you then."

Hope watched them glumly. Her time with Bitty had originally been little more than a distraction to pass the time during her confinement to the active world. It wasn't until afterwards she realized that she had found sanctuary and built up a little piece of home with Bitty. She wished she could sit next to Bitty while she read, or while she knitted in her chair. Instead she had to go back to Doreen and her complaining. She stood outside the house one last time and wished she could go back, that Bitty could've seen her earlier or that she could have felt something sooner. But it was too late now. Her only option was to move forward and see if maybe she could make it back to the Windy Place.

She returned to Lyle's house. She was still trying to lie low and avoid detection so she cautiously looked around to make sure Lyle was gone. Lyle was playing down the street so she was able to move around freely. She found Doreen and Ernie in the kitchen.

"You're not drying them enough. They'll get water spots on them," Doreen griped. It was more of the same as far as Hope was concerned. She hovered in the corner in hopes Ernie would do something entertaining.

After Doreen snapped at him, Ernie put on a clownishly serious face and dried the plates with an intense look. Hope wasn't sure what he was doing. It seemed like he was trying to provoke Doreen.

"You think you're funny?"

Ernie mock scowled back. "Absolutely not. This is serious work. I'm a serious man."

"You know, I used to wonder where Lyle gets his silliness— it's clear he's his father's son."

"Nonsense. He dries as seriously as I do. It's in the genes."

"What on Earth are you talking about?"

"No time for idle chit-chat. I've got moist things that need to be not moist."

"Ernie, for goodness sake."

"Sorry, honey. I can't hear you. There is water out there. It's taunting us."

Doreen shook her head, "Really, Ernie."

Hope was expecting Doreen to blow up, but she turned to face him, hips cocked slightly, hand on her hip and a coy smirk on her face. "Is that so?"

Ernie grinned and kept drying his plate. "Yes, ma'am."

Doreen walked over to him slowly and rested her arms on his shoulders. "You're a silly man, Ernest."

"Not at all, I'm just devoted to my craft."

"Oh?"

"I'm offended you have to ask."

Doreen teased his hair with her fingertips. "Well you have been known to joke around before."

Ernie took on a look of indignation. "I never!"

Doreen just grinned and swayed with Ernie as if they were dancing to a slow song only she could hear.

"Well if that's true, I have a little confession to make."

"Oh?"

"Mm-hm."

"And what would that be?"

"That I know of something that's a little damp right now that you should take care of."

Ernie gave a look of exaggerated shock. "Now, now, what would your mother say if she heard you talking like this?"

"Oh she'd be cross."

"Just cross?"

"*Very* cross. I might be in serious trouble if she were to find out."

"Well that would be unfortunate."

Doreen smiled with a glint of mischief. "Well we'd better hurry up, so no one finds out."

Ernie broke character for a second. "Lyle?"

"He'll be out for a little while yet. We'll have time as long as you don't need to cuddle afterwards."

"Me? Cuddle? You insult me, woman."

"I'll do more than insult you. C'mon."

As Doreen and Ernie stole away upstairs Hope remained in the kitchen. Doreen had always seemed like she was doing a job she didn't like when she interacted with Ernie and Lyle before, but there was something that Ernie was able to get out of her. It was like he was able to remind her that there was someone she used to be before the schedules, the cleaning, the cooking and being the detail-oriented one in the house. Hope didn't think Doreen would ever be her favorite, but in that moment she saw a softening that reminded her of her mother. Hope had seen her father talk to her mother like that before. Her father had the uncanny ability to annoy her mother instantly and then gently soothe and fawn over her afterwards. It was those moments that her mother seemed the warmest and most vulnerable—not vulnerable in a weak way, but in an open, joyful way.

Hope felt more comfortable in the house after that and even stayed when Lyle was home, although she stayed out of sight, often hiding in the basement or the attic. In time, she started to feel more attached to the family, much like she had with Bitty. She even did little things to help out from time to time. Ernie was always misplacing his car keys and Hope would make sure they'd find their way to a nearby counter when he was. While she kept herself largely relegated to the shadows when Lyle was around, she'd still watch him from inside the wall or peeking through the ceiling at him. Lyle was often in his own little world and when he'd absent-mindedly run into something and knock it over. When Hope was able she would slow the object's fall enough to keep it from breaking or would steady it to keep it from falling over.

Doreen was different. She was so focused on what she was doing that she'd become irritated with distractions or frustrated if things weren't going as smoothly as she'd hoped. When Hope's mother would get like that, Hope would sometimes stand up next to her, resting her head against her mother's waist, not hugging, but just being close. Her mother wouldn't always brighten up, but she'd pause for a moment to give Hope a little squeeze and half smile. Hope would stand close to Doreen and sometimes it felt like Doreen knew she was there. Other times Hope would let a light breeze dance across the back of Doreen's neck to give her a little jolt out of her own thoughts. It wasn't much, but it allowed Hope to feel like she had a role of sorts and she felt as if she had her own rapport with each of the occupants in their own special way.

Hope began to spend more time around Lyle. There hadn't been any sign of the mysterious orange creature since the day in the park with Bitty so Hope felt more comfortable being around him.

Lyle was a quiet boy. Back home Hope wouldn't have thought much of him—he was too quirky and too shy. She would have either ignored him or teased him along with her friends. But watching him she found herself enjoying his little idiosyncrasies. While he could sit for long periods of time watching television or playing video games (often with a zombie-like glazed-over look in his eyes) when he was lost in thought he could almost be like a wind-up toy. He'd examine, play with and, sometimes, take apart something and then, like a switch flipped in his head, he'd move on to something else, in the middle of arranging, manipulating or fixing it. His curiosity was so singular that one day he spent the better part of the morning going from object to object, book to book without any pants on. They lay in heap in his bedroom, one leg turned inside out where he walked out of it in the middle of getting ready.

When Doreen finally came upstairs to see if his room was clean yet, she yelled at him for not even being dressed. Lyle gave her a confused look as if he didn't understand why she wasn't more interested in what he was doing. Hope liked that about him. There were moments where Lyle could see the immensity of the world with wonder—like it was all an elaborately constructed puzzle, or even a joke, and he was close to figuring out why it was all so marvelous and funny.

Like with Bitty before, Hope found herself settling into her own routine alongside Ernie, Doreen and Lyle. During the summer Ernie would get up for work early. At least a couple mornings he would try and get out without waking Doreen so she could sleep in. He wasn't as successful at it as he thought, but Doreen would play possum until he left so he could think he had been clever and thoughtful. Both would get a little satisfied grin when they thought they'd pulled one over the other. It was good-natured and sweet and it reminded Hope of what homesickness felt like.

Lyle would usually sleep until nine, sometimes ten in the morning. He wasn't much of an early riser as it was and even when it was late morning, Lyle would often try to go back to sleep. The summer days were too bright, too loud and too warm and he'd reluctantly shuffle downstairs for a bowl of cereal and television. What Hope couldn't understand was that Lyle seemed in a perpetual state of boredom. He'd wake up begrudgingly, eat with disinterest and then plant himself in front of the television. There was a show or two he watched with interest, but for the most part it seemed like it watched it because there was nothing else to do. Even when he played video games, he tired of them quickly. He had the same bored and irritated look he had when watching television. It was such a stark contrast to those moments when some seemingly random object or event would turn him into a single-minded miniature scientist. What was more, he seemed to actively avoid putting himself into situations where he might find things to pique his interest. Hope was baffled by

110

Lyle's irritable inertness. She tried to snag his attention sometimes when something was going on that she thought would interest him, but he'd inevitably end up staring listlessly at the television.

That familiarity with the daily routine made that particular Wednesday seem all the more out of place. Ernie's alarm didn't go off, but he was still up early. Instead of getting ready for work he went out to the backyard and started cleaning the grill. Doreen made a quick breakfast and then started busying herself making potato salad and cleaning the house. Lyle was up by nine, bounding down the stairs. "Where's Dad? Where's Dad?" Doreen didn't say anything, but gestured outside. Still in his pajamas Lyle ran out through the kitchen and back garage door.

"Can we go buy fireworks now?" Lyle shouted as he saw his dad. Hope realized it must have been Independence Day already.

"I got some stuff to do get cleaned up first to be ready for company. It'll probably be after lunch."

"Aw, can we go now? All the good ones might be gone if we wait."

Ernie smiled with a twinkle in his eye. He always got that look when he was going toy with either Doreen or Lyle. He must've been someone's older brother, Hope thought. Her older brother, Isaiah, got that same look.

"Well, you could help be clean this grill. The less I have to do, the sooner we can go."

Lyle's head dropped , "But Da-ad, I wanna go now," he said softly.

"Listen, there's a lot to do before people get here. Fireworks just need to be picked up before it starts to get dark. You tell me what needs to be done first." Lyle didn't answer; instead he just sat on the back steps, sulking. Ernie seemed to ignore him and kept scrubbing away. After a couple minutes Lyle sighed loudly. "If I clean the grill can we go after?"

"Hm?" Ernie replied as if he hadn't been listening.

"If I clean the grill can we go to the fireworks place?"

"It would help."

"Da-ad."

Ernie shot Lyle a little look, "Ok, but it better shine. Go get dressed first. Your mom will have my head if you get your pajamas all messed up."

Lyle hopped up and jogged inside. Ernie stood up, dusting off his hands and pants and ambled in the house. Hope followed him. He grabbed a glass out of the cupboard and poured some iced tea. Doreen was washing some dishes.

"Where's Lyle?"

"Upstairs, getting dressed."

"You done already?"

"No, just taking a little break."

Lyle came running down the stairs and through the kitchen. Doreen looked surprised by Lyle suddenly clomping through, limbs and shoelaces flailing. "Tie your shoes! You'll trip and break your neck!" she yelled after him.

"What's he doing?" she asked.

"Cleaning the grill."

"He's what?"

"Told you I could get him to do it. I win."

Ernie moved next to Doreen and peered out the back window at Lyle crouched by the grills, scrubbing away.

"You're as bad as him. You want firecrackers as bad as he does."

"Maybe, but I still won our bet. I get to get the Super Family Pyro Pack."

Doreen shook her head. "You boys and your bets. I'm married to a giant child."

"A giant child with the Super Family Pyro Pack," Ernie replied flatly and then took a long drink of tea.

"Be back by one. That's when Jackie and the girls will be getting here."

Ernie yawned as he watched Lyle hosing off the grill to see how much crust was left. "It shouldn't be difficult. He looks motivated."

There was lots of hustle and bustle the rest of the day. Lyle finished the grill and was bouncing everywhere until Ernie took him out to pick up the fireworks. Hope stayed behind with Doreen as she busied herself around the house getting it ready for company.

By the time Ernie and Lyle got back there were already a few guests mulling around the backyard picnic table. There were a few other kids: Two girls who looked to be older than Lyle and a little boy who looked too young for school. The girls didn't seem to like Lyle very much and made a little show whenever he was near to either turn their backs to him or leave the room. Hope knocked a glass of punch into the taller one's lap to show her displeasure.

The adults mostly mulled around with conversations about tiresome grown-up things. Lyle, meanwhile, played by himself, holing up under the dining room table, spying on everyone and playing little hiding games. As the afternoon wore on, it was clear that Lyle was disappointed—he'd been so excited in the morning at the prospect of fireworks and other kids to play with only to find himself excluded from the other children, and wandering from one cluster of adults to another, each with conversations of their own that held no interest and offered no place for him. Ernie, after doing some grilling and chatting with others, noticed his son sitting quietly by the front step, digging at an ant hill with a stick. Ernie dug through the brown paper bag of fireworks and found some sparklers, snakes and smoke bombs and then slipped out front.

Lyle's face lit up as Ernie showed him what he had. Ernie made a serious face with a finger to his lips as if it was a secret to which Lyle nodded dutifully. They started with the snakes, which weren't terribly exciting, and then Ernie let Lyle run around with some sparklers. Lyle danced in the yard, writing words and drawing pictures in the blue-ish afterglow of the sparklers' light. Ernie sat back grinning contentedly as Lyle jumped through the smoke of the little colored smoke bombs.

Later on, in a move that made Doreen furious, Ernie even let Lyle fire off some bottle rockets. She came out and yelled at him but Ernie fibbed a bit and told her that Lyle hadn't actually been holding them. Doreen didn't seem to fully believe him, but she went back inside after giving Ernie a stern look. As soon as she was gone Ernie let Lyle fire off a few more. Ernie and Lyle didn't seem to spend a lot of time together, and when they did they didn't really mesh well, but on that day they both were acting like little boys. Hope even found herself smiling as she watched them trying to play with their fireworks without getting caught by Doreen.

The rest of the day was more of the same. Ernie did more grilling as neighbors and friends filtered in and out. Then as dusk set in Ernie started firing off the rest of the fireworks—although this time Doreen was watching so Lyle was relegated to watching from a lawn chair, not that he seemed to mind. As night fell a much larger display went up and they all sat together watching. Lyle seemed so tired by the end he could barely keep his eyes open. Ernie picked him up and carried him upstairs to his bedroom. He slipped his shoes and socks off, and then his shirt. He left Lyle's shorts on and just put him to bed partially dressed. "I'm not tired," Lyle mumbled.

"Well, just rest your eyes then," Ernie whispered back before setting him on the bed. He slipped a blanket over Lyle's shoulder before saying a quiet "G'night, kiddo."

"Is he asleep?" Doreen asked as Ernie left the bedroom. Ernie just shushed her quietly as closed the door, leaving it slightly ajar.

"He was out like a light. I let him sleep in his shorts," Ernie whispered in the hallway.

"He certainly seemed to have a lot of fun today. You didn't let him fire any of those bottle rockets did you?"

"What? Noooooo."

Hope smiled as she heard the two talking in hushed tones back to their bedroom. She returned to Lyle's room. As soon as she heard the sound of Ernie and Doreen's door closing Lyle sprung out of bed. He grabbed a flashlight and a piece of paper and pencil and then dove under the covers, creating a little pup tent in the middle of the bed.

Hope watched over him as he scribbled away under the blanket. The room was a dull orange color from the flashlight being filtered through his bed sheet. Whenever he moved the walls would ripple with little waves from the light and the material. He seemed very proud of himself that he'd been so sneaky until there was a gruff, "Get to sleep," from outside his door.

He turned off the flashlight in an instant and tried to lie perfectly still. This time the day finally caught up with him. Hope watched him try and fight off sleep before finally succumbing.

Only his head from the nose up was sticking out from the covers. Hope noticed Lyle had a smudge of dirt or ash across his cheek. She instinctively she reached to wipe it off before realizing she couldn't actually touch him. Before she could pull back, however, she felt a burning in her wrist and suddenly an orange, glowing tendril wrapped around it and pulled. She tried to pull away or hide but it was too strong—t was pulling too hard. As she frantically tried to free herself she was enveloped by a blinding light and the smell of lightning.

Part IV: Mourning Would

Hope found herself by her tree—not her tree, but the one she had in the regular world. Except it wasn't the regular world. It looked off—the colors were flat and would bleed into each other, there was no sound and there was the lingering odor of lightning.

This new place was even stranger. Time would stop—everything would freeze in place, and then suddenly move very quickly, or just jump ahead. The sun went from morning to midday and then stopped for what seemed to be hours and then accelerated to later in the afternoon—maybe three or four o'clock. She wanted to explore, but found it incredibly difficult to move. At times it felt like she was knee deep in mud, except she was standing on dry ground. Other times she would appear in a spot she was thinking of and then would just as quickly return to where she'd just been. It didn't feel as if she was fully in control of her own movements. She explored the area. She wandered around for a while, finally ending up back in a tree row across the coulee. She leaned against a nearby tree to rest when she heard laughing in the distance.

A girl who looked a little older than Lyle came bounding through the woods. She was far enough away where Hope couldn't see much beyond that she was pale with reddish-brown hair and wore a bright orange dress. The girl slipped down the incline opposite her and then slipped in between the exposed roots of a tree. It reminded Hope of her own hiding place and her tree in the Windy Place. Oddly, she hadn't seen an opening in the ground or in the tree roots, it almost seemed that they parted for the girl.

Hope heard Lyle calling. She wasn't sure what to make of that. She hadn't seen him with the girl before, but given how everything worked here she didn't know what was to be believed.

Lyle kept looking for the girl in the orange dress and calling out. Hope could see the girl poking her head out from beneath the tree, but saying nothing. Just when it seemed Lyle was frustrated to the point of giving up she said something to him and slid out from under the cover of the roots.

Lyle seemed very comfortable with the girl, which was very strange to Hope since he'd always been quiet and awkward around girls. She couldn't hear what they were saying, but Lyle started looking in Hope's direction. The girl didn't seem interested in what he was looking at, and sat back against another tree, playing with a leaf.

Hope wondered what he was looking at. She looked to either side but there didn't appear to be anything of note. He didn't seem to be looking at anything in particular, but something in her general vicinity. He turned and muttered something at the girl, who didn't give any indication that she was even listening to him. Then he suddenly locked on to Hope with a laser focus. She felt a strange connection to him and for a moment she found herself staring directly back at him as they both saw each other for the first time.

Hope felt unsettled, almost exposed, by being seen, but didn't look away. It was almost a relief. She still wasn't sure what this new place was, but she liked Lyle and was glad she didn't have to hide anymore. As they stood on opposite sides of the coulee she felt like there was something personal between them. She thought about calling out to him; the thought of making contact was strangely terrifying and comforting all at once. He turned his head to say something to the girl.

As soon as eye contact was broken, Hope was enveloped by a roaring wind sound and the smell of burning air. She felt as if she was pulled away violently from the scene. She didn't feel anything physically and it was hard to tell if she'd been yanked away from Lyle in the alternate world or if it had flown away from her.

As she tried to get her bearings, Hope felt disoriented, but at least could move freely again. She was in a flat, grey place and there was nowhere to go. The smell of lightning was still there but there was nothing to see: no color, no objects; she couldn't even see the ground, per se, but was still standing firmly on something.

"I was wondering when we'd get a chance to talk."

Hope spun around to find two figures standing behind her. One was the girl Lyle had been with and the other was a woman who could have been her mother. There was something off about them, though. They seemed almost plastic and doll-like.

"What are you?" the girl asked. "You're not supposed to be here. Why aren't you back at your tree? That's where you came from, right?"

Hope didn't answer but walked towards them. The girl seemed to be speaking, but her lips didn't seem to match her words.

"We're not afraid of you, if that's what you think," the older woman said. "Coming toward us isn't going to make us run away."

The woman's mouth seemed to be doing something similar to the girl's, but that's not what had caught Hope's eye. It was if there was something behind the two that was speaking.

"Why don't you just sit down and we can talk?" the woman offered. She looked at the girl and they both sat, cross-legged and looked at Hope expectantly. "Now, do you have a name?"

Hope paused and looked at them. She wasn't scared by the two, but was curious about what was going on. Behind the two there seemed to a very faint figure bleeding through the pervasive grey of the place.

"Hope," she answered as she kept walking.

"Do you see something, dear?" the woman asked. Hope walked towards the orange form.

"Ah, she is something different," the girl said. "What do you see?"

Hope got closer and the silhouette began to bleed through and take shape. The woman and the girl stood up and walked up on either side of Hope.

"That's my actual form," the woman said. "Or at least as close to it as can be seen."

"I use these forms so that he can understand," the girl continued. "Do you know about the Narratives?"

Hope said nothing but reached out to touch the orange form. She couldn't see any eyes or a mouth, but it moved in a way that indicated it was studying her as well. Hope's hand hit something very solid that was between her and the form. The form mimicked her motion and placed what looked like a hand against where Hope's was.

"You can't touch me, I'm afraid. But the fact you can see me is very curious. I'm still out of sync with this Narrative, you see," the woman said. "I'm sorry I can't talk directly to you. I have to use these analogs for now."

Hope sat down cross-legged in front of the orange figure. The two figures mimicked her and sat down on either side of her.

"Well, since I have to use one of these to communicate, do you have a preference which one I use?" the girl asked. Hope didn't say anything, but looked at the woman. She looked to be about her mother's age. The woman turned her head and smiled at Hope. "Well, it's settled then."

The girl disappeared and it was just Hope, the woman and the orange figure. The woman put her arm around Hope's shoulder. It was the first contact Hope had felt since she found herself in the Windy Place. It didn't feel like a normal touch—there was no substance to it. It felt like pressure and static electricity where the woman's arm and hand rested against her. It wasn't something she would have considered pleasurable, but Hope hadn't felt anything for so long that even the unnatural, tingling sensation felt oddly reassuring. Hope rested her head against the woman. The woman looked down at Hope and smiled. "Well it seems like we've found each other. I must admit, I've been lonely at times waiting here by myself. My name is Nicola."

Hope let her eyes close as she felt the woman's hand brush over her hair.

"Let me tell you a story of another place far away from here and you tell me if you've heard it before," the woman whispered to Hope.

*****

Imagine every story, every life, every thought is like a book. There are details and characters and ideas that are described or implied starting from the beginning through to the end. Now imagine that this book is adapted. There are comic books of it, children's adaptations, translations into Swahili, vignettes, stage plays, short films, epic trilogies, color, black and white, operas, anything and everything you can think of. Some are good, some are bad. Some focus on one or two aspects, some try and tackle all of it and some sputter out of the gate and die away quietly. They all tell the same story in as much as they all have more or less the same origins and

123

actions, but they're very different in the way that if you tell a story one way it's a love story, another way it's a comedy, another a tragedy and so on.

Now imagine over time someone realizes all these different stories are all from the same source. They figure out that there's an original story that they all came from and that all the other stories are related in one way or another.

There are three things to look at if that's the case: First, what is the original story—out of all the hundreds and thousands, even millions of stories, which is the one that was the template for the rest? Second, how do all the versions relate to each other? Is there a theme shared between them all, or at least a set of themes that can be used to examine and understand each permutation? And finally, which ones are the best? Now "the best" is kind of hard to determine, since a comedy and tragedy can both be great, but aren't necessarily comparable in a lot of ways.

This is where it gets a little more abstract: imagine that the characters in the stories are the ones who determine which one is the best. In that case, most would choose the great love story or comedy before the great tragedy or the great war story. So "the best" would be the story that leaves all the characters the happiest; the one where goodness triumphs, where faithfulness and love are rewarded and each person is given at least a chance at true happiness. The characters would choose that story over all others and hope that theirs is that story. But in the process they would study the others and learn about the strengths and weakness of each one.

These are the Narratives.

Here you have scientists and writers that theorize about alternate realities. Sadly, you haven't been able to figure out what they are or how to see them or even how to communicate with some of them. Then again, this *is* a Lesser Narrative.

That sounded condescending. I'm sorry. It's not as if you can choose which Narrative you're in, after all.

There is a hierarchy. Obviously the "Greater" Narratives are at the top, then there are the "Source" Narratives, then the "Minor" Narratives, the "Lesser" Narratives and finally the "Archaic" "Primitive" or "Reductive" Narratives. The last three are academic points, really. They either never got started properly, imploded early on or were just very, very unpleasant. There's some debate whether many of them even qualify as Narratives, but that's a topic for another day.

Now I'm from the Second Greater Narrative. More specifically the Neo-Enlightened Golden Epoch of the Second Greater Universal Narrative. In contrast, this is the 14th Lesser Universal Narrative—the Waning Days at that, which is unfortunate. It could be much worse, if that's any consolation. Anything ranked in the top 25 could easily be the next level up for many people involved, there were just some, shall we say, "shortcomings" that kept it from being a Minor Narrative overall.

The Source Universal Narratives are believed to be closest in quality and action to the original Narrative. Of course we call the one we believe originated everything the First Source Universal Narrative. There's some debate whether we've found it or not, but if not, we've found some that are very close to it. If we ever were able to determine absolutely that it was the First, not much would change with rankings or how the Narratives are viewed overall. From studying them all they've pieced together what the First would likely look like and what properties it would have. Think of it as a dinosaur fossil—from what we've learned we can put together what it more or less looks like even if we haven't found it per se. It's a Tyrannosaurus Rex reality.

I mention it because the Second Greater Narrative is actually the highest Narrative we've found. But we've put together enough things and found enough flaws that we're pretty sure that it can be improved on ever so slightly. This is, of course, a controversial finding in some circles. Some believe that being able to identify the existence of flaws indicates that we are the Apex Narrative—if we had no recognition of flaws then we wouldn't be wholly developed, realized individuals. Others speculate that the Apex would be so much greater that we couldn't comprehend it and there is actually a series of Apex Narratives above the Greater Narratives, but that view is largely held by those of religious persuasion who believe that the Apex Narrative is something that must be attained... It's complicated.

The pervading school of thought says that there can only be one improved Narrative above ours. There may be other Narratives that are more tragic or amusing, but those are Narratives that are lesser-ranked overall because, well, frankly living in them would be less fulfilling.

Here's where things get even a little more complicated. When you view the Narratives in terms of protagonists and antagonists, plot points and themes they're all very similar in many respects. However if you look at it in more superficial terms they don't necessarily look all that similar. In your

Narrative people are the primary actors (Although you really should give dolphins more credit... and dogs. Dogs are really quite lovely!) and they come in a few different varieties—male and female, pasty white-ish to dark brownish with several shades in between. There is some variation in features, of course, but generally you're earth-bound bipeds running around fighting and loving and building and destroying.

There are other Narratives where the main actors are nebulous creatures made of gas and plasma. Others where the world is controlled by giant hermit crabs—they are really quite sweet and genuine folks, although they seem incapable of writing a good dance song—is that racist of me to say? Anyway, the point is they all generally think and act as you do in your Narrative, they just may look completely different.

Long story short, I use these analogs to communicate with you and Lyle, but I don't actually look like you. I feel like you do. I think like you (more or less) and understand my existence in much the same way you do. I just happen to be a large, floating orange waxy looking creature with no eyes, mouth, or ears as you understand them. But you already knew that, or at least had an idea of that, didn't you?

It's really extraordinary that you can see me as clearly as you can. Have you ever thrown a sheet over something and pulled it tight? You can see many of its more prominent features but it's obscured by the sheet. The Narratives are divided by a kind of barrier like that. Nothing is supposed to get through between them under normal circumstances but you can press against it hard enough to where you can kind of see through it. That's what you're seeing now and also why you can't touch me. But it's very strange to even be able to see something pressing against the Narrative. It's like a one-way glass in that respect. I wonder if you're actually *in* the barrier between Narratives. Hm... Anyway, we can talk about that later.

The thing about the Narratives is that there are equivalents in them. In most there's a version of me and a version of you. Probably my favorite equivalent of all time was in one of the Lesser Narratives there was a President of a great and powerful nation. He wasn't too bright, but still got elected. Anyway, when we tracked his equivalency in our Narrative he was, well, to you it would've been kind of like a German Shepherd. I mean it's a different kind of creature here, but for the same kind of purpose. It would've been one of the smartest German Shepherds ever, but, you know, still a German Shepherd. I'm not saying he was one of the *good* presidents, either. But still, he did get elected. Anyway, we all got a good chuckle out of that.

Usually it's not like that, though. They usually stick with their approximate species so, in my Narrative, you'd look like me and here I'd be another pinkish biped, probably. Maybe brown-ish. Ooo, that would be something, wouldn't it? I think I'd be good in brown.

Where was I?

Equivalents, that's it. Maybe I should start somewhere else for this part.

I'm from the Second Greater Universal Narrative and I'll be honest, it's very nice. It seems like everyone I know is happy and has had good opportunities in their lives. We get along for the most part and we have enough to get by on. I was raised in a nicer home. I mean we weren't obnoxiously wealthy, but I probably had a bit more than most of the kids I grew up with. I got to go to a university and, while I had good grades, there were some family friends who put in a good word for me which helped, I'm sure.

I did well at university and while I was there I met someone. He was perfectly nice and we got along well. Where I came from, if you meet someone and you kind of mesh you go forward, you know? We had a child and put together a nice little life. We had our work and our time together wasn't unpleasant. I should have been over the moon but I wasn't. It just felt so... empty is the only word I can think of.

My friends were happy with their partners or life choices and as I looked at my life I realized that they were happier than I was. I thought there had to be something I was missing. I tried anything I could think of—spontaneous trips, more time together as a family, more adventurous intimate contact. In the end he seemed fine with all of it, but I just wasn't where I thought—no I *knew*—I should be.

I turned to the Narratives to try and find something I could relate to—some guidance from how other "Nicola"s had done things. It seemed like the logical thing to do, you know? How better to understand how I could be happy than to find a happier version of myself, right?

What I found shattered me. In the other Narratives I wasn't with my partner. In nearly every one I was with Lyle, the little boy you found me with. We grew up together and it seemed like we were always in love. I mean, there were problems, but there always are issues when you're looking at Narratives below yours. But I seemed so much happier in all of them. I saw in them the life I wish I had.

I didn't want to hurt my partner, but I started searching for my Lyle. I tried finding him through record searches and social media—I thought I was close a few times. I even had a brief affair with one of them, but then I realized it wasn't him. Then it occurred to me that there might be another explanation.

I searched news stories and public records and I found him. There had been an accident when he was only two and he'd died. My one chance at happiness had been taken from me before I'd even had a chance to know it…

I'm sorry, I don't mean to cry. It was a very difficult time for me and I still get emotional thinking about it, let alone talking about it.

That was the first time that being in the Second Greater Universal Narrative felt like a prison sentence. I mean, on the whole things were so good for so many people, but I knew that I was destined to be one of the few things that were imperfect and alone. It was the most awful thing I could imagine. And I probably made it worse on myself by studying the other Narratives where Lyle and I were together. I'd see our children and the lives we'd build and the trials and tribulations that we'd endure. I really fell in love with one in particular—it was the Ninth Source Universal Narrative. I'd stay at home, rewatching parts of it, crying. I wouldn't leave my room for days at a time. It was everything I wished my life could be and even though this beautiful world was objectively so much more complete than that one, I envied every moment they got to live in it.

One day I was feeling sad and bored and started looking through some other Narratives and I found one that was just like the one I loved, except I wasn't there. I'd gotten sick as a girl and died. It was like my Lyle only reversed. I watched him in this sad, little world. He languishes alone for so long here. You all do. This is such a lonely place. I don't know how you bear it as well as you do.

It seemed wrong that there was nothing to be done except watch us both be miserable. We were missing each other and being together could make things so much better for both of us. It was so unfair and it seemed so... arbitrary, I guess. Do you know what arbitrary means? Like something that has no real reason for happening other than *something* needed to happen—no rationale behind it. Does that make sense?

I should explain another thing about the Narratives—there are very limited means of communication between them. It's almost exclusively limited to other Greater Narratives—the others usually don't have the technology or awareness to even know about other Narratives. They don't tell us about all of the communication, but a lot of it is information sharing about the nature of the Narratives and things like that. "Science Geek Stuff" is what I always called it. It takes a ridiculous amount of preparation and power to do it. They manage to create a kind of temporary neutral space where they meet between the Narratives.

Supposedly in one of the Narratives where they'd made some advances in Narrative theory they managed to create a portal and crossed into each other's Narratives. Unfortunately, something came across with them. That's how the Ninth Greater Universal Narrative became the 101st Minor Narrative and the Forty-third Greater Universal Narrative became the First Archaic Schism Narrative. Every child has to study about it in school—it was horrible.

What they say happened was that the portal between the two was open too long. Imagine two soap bubbles butted up against each other, one larger than the other. The pressure of the greater pushed into the other one—I mean not literally, it's much more involved than that, but it gives you a rough idea what happened. By the time they realized what was happening, the flow was too great and even trying to "turn off" the portal couldn't stop it. It wasn't like a hole in an airplane where things were sucked through—although that would have been bad enough. It sucked the energy of the Narrative through—time and matter were both being spontaneously unmade. Imagine everything you knew and you were being ripped away.

When I was little I stunned a fly and instead of squashing it I pulled off its legs. The leg twitched after I'd pulled it out. Now imagine being that leg and twitching even though you're not attached to anything. That's what happened to everything left in that Narrative. It was the most terrifying thing I'd ever seen or could have imagined.

The other Narrative fared better, but really only in an academic sense. The sudden surge of energy and whatever else the Narrative was made of, hit a critical stage and suddenly expanded as it came in contact with itself. Half of it was blown to ash in an instant. The rest survived, more or less, but was in a state of chaos for thousands of years and even then was little more than a collection of survivors and refugees trying to find a safe place to live.

My teacher would say the only thing that kept it from being classified as "Lesser" or "Reductive" Narrative was how brilliant they had been before and how much we'd learned from them afterwards. He said that their example stood as a warning to the other Narratives and that they were heroes of early Transitional Narrative theory.

The one positive thing that came from all of it was the creation of the First Artificial Primitive Narrative. When the explosion took place, the bond between the two Narratives was fractured and some of the residual energy leaked out creating another "bubble" between the two. At first no one thought anything of it, but as they began to study it, they realized that it had started to develop on its own. It was an incomplete Narrative, but it showed that it was theoretically possible to create a Narrative from energy from competing Narratives.

This had two immediate effects. The first was that Narratives all established a temporary neutral space between other Narratives when they bridged to each other. This space is actually a little Narrative, or "Bridge Narrative" as they call them, that is harmlessly released after the sides have concluded their business. They're more stable and, if there is a fluctuation, the energy would pump into the temporary space instead of pouring directly into another Narrative. There are all sorts of safety things that go into it, but that's the extent what I remember from school.

The second was the theory of "Narrative Probing". The scientific establishment proposed that when a foreign element was inserted into another Narrative it would bring some of its history with it. Once within a foreign Narrative the object and its energy would either be assimilated into the Narrative, or, if it were to react, the Narrative would expand and eject the object in response. The belief wasn't that the object would explode, but the rejection would create a secondary bubble with the object and everything it had encountered inside and that when it was ejected, it would spin off as its own Narrative. They experimented with it and found that the objects would create temporary shadow Narratives—they would superficially mimic the history and energy of the source Narrative. The energy they provided in their experiments wasn't sufficient to maintain those histories but it appeared that, given sufficient power, the Narrative could be sustained with a full, if not entirely "true", history. In fact, they started doing experiments with Bridge Narratives to see if they could seed histories into them by injecting objects into them and letting them grow. Some of the early results were very promising, in fact.

I've lost you. I'm sorry. Let me put it another way: I understand that there are peoples in your world that, at least at one time, believed every night when they fell asleep they died and when they awoke they were reborn. Let's say that was true—all the memories they had of past days were false, but still seemed real. This would be the same kind of thing— they would have memories of things that happened in the original Narrative, but they wouldn't have *actually* happened in the Narrative they were currently inhabiting. But it's not really about what's true, it's about what you can believe, isn't it? I mean, that's how people get through life here, right?

I'm getting ahead of myself. You ever have an idea that seems so great that you forget that great things just don't *happen* on their own? It sounds silly, I know. I must sound like a crazy person. I've been following around a boy in a Lesser Narrative in hopes that somehow we can have a life together.

I thought—I really did—that speaking in dreams and spending time together in little spurts would be enough. Just having a little of him in my life would give me what I was missing so I could go back to my family at the end of the day and it would be enough. But the more I'm with him, the more it kills me to go back to that life.

I know I must seem ridiculous. There's no way for us to be together. I keep pumping time and energy into this place and there's no hope of anything ever happening. Do you realize what it takes for me to maintain these two forms even in just a dream state? Or to stay connected to him? My partner has no idea but he's going to find out soon that I've drained all our resources, and for what? The fantasy of a life with someone else?

I can't get over you, though. You're able to interact with the forms. None of this is supposed to be possible. They're supposed to be directly tethered to Lyle and only he should be able to see them. Do you have any idea what's going on?

Well, I'll explain a little and maybe that will help. There are two principals at work with them. They're like marionettes—puppets—in a lot of ways. I tell them what to do, but it's tricky. There aren't any "strings" that I can manipulate to get them to move. Have you ever seen a "Wooly Willy" toy? It's a cartoon face, completely bare, in a clear plastic container. It's got all of these metal shavings inside and it's also got a little pen-like thing with a magnet. The point was to "draw" a beard or hair or whatever with the metal shavings using the magnet pen. I'm the magnet pen and they're the shavings. And that's the other part, since I can't enter your Narrative or insert anything the forms are made from energy that's already floating around. I chose them very selectively, of course. I knew what he'd like and I wanted it to be representative of what I was really like at the same time.

So, while I can't enter your Narrative, it's a lot like that magnet—energy of specific types and wavelengths can act to manipulate some things within the Narrative. At first I thought you were just some interference or distortion from what I was doing, but you're not, are you? We've gotten tangled up somehow, but you're clearly acting on your own.

…I just had a horrible thought—I haven't hurt you, have I? Oh my God…

*****

Hope didn't move or say anything. She felt the woman's form go limp against her. She opened her eyes and saw the orange figure—Nicola, down on the ground, slumped against the barrier.

Hope sat up and leaned against the barrier next to Nicola.

"It didn't hurt that bad."

The woman's form still sat, slumped over like a rag doll. Nicola didn't seem to move, but stayed curled up against the invisible barrier opposite Hope. They both sat there, saying nothing. Hope wasn't sure what to say—she'd been torn away from the Windy Place and had spent so many years trying to get back. But instead of feeling the desperation to return home, she felt pity for Nicola. Nicola didn't seem as if she meant to hurt anyone and the particulars were more complicated than Hope had any desire to decipher. Nicola just seemed like a very sad person who had perhaps gone too far in her attempts to be happy.

The form of the woman, still slumped over unnaturally next to Hope began to speak again. It looked particularly eerie because she looked almost inanimate with her strange posture and dull, lifeless eyes, but her mouth was moving.

"They warned that there might be consequences. They said the energy being emitted could disrupt time on a small scale, but I didn't listen. I thought it would be minor if I was just attached to one person. I could see that things had changed —little moments and memories disappearing. Did you see any of that?"

Hope remembered in the Windy Place how the Memories the orange blob had touched would disintegrate. She hadn't been sure what had become of them, but it seemed the Nicola knew they were gone.

"What happened to them?" Hope asked

"They're gone. Like they never happened."

"I don't understand."

"Did you ever remember something but the more you thought about it you realized that you remembered most of it, but a part of it was just gone? Or you knew you'd talked to someone, but for the life of you you couldn't remember what they looked like or what they said? Your memory of it is more about the course of events instead of remembering the actual thing. It's like that. I mean, not all of it was me. People do forget things, that's normal. The Lesser Narratives tend to be more susceptible to degradation overall, too. Again, part of the reason they're 'Lesser' I suppose."

"I saw that."

"You saw what?"

"I saw the Memories fall apart."

Nicola raised her head and tilted it curiously at Hope. She raised herself up and sat down facing Hope directly through the barrier.

"How did you see that? I can't even see that, at least not directly."

"They were in the Windy Place. The Memories were everywhere there. I could see them and touch them. When I touched them I got to see them. I could see all of them and I could go between them. I could travel the Memories, but I could always come home. I could always get back to my tree."

"Your tree?"

"That's where I've been trying to get back to. It was there when I arrived. It kept me warm."

"When you arrived? I don't understand, dear. Where did you come from?"

Hope told her the story. She told her about her mother and father and life on the farm. She told her of running through fields of corn and catching lightning bugs at dusk with her brothers. Hope told stories of Christmas and riding with her father in the sleigh over white fields of snow. She told her about her mother and father and how they'd tease each other and about the chickens they kept and how Hope had to collect the eggs every day so they could sell them at market. She talked about how the thunder would shake the ground and echo across the open fields in the summer and how she'd tried and close her eyes tight and pull her grandmother's quilt up to her ears to try and make it go away. Then she told her about her secret place beneath the tree.

She told her about the day of the thunderstorm and the den collapsing and then being in the Windy Place. She described the Memories she saw and the lives she'd followed before seeing the orange blob.

"So, was that me?" Nicola finally asked. "The orange thing, do you think that was me?"

"Probably."

"And now you're stuck to me? Or do you think you're tied to Lyle?"

Hope shrugged.

"I suppose there's no way to tell. But now you can't get back to your tree in the Windy Place? Have you tried since you were brought here?"

Hope shook her head.

"Don't try it yet. I don't want to risk making anything worse. I've still got a connection to Lyle, but obviously I'm not with him right now. I pulled back because of some fluctuations—I thought if I tried to reestablish the link it might clear things up, but I think that's what pulled you in.

"I'm terribly sorry, Hope. I'll do whatever I can to make it right, ok?" Nicola paused for a moment as if debating what to say next. "Can I ask something of you? I know I've already imposed upon you more than anyone could have ever imagined and I feel guilty even thinking it but… if the only solution is for me to lose my connection to Lyle would you, I mean, would it even be possible that you'd wait? I'm sorry to even ask, but I've come so far to be with him and if it's not too terrible would it be ok if I stayed? I mean just for a while?"

Hope didn't say anything. She felt bad for Nicola, but she didn't belong there. Neither of them did, really, although if Nicola's presence wasn't destroying the Memories Hope wouldn't have had much of an opinion about it. After a long silence, Nicola sighed. "It's ok. I don't blame you. I really shouldn't have asked you, anyway."

The woman sat back up to a normal position. "Ok, let's see what we can do here for you."

The woman reached out and touched Hope, or as much as she could be touched. She ran her hands around her body, as if she were trying to sense something. After several minutes, she crossed her arms with a slightly perturbed expression. "I don't know what to say. I don't know what you are. This is all very strange. Do you think you could try to go back to the Windy Place—see if that does anything?"

Hope nodded and closed her eyes and tried to release the Memory. This time there was a snap like lightning and the smell burned her nostrils. She felt the wind blowing over her again and then it felt like the room shifted violently.

"Oh dear God," Nicola whispered.

Hope opened her eyes, head spinning from the sudden tilt that had shook the room. In front of her was a giant fissure in pervasive wall of grey and beyond it she could see Memories rising and falling. She could feel a draft coming through it and, as she looked into it, she could see the faint silhouette of the white ash.

"Wait, Hope, stop!" Nicola cried out.

Hope turned to the woman and saw her skin, hair, clothes—all of her—blowing away like ash in the wind. Hope recoiled in shock at the sight. The fissure snapped closed as her focus was interrupted. With the opening closed, the wind stopped and the woman's form stopped disintegrating.

"What was that? Was that the Windy Place?"

Hope nodded.

"I'm sorry I yelled at you. I just wasn't expecting... *that* to happen. The woman and the girl are comprised of energy and remnants and particles from this plane. The energy I'm putting through brought them together. I have to use what's around because I can't put anything through, like I said before. Whatever you opened up was unmaking them. I wasn't able to stabilize their forms and they were being drawn into that other place.

"I overreacted, I'm sorry. But I may have figured something out. I'm attached to Lyle so I'm only able to follow him, but you seem to be able to go anywhere and see anything. You somehow got tangled up in my connection, but if I disconnect from him, it should leave you alone...

"If you'd let me I'd like to attach to you. If it works you'd be free, I could move about and if nothing else you'd have some company. Would you be willing to try that? If it doesn't work I'll let you go, no questions asked. I know you don't have any reason to trust me, but hopefully disconnecting from Lyle is a sign of good faith."

Hope thought for a moment and then nodded. She didn't know half of what Nicola was talking about, but not being trapped sounded good and having Nicola around didn't seem so bad. She'd liked being able to cuddle in her lap. Her time alone in the Windy Place seemed so long ago now. The warmth of the tree still felt like home to her, but her time with Bitty, Lyle, Ernie, Doreen and now Nicola made her feel connected in a way the tree hadn't. She liked watching them, spending time with them and, in the case of Bitty and Nicola, being able to interact with them. She didn't think it was better than the warmth of the tree, but it was different and good in its own way.

"Ok. I don't know how long this will take—if it even works. If I don't see you again, thank you, Hope. I'm sorry again for what happened but I'm glad I got to meet you," the woman smiled. "Alright, here we go…"

Nothing seemed to happen and then suddenly there was violent flash of orange light and a monstrous clap of thunder. Hope closed her eyes tight and covered her ears as she crouched down and she felt thunder reverberate through her body. It went on and on and just when she didn't know if she could take another second of it, it was gone. All she felt was a gentle breeze running across her exposed shins.

She opened her eyes and everything was grey and peaceful. Memories danced in the distance and faded away silently. And through the haze the great white ash stood as if nothing had ever happened.

Hope ran to it, smiling so hard her face hurt—which was a new sensation in and of itself. She ran her fingertips across the bark, feeling them trip and stumble across the rough surface as she walked around it. She let the friction take hold and let her hand act as an anchor as she let her body fall across the trunk in a one-armed hug. The warmth from the tree radiated from her hand, up her arm and up through her stomach and chest. She closed her eyes and relished the feeling. It almost felt like she had remembered it, but there was something slightly off.

When she'd first come to the tree she'd been alone, unfeeling and detached. Now she'd seen so much. She'd spoken with others and been a part of families, even if they hadn't really known she had been there. She was no longer a passive observer, but had been an actor in those far away lives.

The warmth radiating through the bark across her skin was reassuring, but deep down part of her wanted to go. She didn't even know where she wanted to go to but she wanted to *do*. She wanted to *be* something, somewhere. She wanted to mean something to someone. As much as the tree felt like her center, a little part of her felt like she no longer belonged there.

"Let's start back at the beginning. I'm talking about way back in the beginning—back in the Garden. Now we all know the story: God says you can have it all—now let that set in a second. God let us have everything our hearts could ever want. That's how we started out. We didn't earn it. We didn't deserve it. It was just what He gave us.

"Now there was only one condition to all this and it was easy. We're used to conditions being on things all the time—heck I can't turn on the TV without being told 'void where prohibited' and 'some exclusions may apply'. It's just the way the world works and the expectation is that we will fail to meet the conditions of our lives. The conditions we have are usually along the lines of 'be at least this good, or else' or 'try and make sure someone else is happy with you, or else'. In the end the conditions we give ourselves require us to be perfect—or just very lucky, I suppose. And that's the thing; we're not perfect. We are frail creatures and it is in our nature to falter.

"But the condition God gave us was not 'be good enough for my love.' It was not 'always make the right decision' because our knowledge has never been infinite. People always say to me, 'Pastor Dave, God expects perfection from me and I am just a lowly sinner. How can I be saved if I am imperfect?' And I say, 'No, my friend. We are not expected to know everything. We are not expected to know the full consequences of all our choices. God wishes us to be redeemed. He wishes us to be holy, but He never said "know as I know" because while he may be a righteous God, a demanding God, even a harsh God, he is not a cruel and unfair God.'

"You see, this is revealed in the one condition we were given back in Eden. The first thing you need to examine is the condition itself—it was not what we *had* to do. We were not told to strive for perfection. We were not told to be perfect. We didn't have to *do* anything. We were told to not eat of one tree in the Garden. I think you'll agree that under normal circumstances it's much easier not to do something than to have to do something. It's easier to *not* murder someone than it is to love our neighbor. It's easier to *not* lie, cheat and steal than it is to feed the hungry, clothe the naked, visit the sick and the prisoners. We were asked to do the easiest possible thing because God didn't want to see us fail. He wanted us to be set apart with Him for eternity.

"The second thing is what we were being kept from—fruit from the Tree of the Knowledge of Good and Evil. Now I can hardly say it better than that old wily serpent: 'You will not certainly die, for God knows that when you eat from it your eyes will be opened, and you will be like God, knowing good and evil.'

"That doesn't sound so bad, does it? I'll be honest, I pray everyday that I'll know good from evil and act in love as God would have me love. That knowledge is a blessing to me. But that's the thing—we obsess about what we think will make us happy and how our lives should look. We need to take time to thank God for the blessings he *hasn't* given us. With each blessing comes an expectation—a responsibility. Now they are good responsibilities. Those of you with children out there know what I'm talking about—your blessings come with a lot of work.

"I know it's counter-intuitive but we need to be grateful for things we're not asked to do. We must trust that God gives in His time and when we're ready. Sometimes we'll never be ready for a particular blessing. Instead of being upset and asking why we're not getting what we desire, we should thank God that He hasn't given us something beyond what we can handle.

"So let's look at what they received in the Garden: God didn't create anything corrupt. There was no evil in the Garden. Even the serpent spoke the truth—the fruit wasn't poison, they did not die from consuming it. What that fruit gave them was a blessing—the most wonderful, horrifying blessing ever created. We were made like God—able to know right from wrong, good from evil.

"Now I know some of you are saying that I'm blaspheming by saying we were made like God, but it's true. Let's look at the story of the Tower of Babel. Everyone remembers that they built a tower and God confused the language, but no one remembers why. It says right in Genesis: The Lord said, 'If as one people speaking the same language they have begun to do this, then nothing they plan to do will be impossible for them. Come, let us go down and confuse their language so they will not understand each other.'

"Now that's an image you don't hear a lot of preachers preaching about—you don't hear us talking about how nothing can stop us humans very often and we never talk about how God thought we needed to be stopped. We talk about the great flood where we were nearly wiped out, or Revelation where we'll be judged, the punishment of Sodom and Gomorrah—we all have heard those stories. But we don't focus on being a force that God himself thought needed to be slowed. Before the flood it says God said 'I will not contend with humans forever, for they are mortal.' I mean, it sounds to me like God is saying 'I can just outlast them,' not 'they are weak, pitiful creatures.'

"Make no mistake, God is still God and as the flood waters of Noah's day, the fires of Sodom and the final judgment before the throne tell us, He is still the Lord of all creation. But we were created in His image and we have the capacity for so many amazing things.

"You might be asking yourself, 'Why is Pastor Dave going on this tangent. What is he on about now?' and I assure you, this isn't a tangent. Do you remember Moses and when he saw God? Moses was only able to look upon Him as he passed by and even then what he saw was so great that he glowed—he shone like the sun itself and the Israelites were afraid of him because of it. God only allowed a passing glimpse of Himself to Moses because that's all he could handle. In the same way, we are able to handle the knowledge of good and evil. It was a blessing just as Moses seeing God passing was a blessing. But like that encounter with Moses, we were changed by it. We did not radiate with holy energy, but instead we were suddenly burdened with the knowledge that there was something outside of perfection and, because we knew of it, we could then be judged by it.

"We are truly like God in that we have the capacity for this understanding. We can be unstoppable if we work together. But we are mortal and instead of being able to go about our lives in peace and love we must now contend with the reality of being creatures apart from God. Because that's what knowledge of evil is—knowing that there are thoughts, actions, consequences that exist outside of the goodness God desired for us. And because we are only *like* God and not actually God, we will fail.

"For you people who like statistics think of it like this: God is the singular answer to all the problems we face. When faced with evil and darkness and the possibility for failure, He is the only one who has never failed. The only thing we, as creatures who understand the difference between good and evil, can do is try and emulate His actions and His heart. We will never be the perfect thing we were made after and now, because we are born into an existence where we know sin, we are cursed to lives of frustration and failure. But we can have hope because we can look to that singular, perfect example—an example that made a way for us to be reconciled to God through Jesus. Through our belief and through His unfaltering grace, we can someday be brought into that singular, perfect reality that is God.

"That's who Jesus was—He was us, *like* God, but still God by his perfection. And through His perfection He was also one with God. And by Him suffering the punishment and death that we all should suffer through the natural consequences of our sinful nature, He has offered payment for us to be like Him and viewed as Him. He degraded Himself to die as a sinner so that we could all be viewed by God with the love He could only give his Son. That's the beauty—Jesus didn't make us better, he made it so we could be accepted as we were by God. We're not perfect creatures because of Jesus, but we are *forgiven* creatures because of Him.

"And our final reward is being able to share in that perfection with Him. We are granted access to that singularly perfect reality that is knowing and being a part of perfection. People ask me 'What's Heaven like, Pastor Dave?' and I say, 'Look out your window. See the beauty we've been given already. This world wasn't given to you as an individual, it was given to us as a people. Heaven will be all of us, together, knowing that there is something else, something lesser, something evil in the universe, but knowing that the world we live in is separated from that frailty. It will be all of us together, working towards tasks great and small knowing that it is the right thing and knowing that instead of confusing our language, God himself is cheering us on because all we are and all we do is in accord with His perfect, loving desire for us. And we will be praising Him through our actions and our love and through that He will be able to see us joyfully fulfilled as his children. We will be able to please Him and make Him proud as only children can for their father.

Amen!"

Moses' eyes were closed as played through the verse of the "Nearer My God to Thee" and held the final chord and allowed it sustain and fade gently.

"Aaaaaaand we're clear… That was one of the good ones. That's one worth saving."

Part V: The Sunset at Patmos

Once or twice a week after the broadcast, Irvin would buy Moses breakfast at a little 24 hour joint. The food was decent, but the restaurant itself was rather run down. The Formica table tops were worn down to white patches where elbows and forearms would rest. In a few spots it was worn down even further to the deep chocolate brown material beneath. The coffee cups were brown with a white interior. They were ceramic but had a strange plastic-y finish that made them look waxy and cheap—but in a good way. The silverware was flat and unadorned and the plates were glossy and off-white like they were made from the same stuff as toilets.

It wasn't exactly a place where you'd use the word "ambiance" in a positive way, but it suited Moses. It had a certain earnest and pedestrian feel that he admired. Not to mention the cooks seemed to find nothing better in life than to dish out huge piles of eggs, hashbrowns and meat. As Irvin was fond of saying, "The place may be from the 60's, but at least the portions have been adjusted for inflation."

Irvin would always order coffee and dump in three or four packets of sugar. He'd order the steak and eggs if they were on special, otherwise he'd find some sort of omelet. Fortunately, the steak and eggs were on special that day.

Moses settled for black coffee and the Farmer's Breakfast— biscuits covered by hashbrowns, scrambled eggs and country gravy with sausage. He ordered it every time and was only ever able to finish half of it. The half he did finish would sit in the bottom of his gut like quick-set cement for the entire day.

Little was spoken at the beginning. Both men were exhausted from the previous night's show and would drink their coffee in silence. When the food came they'd dive in and then after the initial pangs of hunger were satiated Irvin would offer the first bit of conversation.

"You were really playin' it, last night," Irvin said as he cut a bite of steak.

Moses nodded and mumbled a "thanks" with a mouth full of biscuit and hashbrowns.

"I was curious; you ever listen much to what I say or is just the music for you?"

Moses nodded as he chewed both as an indication he was thinking and to say he had to chew and swallow before replying.

"I hear bits and pieces, mostly. I mainly try and think of music that fits the mood of what you're saying, though."

Irvin nodded as he took another bite of steak that he quickly followed with a scoop of eggs.

"You seemed a little more interested in some of the stuff from tonight. At least it seemed so to me."

"Maybe. Some of it reminded me of stuff I heard my father talk about. Some of the stuff about heaven was like stuff he was interested in."

"Now you know me, I'm not one to pry into a man's past—I figure that business is between you and God. But I am curious how you ended up here. I don't think you've ever really talked about growing up before or anything. Course, if it's something you don't care to share, that's fine, too."

Moses kept pushing around chunks of biscuit and eggs around his plate but didn't give any indication that he'd even heard Irvin. After finally managing to get some of his quarry stabbed with his fork he paused before lifting it to his mouth. "Well, not much to tell, really. Brought up the same as most, just been travelling a long time."

"I was just curious. You know what they say: still waters run deep. I get the feeling you're a pretty deep guy," Irvin said with a laugh. "It just caught my eye. I mean, we get on pretty well I think, right? Just made me wonder what I could've said that took you back somewhere."

"It's not that I won't talk about anything—"

"Never said it was. Figured if you ever had something on your heart you wanted to share, you would. If not, I hoped you'd know me well enough by now that I love you like a brother in Christ, even if you don't fully subscribe to all of it, you know?"

"Yeah. I appreciate that."

"Sorry, didn't mean to interrupt. You know me by now, I never mean any harm, but I can be nosy sometimes. I can shut up and let you eat your eggs if you want."

"It's fine. Just been a lot of water under that bridge, you know? Hard to start anything without telling everything."

"Well, I got the time if you got the will."

Moses didn't say anything. He fiddled around with the remaining half of his breakfast, moving it from edge to edge on the plate while contemplating whether he had room for one more bite. The food already felt like it was congealing at the bottom of his stomach. He looked up and locked eyes with Irvin. Irvin's light blue eyes came back with a surprising steely quality. Moses had learned long ago that for all his light-hearted, good-natured "aw shucks" presentation, Irvin could be singularly focused when he sensed there was something interesting going on.

"You can't unhear some things."

"Only the good Lord judges and He's already said He's willing to forgive you. I've heard it all and if there's one thing I've learned, it's that when we listen with compassion and open hearts, that's when the truth of a man's experience can come through."

"I didn't mean like that. I'm not worried about me."

"You think I'll be in danger from something you'll tell me?"

"No, but if you believe me… well, there's no turning back."

Irvin chuckled and looked at Moses a little incredulously, as if he suspected Moses might be toying with him. Moses' expression didn't change at all as Irvin studied him. Irvin finished off his coffee and leaned back in the booth and crossed his arms. "Well, you got my attention now, my friend. Can't hold back now."

Moses took a deep breath. "Alright, but you can't say I didn't warn you…"

*****

It was the only place I ever knew growing up—we'd actually moved there from a more working-class area, but I was too young to remember. My father said that was part of the problem—that my life had been too easy. Maybe he was right. Then again, it's not as if, other than having less money to start out with, his life was difficult.

He liked to act as if everything he'd ever gotten was something he had earned. But his family did well enough that he wasn't conscripted for the Security Forces or forced to do his research fellowship for a military research project or the like. His career trajectory went from "working class interesting" to "lower-upper class dull" honestly.

I can't be too harsh on him—at least he *did* something and managed to accomplish most of his goals in life. Just because I think his goals lacked imagination doesn't mean that he still didn't do better than I have. Growing up I never followed through on anything. I was happy to take whatever considerations were given because of my father's status, and often had the nerve to ask for more. I was young then, not that that justifies it. I was an asshole. That's a more substantive explanation than my youth.

I got no one to blame but myself for how it all turned out. It's fine, though. I'm at peace with what's happened. I wish I hadn't hurt some of the people I did, but that's why I keep going on now—so that I can be able to look them in the eye again someday and tell them I'm sorry, and that I learned my lesson and now I'm the man they always believed I could be.

I suppose that's all pretty vague, though. You're a good guy. You've been a friend to me when I had none and while I don't believe in everything you talk about, I do believe that you do your best to live by those principles you preach about every night on the radio. I've been a lot of places and seen a lot of things and that's rare—it's not "practice what you preach" with you so much as "preaching what you practice". I knew one other person back home who was like that. He was the only person to help me out back then and the only person who talks to me now. I'll call him B.

Now this is going to sound all conspiratorial, but it's true. I can't give you some details because I'm afraid it might affect your safety. I know you're not afraid of anything, but just listen and you'll understand by the end, ok?

It would be easy to say that I fell in with a bad crowd, but that wouldn't be truthful. I was the bad crowd. People fell in with me. I wasn't the one selling drugs or beating guys up or stealing shit. I was the guy who knew the dealers, the thugs and the thieves and I was the one who knew where they could sell, who they should intimidate and what was vulnerable. In the end they painted me as the mastermind of some big criminal enterprise, and that wasn't the case— honestly, it wasn't. That would have been way more work and planning than I was willing to do. But I knew enough, had enough clout and was owed enough favors that if I needed drugs, someone's ass to be kicked or wanted something someone else had, I could get it by asking and making an introduction here and there.

I mean, it was great. I'm not gonna sit here and lie to you and say I was suffering or had some deep unfulfilled void in my life. I was on top of the world: I had money that I didn't have to earn, I got respect without really having to do anything and I wasn't responsible for any of it. I didn't answer to anybody. I didn't have a crew or organization or anything that I had to oversee. It was all about me, all day, every day. I was useful to a lot of people, but not a threat to any of them—I was the golden goose, man—treat me well and I shit gold for you.

I guess in some ways I was like my father. He aspired to a higher social class than he came from and to be treated like he belonged there, not some coattail hanger, you know? Well I wanted to walk with the best and the brightest and belong, too. Of course you need some sort of currency to travel in those circles. My father had knowledge and a special kind of uninspiring brilliance. I had the angles.

I had access to enough money and prestige where I was able to move around as a peripheral character in that world, but I would've never made it any further. If you look like you have to work to be part of that circle, you've already lost. The hardest part was to manage and juggle all the supply and demand things—not just goods, but socially being "the right guy to the right guy at the right time" sorta stuff—I had to do all that and make it look like I was able to take a nap out of sheer boredom at the same time. I was a day trader of personal currency, just not my own.

Let's say you have "Debutante A" who wants to be seen with a billionaire philanthropist at the big event of the season. Meanwhile you've got "Social Climber B" who wants to be a sidekick of the Debutante so they can land their own reality show and finally you've got "Player C" who wants an epic piece of tail to add to the trophy collection of personal conquests.

You've got to figure out who you're going to help, who you're going to misdirect, who you're going to ignore and who you need to break into a million tiny pieces and send down the river. No one was better than me. In that last scenario, Social Climber B ended up on a sex tape and a one-way ticket to D-list obscurity, but not before getting me in touch with a big-time producer who had a taste for the exotic. Debutante A got to the event, but only because she brought her sister who I arranged to meet up with the billionaire's son—I used to get holiday cards from them every year. As a result of that connection I ended up with a source to help other associates of mine launder money as well as some start-up capital for a few other up-and-comers. And Player C, well, I had him eating out of my hand with little difficulty. His little black book alone kept me insured and protected for years while I worked my magic.

That social world moves quickly, but most of them can't see beyond the next 15 minutes. I could see moves days, months, even years ahead. You know that old poem, "For want of a nail"? Well, I bought, sold and traded a lot of nails in my day and then bought up a lot of cheap, prime real estate when the kingdom went belly up. What's more, I didn't have any enemies—or at least any that were still worth a damn by the time they hated me. I was just a guy everyone liked who had a lot of nails, you know?

I suppose I was able to see the angles on everything except myself. I could see the consequences of other people's actions. I could strategically amplify or transfer them as I needed, but I always knew there were consequences. The effects weren't always major and sometimes didn't even directly affect the ones who set them in motion, but they were always there. I got to the point where I thought I was immune to the ripples and aftershocks. You can't see it when you're focused on manipulating others and trying to live it up in the moment, but all of those actions just build up behind you. By the time you realize it and have to try and stop it there's so much inertia that it's too late. Suddenly you're getting battered down by devices of your own creation and there's nothing you can do to stop it—it spirals all out of control, running you over in the process.

Then again, I also thought there wasn't a problem that I couldn't somehow buy my way out of. I thought everything had a value I could assign to it. I suppose given what I was doing and who I was with, that was true in a lot of ways. Have best friend? That's worth X amount of something. And if you crush them in the process? Well you can either buy them back later or buy a new best friend. It's all the same in the end, as long as you acquire everything on your list of accoutrements, the names don't matter.

D was the icing on the cake. I'd made my way up the ladder. I'd manipulated friends and foes alike, bested everyone in my path and D was the prize. You ever wonder what those guys who climb Everest feel like when they reach the top? That's what I felt for D—I had been vindicated, and reached the pinnacle of what I had wanted to attain and for my trouble I got the most beautiful, wonderful, kind and decent soul in the world to fall in love with me. I'd conquered all of it; it was mine by right. I'm ashamed to admit it, but D was the spoils of war to me, at least at first. D was what others wanted but he was mine.

Yes, I said "he".

It drove my parents crazy. Of all the horrible things I did— the lying, cheating, backstabbing—the one thing they weren't able to get over was D. That's pretty fucked up, right? The one person who kept me from being a total monster was the one thing they held against me.

Now I know you may not approve given your beliefs and all, but you always seemed the type that was willing to let his god do the judging, so that's why we're having this conversation. I'm not ashamed of him and I won't apologize for loving him. If your god hates me for it, so be it. I've done enough to deserve his hate, anyway. But I'd rather be hated for something that made me a better person than to be loved for doing something I hated myself for. That's all I mean to say on that. Like I said, you're a friend and I trust you'll continue to be so, regardless.

My parents would always bail me out if I got into trouble or would use their influence to make certain things disappear. But as soon as D came on the scene they thought it was in my best interests to make me "suffer the consequences of my actions". I guess before that, they weren't able to believe that I was a "bad kid" or that anything that happened wasn't some sort of misunderstanding or persecution. Maybe I just got worse at selling them those lines. I don't know. I can say it was inopportune timing when they decided that I needed to grow up.

D was there for me. He didn't like some of the things I did and we'd fight about it. We'd have terrible screaming matches and I'd leave for days at a time sometimes. I thought that I didn't need him and if it came down to it, I could buy, barter or steal someone else I cared about as much. Hell, might even be a girl so my folks would leave me alone, you know? I'd go out and hook up with whoever I felt like at the time, because, at that point, I felt like D was beneath me—like I was doing him this big favor by letting him be near me.

I suppose it didn't help that when I'd get back from doing all that D was still there waiting for me. Part of me thought he was pathetic—I'd *never* come back if he'd done that to me. What kind of damaged person stays around when they're being treated like shit, you know? But the other part of me felt—I don't know what words to put to it—my soul flew for joy when I'd open the door and he'd be there. I mean, part of me was terrified that he'd be gone. I've had a long time to think about it, and it seems like I didn't think I ever felt like I deserved to be happy. I mean I was an asshole, but there was a part of it that was me testing him. Kinda like I was telling him "See, this is why you shouldn't love me—I'm horrible and unlovable. Can't you see that?" I was afraid he'd figure it out on his own someday and when that day came, it would break my heart and everyone would know that I was a worthless fraud.

160

I've been around. I know a lot of people go through that sort of thing when they're younger. But when it's happening to you, you really think sometimes that everything good about you is just a reflection of someone who is so much more beautiful than you could ever be.

Anyway, you either have to learn to accept their love as a gift or you have to keep fighting the world at every turn over every little thing—at least that's how it was for me. The day I was able to believe D loved me was the day I stopped trying to control every little thing and I was able to love him back the way he deserved. He got me to the point where I thought that maybe life was good enough as it was and I didn't need to keep playing the angles every second of every day—there was something else in the world worth my attention besides the great imaginary chess match I was playing against the world.

Of course, that just doesn't happen overnight. It took a while for me to let some of those things go, and in the meantime I was still very much a player in that world.

I can even tell you exactly when I knew that I needed to have D in my life. I did all sorts of crazy things back then. It was after one of our fights and I was on the second or third day running wild. We were all out doing anything we could get our hands on and at some point I just took too much. I honestly don't remember anything 12 hours before it happened because we were going at it hard. I passed out and apparently I was in pretty rough shape. No one wanted to call the ambulance because the cops would show up and it would be bad for everyone, or at least everyone who wasn't in a coma. So they left me there for a couple hours—might've been longer, a couple hours was as much as anyone would own up to. Finally someone goes through my stuff and finds D's number and calls him.

Now the fight that led up to this was particularly ugly. I said some things. He said some things. I said some really, really awful things and told him that I was going off to fuck someone we both knew and that he needed to have his shit gone by the time I got back. And then I went and did exactly that. I mean, it wasn't an idle threat like "I'm going to say some stuff to hurt you and that's how I'll get back at you," it was a "Fuck you, I'm going to hurt you the worst way I know how and I want you to know I'm doing it because I know it'll hurt you the worst way I know how." It was really one of the worst things I've ever done to anyone, let alone someone I cared about.

So when we were out partying, we were way out of the way at this kind of resort/enclave kinda place where the rich and privileged could go live out their dirty little fantasies and indulge their more wanton desires with impunity. It was hours to get home from there. Well, they call D and tell him I'm out and that someone needs to come get me otherwise they were just going to dump me along the side of the road somewhere.

Well, I don't know how he did it, but D got there. The place was a fair distance away, but also intentionally hard to find. He made it in record time—I didn't think it was physically possible. I woke up in the hospital two days later and the nurse told me all about it. As soon as my parents found out about it they came, as you would expect. They also barred D from visiting me, which I suppose you would also expect.

The funny thing was, I wasn't glad I survived. I mean, I wasn't suicidal or anything. It just wasn't the first thing that occurred to me. My first thought was elation that he'd come back. I was so... I don't know, *relieved*. It's hard to explain. I'd been at my worst and he'd come back.

I got out of the hospital the instant I could—doctor's orders be damned. I couldn't get home soon enough. I knew it was probably too much to hope that D would be there; I knew that he had to have left. If he'd stayed there's no way he could've looked me in the eyes afterward. When I got home all his things were gone. There wasn't even a goodbye letter, just his keys on the table.

It was sad, but I knew it was the right thing for him—for both of us, really. Things were bad and needed a lot of repairing, but it was a starting point. I knew he loved me and I had to show him that I could be the person he deserved. It was up to me to prove it—to make things right.

But that's the problem with life—there's what you need to do and then there's what you're forced to do.

Maybe that's not entirely accurate. Everything that happened was because of choices I made—nothing was forced on me. But after enough history, the momentum can leave you where you're only option is choosing the best of a number of bad choices.

After I got out my parents hired B to be my personal assistant. That's what they said, at least. He was supposed to spy for them. I guess the last incident along with their reservations about D made them suspicious that not all was well. I was in a strange situation—I had lots of influence and was able to do well in trading favors, but I didn't have much in the way of actual currency. Besides, it's hard to get a place when you can't really say where your income is coming from —partly because you don't know month to month, and partly because the income you do know about, you can't really go around advertising. I had been staying at my grandmother's summer home, but when my parents told her about D, she barred us from returning.

My parents had a condominium that they used to holiday at, but they hadn't used it in years. They were in the process of selling it, but after D left they thought it would be an effective bargaining chip—and they were right.

The deal was this—they'd keep the condo and I could live there, but I had to keep B on as an assistant and if I got into trouble again, they could sell it. If their choice of spies had been a complete stranger to me I may have called their bluff, but I'd known B since I was a kid. He was six or seven years older than me. At that age that still seemed like an eon, but he was alright. He'd actually known about a lot of the stuff I'd done before; we knew many of the same people. In fact, he could've gotten me busted a bunch of times before if he'd had the inclination.

It's hard to describe him. He moved in that world because it was his job. He was the dutiful employee who would pick up his boss' dry cleaning. His title, well before he started working for me, was never "personal assistant". He was just a guy who liked his work and didn't seem to think anything was beneath him, even if when he was sent on trivial personal errands. He'd go about his business, not make waves, and just kind of be in the background of everything. I can't tell you how many times I saw him around and didn't even realize it was him until later.

He was a terrible spy. There are two kinds of people who seem to fall into those jobs—the person who hangs on to everything and is just waiting for the right moment to tell anyone and everyone what they saw, and the person who says nothing, regardless of what they saw. B was definitely the latter and it had served him well. You can't move in the circles he did if he talked. More to the point, you couldn't have the bosses he did—many of them vile and tempestuous entitled assholes—without both perspective and a strong personal sense of responsibility. I mean, those guys loved him and they didn't love anybody. Integrity, honesty and silence were more valuable traits for someone in his position and the first two were practically extinct in our circles.

I remember that first day; we sat down and I told him, "I have things I need to do. If you don't want to lie, I can tell you when you should leave. I know you, and I know your reputation. I think you're a stand-up guy and I won't dump on you or treat you like shit. Guys like you are worth their weight in gold and I don't mind saying it. If you work with me, we both can make out pretty well. I'll respect what you tell me you can and can't do. I'm not greedy, and I'm happy to share the benefits of what I do with you if you're on board."

He thought a minute and then he said this—and I'll always remember how he said it, with this really soft, even tone in his voice, "You're involved with a bunch of things I want no part of. I think the consequences of your actions could follow you for years to come, but at the end of the day, it's not up to me to tell you how to live your life. If you can sleep at night, then that's your thing. I'll be honest with your parents about what they ask, but I won't speculate, answer rumors or nose around in your business. If you've got work for me to do, then I'll do it. I'll tell you if I don't like something and if there's ever a day that I think you've gone too far, I'll walk away. But that's it—I'll just walk away. You don't have to worry about what I'll say or do. Just as you'll be judged by your conscience, I'll be judged by mine. I trust that if it comes to that you'll let me go about my business and not hinder me from making a living. In the same way, your actions are your own and as your employee, they're for you to share as you see fit. I have no interest in sharing anything beyond what I've willingly done for the reasons I've chosen to do them. If that's acceptable, then I think we have an agreement."

So we had an understanding and we set right off to work. I'd originally intended to find D, set up some consistent, semi-legitimate kind of work and settle down. The problem with consistent and legitimate work is that it didn't seem to pay as well and it wasn't nearly as interesting as what I had been doing.

On the first count, D wasn't particularly hard to find. He was still around, albeit avoiding his usual haunts for the most part. Our mutual friends were picking sides so there were plenty of people telling me to just stay away and let D move on. It was a compelling argument, really. The thing about trying to be better for someone is admitting you were bad for them. I wanted D to be happy and part of that process was admitting that I might be a hindrance to that. But you have to make up your mind early on whether your fear of hurting someone is real enough or if you're willing to commit and take on all the pain you caused head-on. I chose the latter, obviously, but it was by no means a snap decision.

166

The other part of it is that I couldn't bully my way back in. I mean I probably *could* have, but that's not what was best for D, or for me. D had to take me back and I had to prove to him that I was worth forgiving. Our relationship up to that point had been about intensity and bluster. I had to learn patience, empathy and forgiveness.

While all that was going on I was approached by Mr. Halford. I usually catered to middle-tier celebrities, kids of the ultra-wealthy, people like that. Mr. Halford was different. He was one of those guys who was so rich and influential that you never heard about him. I worked with all sorts, but I was still generally pretty selective about how much I worked with some people. I usually avoided contacts with anywhere near the clout Mr. Halford had. I learned early on not to fuck around with those guys.

I had one contact—nice enough guy, never talked about his connections, dealt in some drugs, girls, but usually tasteful on both fronts. He always said that his job was to "provide an experience" so he always had good product, didn't deal with junkies, kept it all clean and respectable. The girls were always well protected and did the work voluntarily. If they wanted out, he let them walk with no threat of anything as long as they kept their stories to themselves. People—employees and clients alike—really enjoyed working with him. We had a couple mutual projects and he was shrewd, but never screwed me. He always thought there was enough to go around in our line of work and everyone could end up happy as long as no one got greedy. He was really into balance and the ebb and flow of the universe, that kinda stuff.

He was approached by one of those big-time guys. They always had something particular and exotic in mind, but from what I heard, the request wasn't anything way out of left field or anything. He set them up, did his job and everyone seemed happy. Then two weeks later—poof!—he was just gone. No one knew what happened to him. He didn't tell anyone where he was going, or what he was doing—just gone into thin air. Five days later his body showed up in a trashy hotel. They said it was a drug overdose. But he never touched the stuff—it messed with his sense of balance and harmony, he said. He was literally against using it for religious reasons.

It thought it was suspicious so I asked around, called in a few favors—you know, did my thing. They had him taken out. Like I said, he didn't talk. He didn't cause any trouble, but he wasn't powerful. He didn't know enough of the right people to keep him safe. He wasn't even a "liability" in most reasonable interpretations of the word since he didn't know enough about anything to make him dangerous. But it just seemed like it might be less inconvenient to kill him than to let him go about his business when he potentially knew a little about something unimportant.

I've seen a lot of shit. I've seen and heard of guys getting taken out because they knew too much or were talking. But this guy, he was killed just because to them, him being dead or alive didn't matter one iota. They did it because they could and because, unless you were one of them, you didn't matter.

So when Mr. Halford came looking for me, I tried to stay away. I didn't need that kind of trouble and I didn't need to worry about being squashed like a bug just for being near the wrong guy at the right time. But when one of those guys wants something, they usually get it and Mr. Halford wanted me for some reason.

I'd been dodging calls and invites for three or four days. I thought it would be a good idea to get out of town for a few days in an attempt to drop off his radar. I was trying to convince D to go with me as a little getaway—just the two of us and it sounded like he was thinking about it. I was going to meet with D and make my final pitch, but I hadn't gotten but two blocks away when I was stopped by the police. They took me into custody but barely spoke a word. I was panicked—trying to stay cool because I didn't want them to think they had me on something—trying to figure out which of my transactions they could've caught me on.

They didn't book me or anything. They took me straight back to an interrogation room and left me there. After about an hour of shitting myself and trying to figure out what was going on, the door opened and Mr. Halford walked in. He wasn't let in by an officer, he just waltzed right in like he owned the place. He pulled out the chair opposite me at the table and sat in it, leaning back. He looked very relaxed, almost amused, but didn't say anything.

I knew enough not to say anything—they have all those rooms set up to record everything. So I just sat there, trying not to look him in the eyes. He never so much as flinched, a strange little half smile on his face, also saying nothing. It was incredibly unnerving because I knew I was screwed one way or another. Either Mr. Halford had given me up and was going to watch to see if I cracked, or he arranged for me to be there so when I was beaten to death by the cops they could say I was in custody and resisting or something like that.

It felt like an eternity and I could see he was just eating it up. I didn't know what he was trying to do, but I wasn't going to speak first. I wasn't going to even acknowledge he was there if I could help it. There was a light knock at the door and an officer came in with a cup and saucer and handed it to Mr. Halford. He took a small sip and gave a little nod of approval. "Very nice," he muttered.

"Is there anything else, sir?" the officer asked him.

"No, no. Just a little privacy for me and my companion here," he answered, nodding at me. The cop nodded and closed the door quietly behind him. I'd seen a lot of cops in my day, but I'd never seen them act like butlers before. It reminded me of one time when I went to see my father at work when I was a little boy. He showed me around and looked all important and then another man in an immaculate suit stuck his head in the office and told my father he needed something. In an instant my father went from the celebrity scientist, smartest guy in the room and all-around guy-in-charge to just another jerkoff with a boss. It was really strange to see him change roles so quickly like that. Anyway, that's what seeing that cop act so subservient and quiet reminded me of.

"You're disciplined. I respect that," Mr. Halford said abruptly as he stirred his drink. "It's a valuable trait, especially for someone with your aspirations. I've done this a number of times and you're the first who held his tongue. Granted, many of them tried to ingratiate themselves or sell me on some scheme immediately. But you know better, don't you? The rabbit in the lion's den is safest when it remains perfectly still, yes?"

170

He pulled the chair in a bit so he was sitting normally at the table. He folded his hands and looked at me intently, "And you know you are a rabbit, don't you? That's good. I appreciate someone who understands the hierarchy of our little world. Rest easy; this lion has no interest in having rabbit for dinner," he chuckled. It was creepy, but I also sensed that the game wasn't over—he was still testing me to see if I'd rattle. I sat up and looked at him directly, but didn't say anything. I was scared, but I did my best to look disinterested, not angry, not afraid and definitely not curious.

"Am I boring you, little rabbit? Perhaps if I roar a little you'll be impressed," he said, still smirking a little. He gestured to the one-way glass. A moment later there was a knock at the door and it opened a crack. Mr. Halford stood up and took a bottle of water from an unseen person. He then took another one and gestured it to me, offering me a bottle. I could hear from the hallway outside D saying "I don't know what I did. I haven't done anything. What am I being arrested for?"

I felt my heart start to pound, but I knew I had to keep it together. I nodded and reached out—still sitting down—to take the bottle. He smiled and brought it to me. "Sorry about the commotion out there. I suppose that's the risk you run when you have your meetings in places such as these."

I opened the bottle and took a slow drink from it. "It's no bother," I told him. His grin never changed, but he did study me intently. He knew I recognized D's voice and I knew he knew.

"Thanks for the water," I told him.

"Of course." His eyes changed. Before he looked like he was toying with me—almost playful and condescending. After hearing D and taking the water though, he was really looking me over—as if he was finally taking me seriously.

"How do you know I didn't poison the water?"

"I don't. But it seems unlikely."

"Oh really? Why's that? It would be quick and tidy and no one would say a thing about it if you just keeled over in this little interview room. Seems like a perfect plan to me."

"Perhaps. But there are two reasons why I don't think you did. First, it would be a very clever, deliberate way to do it. In another setting I could see it. But here? There's no one here who would be impressed. Killing someone like me in a place like this is easy; something that involved here would be a wasted effort. You don't strike me as someone who would go through all that for nothing.

"Secondly, you know how to motivate people and get them to do what you want. You've got money and power and if you wanted me dead you could have it done. You could probably strangle me with your bare hands in the middle of the street and no one would say anything. The reason I'm still here isn't because you value my life or because of your scruples or any of that kind of bullshit. I'm here because there's something you want from me. You have ways of making people dance when you tell them to dance, and I'm sure I'd be no exception. But you haven't asked me to do anything. So it seems you want to know what I'm made of. You want to see if I'm afraid of raw power, or the police or if I will bend when people I care about are involved—the answer to each is 'yes', by the way. I'm not some secret agent. If you squeeze, toothpaste comes out, pure and simple.

"But you know that about people. You know that poise and posturing is all empty when you've got someone tied to a chair and there's a blowtorch and pliers sitting around. Or a nice stiff drink. Either way. I'm nothing special.

"But I am relatively anonymous. I know that I'm a rabbit, as you say, and I know that this is the lion's den. I've got nowhere to run or hide and fighting? Well, that's just foolish.

"So I think you want to see if I'll play whatever part you want, and it seems like that part means staying in the lion's den, or worse. And if I stay perfectly still, I might just last another couple minutes. It's something about those couple minutes that you want. Figuratively speaking, of course."

He chuckled approvingly. "Well done. You certainly have a nose for this kind of thing and a flair for metaphor—a double rarity. It's little wonder you've excelled in your current vocation. I'm glad we have a tentative understanding of one another. It does save me from having to resort to more vulgar displays of power, something for which I imagine those close to you will owe you a great debt, were they to find out.

"Besides, I've never been one for the posturing and such. I suppose that's why I chose you. The less I have to impress upon you, the more we can get done.

"I'm sure this sounds all very sinister, and it can be. But I suggest you look at this more as I've selected you as a retainer rather than being extorted or forced into anything. There are many advantages to this particular arrangement for you, not the least of which is access to those in my circle. Your days of peddling whimsy to the entitled children are over. You will have access to the true halls of power on a level you've only dreamt of. You'll even get to learn the secret handshake... No, really—that's a thing.

"I've had my eye on you for some time and if you don't believe anything else I've said, believe that we have this one trait in common: we are both so *bored*. You play those simpleton trust fund kids with such ease and now there's no challenge left. You annoy your parents with your carrying on and your oh-so-scandalous relationship, but even that manufactured drama is passé. And your beloved D—you know as well as I do that the novelty and intensity will wane eventually. After that you'll be looking for the next person who will be able to spark a fire in your gut. It won't last, not because you don't have feelings for him, but because it'll become so *ordinary*. For you and me ordinary is the same thing as prison. We are great at what we do because we can't help but raise the bar. Besides, settling would be so painfully dull."

He said all that and then just looked at me. I wanted him to be wrong more than anything. I wanted there to be a happy quiet place for me and D where things could just *be*. But I knew he was right about me. I wanted to be better for D; I wanted to be as good as D believed I could be. But impressing him, while difficult, seemed attainable. And once I'd done it, as much as I wanted it to be different, I knew that I'd need something more.

I remember in one of your sermons you said that God speaks in ways we understand, but the Devil speaks in ways that make sense. It was definitely like that.

I'd like to say I didn't have a choice, and maybe in some sense, I didn't. But even if I had, I still would've accepted that offer.

For a while I seemed to be living a charmed life. Convincing D that I'd changed my lifestyle was deceptively easy when suddenly I was surrounded by legitimate businessmen and the upper crust of the upper crust. Mr. Halford had arranged that I'd take over a consulting company he had a controlling interest in. I had all the trappings of legitimacy but at the end of the day my job was the same: find information, exploit connections and bring together buyers and sellers.

I moved out of the condo and got a place in a neighborhood I had no business being in. Part of that was at Mr. Halford's direction, but I loved the conspicuous consumption. Our neighbors initially looked down on D and I, but having Mr. Halford and a few business associates over for drinks took care of that. They may not have respected our money, but they sure as hell respected my position.

That's what I had always been looking for—seeing those arrogant motherfuckers squirm when I was around because they knew what I could bring down on them, or worse yet, what Mr. Halford could do if he felt his retainer wasn't being afforded the requisite deference—it was everything that I had ever dreamed of. Looking back, I suppose that for all the changes I promised to make for D and myself, the only thing I'd done is gotten better at juggling my two lives.

I hired B on as my assistant at the company and for a while it seemed like I had everything in place. I had D at home. I had B, who I trusted without hesitation, handling a lot of the day-to-day things. Mr. Halford, for his strange demands, left me to run the business as I saw fit. As long as everything got done, he wasn't interested in the details.

The job itself was challenging. Most of the time it was like building some super-secret weapon for the military: I didn't know what the ultimate goal was, but I was given one specific task to complete that would be combined with the efforts of some others in Mr. Halford's employ and would result in… something. I suppose one of the problems of being the cleverest guy in the room is you don't always know when it's smart to stay dumb. I could've learned that from B, he was perfect at focusing on a single thing and intentionally not knowing anything else.

I remember once I was supposed to go to an abandoned farmhouse in the middle of nowhere. I was supposed to arrive in the morning and then wait there until dusk. If a girl showed up I was supposed to tell her "alphabet". If a man showed up I was supposed to give him this little hand crafted wooden box—no idea what was in it, if anything. If no one showed up I was supposed to set the car and the house on fire and walk home.

It may have all been a test, I have no way of knowing but it took me almost the entire night to get back home after setting the fire and leaving. That's the thing—it was a big game for him, same as it was for me on some level. I can say that I got paid a lot for that job, more than most.

That was the strangest one, but they all had a cloak and dagger element about them. I was always on, always trying to figure out the angles. You start to make connections—certain guys you run into, you figure out who they work for. Some locations were used for certain kind of transactions. The farmhouse had been a drop point for stolen information and drugs, for example. So I tried to figure out what was going on based on the players, locations, what I was asked to do and when it happened.

I got pretty good. I was supposed to bring a cake—like a birthday cake—to an alley behind a club and give it to this guy I'd met a couple times before who worked for a shipping company. Before it went down I told B, "someone's gonna be dead in the next two days." And I was right. A mid-level enforcer was found in a trash compactor two days later—been there about a day. I was able to figure out different pieces of the puzzle most of the time. I was tantalizingly close to figure the whole thing out a few times.

I think Mr. Halford knew I was figuring things out. He made a couple cryptic comments about events afterwards like he was teasing me with insight into what had gone down. He seemed kind of tickled when I was able to counter with a little something about it—how the message was communicated or who was involved or why something had been done. It was probably hubris that made me think he was impressed. Looking back, he was probably pleased in the same way a pet owner is pleased when they teach a dog to do balance a biscuit on their nose. Maybe he really did trust me with that information. It's hard to really know after the fact.

I was making inroads all over the place and began doing a little freelance work here and there for other players. There was a gentleman's agreement that the members of the inner circle could utilize the others' guys from time to time as long as it didn't interfere with their other duties. I probably took that a little far—I started networking with some of the other guys directly.

It was a nice little arrangement. If I had two jobs on opposite sides of town, I could swap jobs with another guy who would handle the one in his territory and I'd take care of one of his that was closer to me, for example. I could take care of both and be home in time for dinner. We'd both save a trip, everything was done nice and tidy and no one was any the wiser. It also let us set up an internal pool to bid on certain jobs. Let's say I had a job in a nice vacation spot, but the job would take three days, but paid well. Sounds great, but it was D's birthday and he was getting suspicious of my activities so some time off would calm the waters. I would open it up to the others, they could get the nice vacation and the pay (less a percentage "finder's fee") and everyone ends up happy. It gave some of the guys coming up a chance to show their mettle; it gave established guys a chance to control their workflow a bit more, and it gave me a chance to see all the moving pieces and a glimpse of the bigger picture.

Some guys would end up giving away almost their entire workload. I used it more selectively. It helped me with some flexibility when I needed things to appear normal for D, but it also gave me a chance to get to know the other players involved. If there was one guy who was suddenly getting a lot of work from one of Mr. Halford's competitors I made sure meet him and get to know his operation a little bit. I had no interest in running the game—if that rumor had started I'm sure it would've been interpreted as a power grab and I would have disappeared one night never to be seen again. I was sure interested in knowing how to play the game better than anyone, though. It wasn't a secret, but all the same I was sure to drop a convenient tip to Mr. Halford or the inner circle guys when their business interests would benefit. It kept everyone happy, the higher-ups got the work done, got the benefit of occasional insight to what the others were up to and the guys doing the work got a little freedom. Win-win-win.

Or at least it should've been.

The way of maintaining secrecy in the system was that no one knew what anyone else was doing. The thing with the cake, for instance, worked because I was pretty sure I was delivering a request that a hit be approved. There were other people advising of the target, the means, time and place, arranging payment, making sure it was suitably clean or messy —all the details. I knew enough to know how things worked and that depending on who was doing the asking, whether the request would likely be approved or not. But I didn't know the who's, why's, when's or where's of it.

Other people and their little assignments added their pieces to the puzzle and in the end no one knew too much and could only have suspicions. It was a good system. It kept those directing it shielded behind multiple layers of protection. It kept the messengers safe because you never knew what you were delivering, or if you were just giving a birthday cake to a guy on his birthday. And it kept those who carried out the orders safe from angry employers—you can't be suspected of cooperating if you don't know who's ordering you to do something or why.

It was evening and I was just about to head home when I got the request—deliver an unmarked vehicle to the reservoir on my side of town. Nothing stood out about the job: pay was normal, no special conditions. I'd done dozens, if not hundreds of these kinds of jobs before. I called B and had him get the vehicle. While I was arranging that, a job came through the pool. Another rush job, this one that appeared to be a payment drop. Then a third job came through. That was the one I should've just ignored. I could've had B deliver the vehicle. I could've have done the payment drop and no one would have thought anything else. The third job was delivering a message to a contractor.

Part of me was excited to realize that I had three pieces of a puzzle so instead of just doing my job I started looking them over. I knew enough of Mr. Halford to know that the vehicle likely had specialty equipment for whatever was supposed to get done. The payment to a contractor indicated either a robbery or a hit. However, since it was a rush job you could pretty much rule out a robbery—no contractor I knew of would do a rush job on something that involved.

The message confirmed a hit, but that wasn't the part that was the problem. It was the "who" that was the problem. Each of the inner circle guys had a codename. Mr. Halford's real name wasn't Mr. Halford—that was his codename. I don't know how they were chosen or assigned them and it didn't matter. The messages followed a pretty strict protocol —person requesting the job, then there would be a time and place encoded, type of job (also encoded) and finally subject identifier. Looking at it, you'd never know what it was for— the specifics were always encrypted with different cyphers. But when you know other details you can figure out more. What I realized was that there were two inner circle names in message. Mr. Halford at the top and another inner circle guy as the subject—Mr. Halford was ordering a hit on one of the inner circle. That was why it was a rush job—the inner circle guys—would know about a job in the planning, even if it didn't involve him or his guys if it was out there for any length of time.

Now I've made Mr. Halford sound like a scary guy, and he absolutely could be. But in that group, he was mid-level, and the name I saw in there was a top-tier guy. There was no precedent for something like that in the system. Historically anyone who crossed one of the inner circle was taken care of quickly and usually in a way that sent a message.

The anonymity of the system couldn't protect anyone from retaliation if the hit didn't work. Even if they did manage to kill him, there was no indication that there was even a consensus against the target or for Mr. Halford—there weren't defined factions within the organization itself. All of it could end in a civil war at worst. At best it would result in the purging of most of the contractors. With the pool it was impossible to tell who all was aware of any specific piece of the puzzle, which meant everyone was at risk of being eliminated as part of the clean-up. And "clean-up" in this case likely meant friends, family, business associates—basically anyone standing too close.

And in the *best* best-case scenario after a successful hit a handful of patsies would be singled out as having arranged the coup by Mr. Halford and he'd have them eliminated as both the only possible witnesses to what he'd done and as the perpetrators. In either case, I wouldn't fare well.

I tried to think up options. I could notify the intended target and hope he could deal with Mr. Halford swiftly. Of course with Mr. Halford gone, so was my protection and since I knew too much, I'd likely be disposed of. I could tell Mr. Halford I discovered what he was planning and try to leverage that into protection. That would be a move that smacked of desperation and that seemed to be the one thing that would earn his contempt faster than anything else, again leading to my likely demise.

The authorities were puppets. Contacting them would have no better result than approaching one of the higher-ups and would have the added downside of me being labeled a snitch, which would not only guarantee a death, but a painful one at that. If I ran I'd be essentially volunteering myself as the patsy and with their resources it would be only delaying the inevitable. I was stuck and worse yet, I knew I was stuck. If I hadn't put it together there was at least a chance I could've survived the purge, but I had no options.

B came back to the office after dropping off the vehicle and found me there. I told him everything. I think he would've preferred not knowing, but he was in the same boat as me. After I finished neither of us said anything for a while.

"What do you want to do?" he finally asked me.

"There's nothing to do. There's nothing that can be done."

"There's always something you can do. Might not mean anything, but you don't have to just sit and wait for something to happen."

"You don't get it. There's no way for this to turn out well. I'm fucked. We're fucked. There's no way to make this better. There's no way for me to work this out."

"Well, there are times when you just have to take what's coming. But that's not the same as not having anything you can do."

"Shit. I did everything I could to get ahead and be the best at what I do and this is how it ends and you want me to do what, exactly?"

Now B was always composed and said as little possible. Even when he wasn't happy about something he'd never raise his voice. That was part of what made him so good at what he did—he seemed unflappable. All of which made it all the more unsettling when he—it wasn't a yell, exactly, his voice got louder and quivered a little, more forceful, I suppose. It was the most assertive I'd ever seen him.

"You need to sit down and listen for two goddamn minutes. You hear what you're saying? To hear you say it, the only person who's going to suffer the consequences here is you. Get your head out of your ass. This affects me. This affects the guys we work with. This affects D. Is the worst thing you can think of really what's going to happen to you, personally?"

"No, but there's nothing I can do about—"

"You're the only one in a position to do anything right now. You make it your livelihood to figure out everything. You just need to accept that to win sometimes means limiting the damage."

"Are you really going to lecture me?"

"I am, and you're gonna listen. You've reaped the benefits of this life and now you're acting as if you didn't know that this was a likely outcome. You had to have known that something was going to happen eventually. You always have a plan of some sort."

"What plan? There is no happy ending to this. I'm not getting out of this alive."

"Fine. You're right. You're probably not getting out of this. But that doesn't mean there isn't a play."

"What do you mean?"

"I mean that you could at least try and protect the people in your life."

"What? Give myself up? That's not going to do anything."

"C'mon. You know how things work better than anyone. The system isn't designed to let you win, but that kind of thing never bothered you before."

"Blow it all up?"

"That would be one way."

"How?"

"I have no idea. That's your department. I just work here."

"It would have to be big."

"It would have to be huge."

"Are you in it with me?"

"I'll do what I can."

And that was it. It took the entire night but I came up with a plan. I had to do it myself—I was the only one with the access and if I brought anyone it would only stir up suspicion. I sent B to my dad. Someone had to know what was going to happen and why. My father was a pragmatist and if anyone could divorce themselves from the particulars, it would be him.

I went to D. I gave him B's contact information and told him to run. I gave him everything I had. It was sad that after everything I'd done and all that I'd accomplished that the sum total of what I could muster on short notice was so small. He was scared and didn't want to leave. I was afraid he suspected that I was just trying to get him out of the way for some new fling, but finally I convinced him that he had to go as far away as he could. I promised—well, I lied—that I would be there soon and that B would make the arrangements for us to be together when it had blown over.

There was a moment where I wanted to tell him how scared I was and that there was nothing else I wanted than to go with him. It was a moment where it was so clear to me how I'd squandered everything. I'd let the stupidest things take over my life and after all the promises I made about making things better and being a better person it turned out that nothing had changed, not really. The only choice I had left was to make amends in a way that might never be understood. That was the hardest thing—when I was finally doing something selfless out of love for D I had to accept that it would appear that I was being my most selfish. Irony is the universe's way of giving you the finger.

I watched as D left and then I got myself prepared. I knew what I had to do. I had been right; there was no way to get out of it. There was no way to reason or trick my way through. The system was coldly rational. There were precedents and codes—there were rules.

The only way to get around the consequences of such a mechanism is to do something so far outside normal, so completely incomprehensible, that it shocked the system itself. I had to become such an outlier that I couldn't be dealt with by any normal set of rules.

I contacted Mr. Halford and set up a meeting for that evening. He didn't seem to suspect anything, or if he did he thought I was trying to make a deal. It didn't matter what he thought, though. He was at the dinner club where all those guys hung out at. It was the kinda place you see in movies or on TV that you think are completely made up because there's no way any place could be that stuffy, pretentious or ostentatious.

I was late arriving. I was ushered in to a dark sitting room. There were a few others mulling around at dimly-lit tables, but Mr. Halford was sitting by himself. He gave me a little bemused smile as I was shown my seat.

"You're late."

"I had to make a stop on the way."

"Hm? No trouble I trust."

"No such thing as trouble, just inconvenient opportunity, right?"

"Ah, you and your little sayings. Maybe someday you'll put them all down and you can sell them to a bunch of bored housewives. You'll be richer than all of us."

"Maybe. But all the really interesting sayings you have to leave out."

"Why's that?"

"Because the really interesting ones reveal more truth than we want to admit."

"Oh come now. Don't be so dull. You're not going to hide behind the 'masses can't handle the truth' argument are you? I expected more from you."

"No, no. The masses aren't nearly interesting enough to hide the truth from. They'll find ways to hide from it all by themselves. I think of it more like a game. In most games you can play the game or play your opponent. You do a bit of both, of course, but I've always found playing my opponent is more fruitful than playing the game."

"I see. Well, I suppose I've benefitted from that approach as well."

"If you have, it's been a long, long time. You're in the position where you control the pieces and the players. If you play either the game or your opponent on equal footing it's out of boredom. Most of the time you're involved in a much larger game."

"You flatter me."

"Not at all. I don't flatter anyone. That's one of the reasons you acquired my services. You know I check the angles and make the best possible move I can and, more often than not, I show a nice profit. So what do you think I would do, hypothetically, if I found that every angle had been cut off, every avenue closed and I was in a no-win situation?"

Mr. Halford sighed. He seemed bored already. "I suppose pack up, cut your losses, same as anyone."

"Well, that's fine if it's only money, or merchandise or even a reputation. But what if it's life and death kind of stuff?"

"I'm tiring of this. I know you're trying to be clever, but I really haven't the energy for cryptic analogies tonight."

"I know about the hit."

Mr. Halford shrugged indifferently.

"I suppose you've already got clean-up orders sent out?"

"If there were some unfortunate chain of events that were to befall one of my comrades, then I'm sure there would be people ready to go on a moment's notice to ensure order was restored and all culpable parties were dealt with. But I don't handle the straightening up. There are employees for that sort of thing."

"Yes, let them clean each other up."

"I'm actually disappointed in you. What is this? Is this supposed to be shocking? Are you trying to scold me? Or is this your attempt to plead for some sort of deal? I really thought better of you. I thought with you I'd at least be spared your plaintive mewling when I was done with our arrangement. I suppose I should only expect so much from people of your class."

"Oh, make no mistake, I'm not crying. And I know better than to lecture you. I guess I just wanted to get your thoughts on everything before..."

"Before what?"

Two men appeared at the entrance of the room. The valet stopped them. The first man whispered, his face was flush and he was sweating. The valet pointed to our table and nodded and the two men came towards us.

"Before this," I opened my jacket to reveal the explosive vest beneath. He sneered at me, "That won't save your family or your little boyfriend. This will only make things worse for them." It was the first time I remember him not having that smug glimmer in his eye.

The first man came to his side and whispered something into his ear. There was a flash of confusion that ran across his face. He looked to the other man who just nodded solemnly. "But... how?" he said.

"We're not sure, sir. We're tracking down all the information we have. But for now, you should come with us."

Mr. Halford turned to me, eyes wide, sneering in rage and indignation.

"What do you know of this?"

"I know that when you're put in a position you can't win, sometimes the only option is destroy the game."

"OFF LIMITS! That's how it's always been done! FAMILIES ARE OFF LIMITS!" he screamed at me, as he unsteadily got to his feet. The two men with him tried to steady him, still unsure of what was going on.

"Mr. Halford, the only way for the others to survive is to do the unthinkable. And before you ask, yes, it was all me. I apologized for being late, but it took a little longer than I expected."

Mr. Halford lunged across the table at me. His two escorts tried to catch him, but I was ready. I'm not much of a shot, but at that range along with the added adrenaline I had a dead aim. Two shots and both men were down with blood and goo sprayed behind them. By now everyone in the room was scurrying for cover. They had all seen me. And they could see it had only been me.

I grabbed Mr. Halford by the jacket and pushed him onto his back.

"I can see you're having problems with this," I said through clenched teeth as he tried to push me off by pushing at my face. He was old but he was putting up a bigger fight than I had anticipated. "You see, the only choice I had was to do something that made no sense—something so evil and senseless that there would be no other explanation other than I'd gone mad. That's why they're dead. I started with your children, Mr. Halford and worked my way up to your wife. They saw it all. It was the most horrible thing I've ever seen and I had to do it with my own two hands. But I'm almost done. All that's left is you and then afterwards my name will be cursed by all who hear it. Even the people I love will think I became something terrible—and they'll be right—but they'll never know I did it to protect them. Now hold still, Mr. Halford, this is going to hurt."

The first slash took off his right cheek. He raised his hands to defend himself which left his neck open. It was a good knife, but even so, severing a head took more than I had expected. The blood was spurting and after I hit his windpipe there was gurgling and frothy blood bubbles. I kept slashing deeper. I'm not even sure when he stopped moving. I don't even know how long it took. It probably was only a couple minutes but time went out of focus for me. Finally his head came free and I grabbed it by the hair. I walked out the front door. Police and security were just arriving. I stood and held his head up for them all to see.

"Behold! The coming of the Children of the Archaic Schism is at hand!" I yelled and then threw the head at them.

I went back inside to wait. I slipped off the vest. I'd rigged it with a timer just in case things didn't go as planned with Mr. Halford so I thought I'd spend my last moments watching the timer count down. But there was a whisper that came from a back corner.

"There's a way out. Hurry!"

It was B. He grabbed me and then it felt like my brain was exploding. There was a flash and then blackness. When I was able to see again we were in my father's laboratory.

I couldn't stand. Everything hurt and my skin smelled burnt. It was awful.

My father stood over me. "B told me what you were up to. I don't know what you did to get out of this and I don't want to know. I'm sure the news will be around soon enough.

"I've found a way for you to get away from here. It's all in the Narrative work I've been doing. I've found a place where you can go and no one will even think to look."

I opened my mouth to speak, but he interrupted me.

"I can't know anything about it. Not a word. They'll be watching me extra closely because of the nature of my work, of course. The only safe way is that B will be the only one who knows where you are and he'll be the only one who will have contact with you. Any messages you need to get to me, you give me to him, understand? I'll give you two a minute while I get things set up."

It was just me and B again. "I suppose he told you no contact with D?" B nodded. "Can I count on you to get messages to him anyway?"

"Same agreement we've always had. Besides, it's not as if you'll be seeing each other anytime soon. Seems like D has a right to know more than anyone."

"Thank you. You've been a good friend to me. I haven't always been one back but—"

"Don't start that now. Everything will work out as it's meant to. It's been a pleasure working with you."

Now I was starting to get a little emotional. It was all ending and I still didn't know what the plan was. "Do you know where I'm going?"

"I've seen a little. It's about as far away from here as you can get in about every way imaginable. It's kind of—"

"Don't tell me it's kind of 'out of the way' and have that be code for something."

"I was going to say kind of a shithole. But no one will look for you there. You can lie low. You'll figure it out. Just keep to yourself, don't make waves and keep off the grid. I'll make sure you're ok and do what I can, but it's going to be pretty lean living. Hopefully the explosion will make them think you're dead, but given who's involved I imagine that they'll be looking for something definitive. This will probably buy you some time to get lost, but I don't expect this to fully blow over for years.

"Here are your things. There's some clothing and disguise stuff to help you blend in. Let me know if you need replacements for any of it. You take care of yourself, ok?"

And that was it. That was the last time I saw my home. The planet Waffle was often described as "the Green Jewel of the Lamisciate System". If I close my eyes I can still see vast flowing rivers and lush vegetation. Waffle was considered the "nice suburbs" of the Tringol Galaxy and a beautiful place to grow up. I still miss it...

*****

"Get your giggling out of the way. I'll wait," Moses said with a touch of irritation.

"I'm sorry, I'm sorry. You really had me going there. I thought you were on the run from some drug cartel and then you do the whole 'Planet Waffle' thing... Ahhhhh, you got me good, Moses," Irvin said as he wiped away a tear. "Seriously, the whole build up was *amazing*."

Moses sighed. He looked around quickly. The few other patrons were involved in newspapers or staring listlessly into their coffee cup reflections. Their waitress was standing by the kitchen talking to the frycook. No one was paying attention. So, as Irvin tried to catch his breath from his fits of giggles Moses calmly reached up and removed his face. What was beneath resembled a bright purple puffer fish with a couple of antennae-looking protrusions around the cheeks.

"You can laugh, but for all you know 'Earth' means hemorrhoid on some distant planet," the Moses said through his little gasping puffer fish mouth.

Irvin stopped laughing.

Moses put his face back on. "You know, I remember when you were talking about John—the one who wrote the Book of Revelation. He'd been boiled in oil, exiled and then saw the end of the world. I feel like that sometimes—all sorts of horrible things I've seen and done with no one around who knows me. But some days this little world is so beautiful. I picture John sitting on the beach watching the sunset on his little exile island all those years ago and thinking that there was a certain peaceful beauty to all the violence and pain. When it's all said and done, if you're lucky, it's just you and your thoughts on the beach with the ocean washing sand up in between your toes. The world doesn't have to make sense as long you can steal a moment now and then where it all seems to be part of something bigger, something beautiful."

Part VI: Hello to a New Old Friend

Hope tilted her head and looked at him curiously. She'd never heard a grown man make that kind of sound before.

"Oh shit. You're not real. You can't be real," Lyle cried out as he tried to back up and over the back of his chair.

"It's ok, Lyle. She's with me," came a voice to his side. He let out another yelp and turned towards the sound and found Nicola sitting on the couch, smiling.

Lyle's head was spinning. Had they been here the entire time? Was Nicola playing a trick on him or something?

"Shhhh, darling. It's ok. I'll explain everything," Nicola hushed him reassuringly. "This is Hope. She's the one who really made this all possible."

"Who... are you?"

Nicola smiled with a strange familiar smile. "I'm exactly who you think I am. I know it all seems impossible, but it *is* me."

196

"No. I don't know you—you were just by the office the other day."

"Lyle, I know it's a lot to process right now, but you know that you know me. You just have to let yourself believe what your memories are telling you."

"I remember a girl…"

"—A girl that sometimes was a woman. We used to have great fun, didn't we?"

"No, I mean, I don't remember a face…"

"It has been a long time. Do you remember the 4th of July, under the table in the dining room? Or back in the trees afterwards? That girl we saw watching us was Hope."

Lyle crawled out the chair and edged towards the kitchen. Hope hadn't so much as blinked; she just stood watching them with an unnatural wooden kind of stillness.

"Hope, dear, could you give us a few moments?" Nicola asked. Hope looked at Nicola, nodded and vanished.

"Oh Jesus! She really just… just—" Lyle stammered.

"I know. She'll be back, though. She can come and go like that. But I thought she should give us a little privacy so we can talk."

"Why? Why do we need privacy?"

Nicola blushed and lowered her eyes. "Because I wanted to talk to you about the last time we saw each other."

"At the office?"

Nicola's cheeks flushed a deeper red. "No, before that."

She stood up and walked up to Lyle. Lyle recoiled but with the little ghost girl gone he was a little less skittish. In spite of his impulse to run out of the apartment screaming, he remained standing wedged against the breakfast bar. He did feel like he knew Nicola somehow. She kept walking towards him and until she was within a foot of him. The closeness made him anxious, but the closer she got, the more he realized he wasn't afraid of her.

"The last time I saw you you had grown up. I knew your father would be gone the next day, but I couldn't tell you. I knew I should have probably been more restrained but I had missed you for so long. I remember you more like this, but even back then, I could see who you would become and I couldn't say no. You've never heard a woman tell you she couldn't say no to you, but I couldn't. I let you touch me. I know it was only a dream to you but it felt real to me.

"I know your thoughts from your dreams. I know you've always wondered what it was like for me and I can tell you that it was a beautiful moment I've cherished all these years. I loved feeling close to you. I loved knowing what effect I had on you and, in the end, I loved knowing that I was able to please you." Her voice had settled into a breathy whisper by then. Lyle's mouth was dry and the blood had rushed from his head and he had a tentative, rubbery and confused erection.

She saw his eyes gloss over slightly as his head swam with confusion, emotion and awkward arousal. "You remember me now, don't you?" she asked innocently. Lyle gave a tentative nod. She smiled.

"You have to be patient a little longer, Lyle. There's still more that needs to be done, but now we can see each other and talk to each other—"

Lyle reached up to touch her arm and she was gone as soon as his fingers would have made contact. There was only the sound of a quiet sigh of wind and the faint smell of electricity.

"You can't touch her," came the little girl's voice.

"Jesus Christ," Lyle blurted out as he saw the little ghost girl standing in the kitchen staring at him again.

"She's not strong enough yet. If you try and touch her it sends her to the Windy Place."

"Who the fuck are you?" Lyle wheezed, exasperated.

"I'm Hope."

"Yes, but *who* are you? I don't know you. What's the point of you?"

Hope shrugged. "What's the point of you?"

Lyle looked at the girl, irritated and then shook his head. "There's no point to me. None at all. Thanks for pointing that out."

Hope said nothing, but just stood watching him.

"You know, you're a creepy little kid. I mean, there's ghost creepy and then there's you. You know what I mean?" Hope's expression didn't change. She stood motionlessly staring at him. "Yes. Exactly. Just like that. That's fuckin' creepy. Not in a 'I'll drag your soul to hell' sorta way, but in a 'I bet you have a room full of severed cat heads' sorta way."

Hope didn't move.

"You could at least blink once in a while."

Hope tilted her head curiously and then blinked very deliberately. Lyle sighed.

"Sad thing is, I think you actually did that because you thought it would help instead of being even more creepy," he said as he slowly approached her. He tried to be stealthy by reaching his hand out behind her trying and then quickly swatting at her from behind. His hand passed through her and she was instantaneously a foot out of his grasp.

"I'm different than Nicola. I can come and go as I please," she said flatly. She didn't appear annoyed by his maneuver, but disinterested.

Lyle had recoiled instinctively when his hand had swiped through the space she had been standing and now was standing defensively, side facing Hope, cringing as if there were a feral gerbil about to lunge at him. The look on his face combined with the strange contorted stance he was in caused Hope to giggle. As the snicker escaped from her, she stood bolt upright with a look of surprise from the sensation. She hadn't laughed since her days on the farm.

Something had happened to her since she had helped Nicola. She was feeling things like she hadn't since she had come to the Windy Place. Even in her time with Bitty the closest she'd come to happiness was a sense of sympathy and connection, however faint, that they'd shared. At those moments it was more that she remembered happiness than actually felt happiness. But now that was changing and she wasn't sure how much she really liked it.

*****

Hope was curled up in the roots of her tree. The bark would start to slowly creep over her skin, but instead of letting it cover her she brushed it off. The warmth of the tree was inviting, but, try as she might, resting in it didn't seem appealing anymore. There was so much to see and if Nicola was there it seemed like there may be things left to do. Simply stopping and letting it all bleed away seemed like a waste.

Growing up, her mother used to tell her and her brothers that "boredom is just impatience for the lazy." She wasn't sure what that had meant, but she realized she was bored. She wondered if Nicola was ever coming back or if they'd continue to travel together if she did. In the grey distance she saw a faint orange ball bobbing up and down. Hope rose and hurried towards it. As she got closer she could see the ball tailing a Memory again. She was initially confused since Nicola had said that she would be letting go. As she watched it, it began to twitch and throb strangely. She could hear wind and smell burning air coming from the ball and the Memory and then with a sharp clap and a flash the orange ball had turned into the orange form that Hope had seen in the other place.

"Hello Hope. I'm so glad to see you again," the form said. "I'm sorry if I kept you waiting. I had a few things I had to do. I needed to say goodbye to Lyle in case this didn't work.

"Anyway, I'm glad you waited for me. You didn't have to."

Hope walked up to the form. Before she really knew or understood what she was doing she wrapped her arms around its waist and gave it a hug. The form tried to pull back but it was too late. Instead of wind and lightning there was a gentle hum and a vibration.

"Oh! Well, that was unexpected," Nicola exclaimed.

Nicola tentatively reached down and ran her hand across Hope's head. "You're really quite extraordinary. Is it... do you feel that vibration too? This is so... so..."

Hope felt warm. It wasn't like the tree that seemed to be just the right temperature, but almost hot. Closeness to Nicola had an intensity and tension all its own. Hope felt as if she was melting away within it. And suddenly there they were. Nicola was standing there, solid, tangible. Even when Hope had rested her head against the form of the woman before it felt more like wrapping her arms around a column of air. Hope reached out and touched Nicola's hand. She was able to grasp it. She had her own warmth.

"Is this what it feels like to be you?" Nicola asked. "It feels so... detached. How do you live with nothing but your own thoughts?"

Hope said nothing but led Nicola by the hand towards one of the Memories that were rising and falling. As they approached the wind picked up again; Nicola seemed to be experiencing it too and held up her free hand as if to shield unseen eyes. Hope reached out and grasped one of the figures and suddenly they were on a busy sidewalk following a balding man wearing a fedora—bare scalp showing around the brim of the hat—a grey trenchcoat, brown slacks and galoshes with thick, brown, horn-rimmed glasses.

"Where are we?" Nicola exclaimed.

"We're with him," Hope pointed at the man.

"But where is this?" As a large, green car roared by Nicola looked even more perplexed, "Before I had to stay within a certain distance of Lyle. I guess that's not true anymore. When are we?"

Hope shrugged. "Whenever he was when he did this."

"This seems like it was probably a while ago, at least from where I was. You can just jump into these moments?"

"I just came here to show you. I didn't really choose anything."

"I'm not sure I understand. You don't have any control?"

Hope said nothing but led Nicola again to an old, abandoned storefront. She reached out and grasped the door and suddenly its whole history appeared before them. Nicola stepped back, stunned.

"We can go anywhere there," Hope said as she pointed at the history of the building splayed out before them.

"This... this is amazing," Nicola murmured. "It's like you can see any moment within the Narrative as long as you're able to touch it. And you can go from object to object, person to person even when you're viewing something?"

Hope nodded. Nicola seemed so enthralled that she released Hope's hand and walked into a moment of the store. It was strange because Hope was able to see Nicola within the moment now. It was surprising, but Hope supposed that if there had been someone else with her they would have seen her when she was jumping from spot to spot as well. Hope followed her in.

"Did I do that by myself?" Nicola said breathlessly. "We were together and then I reached out and I was here alone. I've been here for—I don't know how long. Is that how time works here? Did you push me here?"

Hope shook her head. "You just went in."

"Do you think I can move about freely here?"

Hope shrugged.

Nicola reached towards a passing man before pulling her hand back hesitantly. "If I try, how do I know I won't get lost?"

"Whenever I want to go back, I just let go and I'm back in the Windy Place."

"The Windy Place is that grey place with the tree, right? How do I let something go?"

Hope looked at her a little confused. "I touch something and go from place to place, but when I want to go back I just stop touching it." It seemed simple enough to Hope, but Nicola seemed unsure. After a moment of indecision Nicola took a deep breath, closed her eyes and vanished. Hope waited a moment and then released the Memory. She found herself back at the tree with Nicola standing there waiting.

Nicola was giddy and laughing when Hope appeared. "I can't believe that worked. This is… there are no words for this. I mean, I've viewed the Narratives before, but I never thought I could view them from the inside. This is wonderful!

"I'm going to try and go back. I want to see if there's anything that I can see that explains this. Is that ok—if I leave and come back again?"

"Ok."

Nicola nodded appreciatively, then disappeared.

The Windy Place seemed so very quiet with Nicola gone. Hope sulked around a bit, but instead of following Memories or visiting places, she preferred to wait. She climbed the tree. It was strange that it had never occurred to her to try it before. She hung from one of the branches, swinging back and forth on her outstretched arms when she noticed something. At the base of the tree was a brownish semi-circle with a white edge. She'd seen them grow on trees back at the farm, but there had never been one on the tree before.

"You'll never believe what I found," came Nicola's voice from the other side of the tree. She peered around the trunk at Hope and waved happily. "Before when I was following Lyle I made the connection and was constantly pumping energy in to stabilize the link as well as trying to negate any interference and trying to adjust for any changes. I pretty much just jumped on and hung on for dear life. But when we connected, we actually *connected*." Nicola paused waiting for some sort of response from Hope, but only got a blank stare in return.

"Ok, let me try this again, did you ever see a rodeo where they rode a bull? That's what I was trying to do. But with you our wavelengths actually synced up. It wasn't just me pumping energy in, you seemed to be giving back and we were able to create a bridge of some sort. That's why I can touch things here. I'm no scientist, but I'm pretty sure that this is a first. Instead of being tied to you, you're bringing me into your world. Do you understand? I still can't do a lot of things, but I can move about freely and I can interact directly with you. It's unprecedented!"

Hope kept swinging from the tree branch. "So what do you want to do?"

Nicola came underneath her and scooped Hope into her arms. "Why don't you teach me what I can do? You know this better than I ever could. Would you be willing to do that?"

Hope closed her eyes. She hadn't been held by anyone since her father held her on his lap while he read to her back on the farm. Even though Nicola was a giant orange creature, being cradled in her arms felt very comforting. For the first time since she'd come to the Windy Place she felt like there was someone who cared about her in the same way she cared about them. She realized how lonely her life had been before. She never wanted Nicola to leave.

"Ok. But can we stay here a little while?" Hope asked quietly.

Nicola brushed a stray hair off her face and nodded. "Of course we can. You know, my little one is about your age. He's a sweet little guy, but I always wanted to have a little girl. I would've loved having you as my daughter." Nicola gave Hope a little squeeze. "Do you mind if I consider you my little girl when I'm here?"

Hope smiled and nodded. "Well that's settled then," Nicola answered.

They travelled all over the place, through different times and different lives all across the world. Nicola's excitement and curiosity at first confused Hope, but the more they were together the more Hope began to remember those feelings and even began to feel little glimmers of them in herself. The more they travelled the more Hope became able to manipulate objects—closing doors, making sounds, even being seen if she wanted to be. Hope explained how she was able to appear to those in the real world—she'd picture herself in the scene and would project herself (for lack of a better word) there. Nicola was fascinated by this and said it was very similar to how she used avatars when she'd visited Lyle in his sleep.

Nicola was unable to touch or manipulate much. When she did she'd be exhausted and have to rest for a while. But in time she did master appearing. Perhaps unsurprisingly, when she did figure out how to manifest a physical apparition it was in the form of the woman that she'd use to visit Lyle.

They kept jumping from place to place as Nicola slowly mastered some of Hope's tricks. They ended up in a dirty, dilapidated neighborhood. Hope used to be able to breeze through places like that without a second thought, but Nicola was repulsed and horrified by the squalor. Hope had always viewed things within the memories as inanimate—moving pictures, not people. Nicola in contrast seemed to feel empathy towards the people she saw. There were children playing in filth and things happening that Nicola said little girls like Hope shouldn't see. Hope looked at the scene before her and saw it as Nicola was seeing.

"I don't want to stay here," she told Nicola.

Nicola nodded, but then something caught her interest, as if something was off. Hope didn't see anything other than some people getting on a bus. Nicola studied one of the men boarding the bus intently.

"Can we go? Please?" Hope asked. Nicola looked down at her distractedly before realizing that Hope was talking and another instant before she realized what Hope had said.

"Of course, dear. I think it's time we go back to your tree, anyway."

They returned and sat under the tree. Hope rested her head in Nicola's lap and Nicola gently stroked her hair as they listened to the distant sound of wind in the stillness. Hope noticed that there were more mushrooms growing around the trunk of the tree. Everything else looked fine. It was just strange to see things in the Windy Place changing

"I need to go to Lyle, Hope," Nicola said as she kept running her hands through Hope's hair. "It's what I came here to do and now, thanks to everything you've shown me, I'll be able to see him when he's awake…"

Nicola's voice trailed off, she seemed apprehensive. Hope didn't want to think about her leaving. She liked moments like the one they were having and thinking about them ending made her stomach knot up.

"I've been thinking about this for a while. I don't know what it might mean, but I'd like you stay with me. It just wouldn't feel right after everything to be with Lyle and not have you with me, too. I know you said you'd help me, and you have— you've done so much, but I'd like you to stay. I know I can't ask you to, but I like to think that maybe you like being with me, too. I don't know how Lyle will take it. He's a good man and I think he'll understand. I don't know. It's like I set out to be with him, but in the meantime I found you and now instead of just being with him it feels like I have the chance to have a little family with you, him and me all together. Would you like that? I mean, you can say no and I'd totally understand."

Hope looked up at Nicola and smiled. She took Nicola's hand and put it against her cheek and closed her eyes. "Just like a family," she said with a soft smile.

Hope wasn't sure how they would find Lyle again. She'd only found him originally because she saw Nicola. She told Nicola she didn't know where to start, but Nicola gave her a little hug. "It's alright. I know where we're going."

And then they were standing together in a small apartment. They stood together in the bathroom looking down a hallway at a man grabbing at himself. Hope was a little unnerved by it, but Nicola smiled. "I always know where to find him. He's my tree…"

*****

"You… you… took off your *face*!"

"I took off my faceplate."

"It was your *FACE*!"

"Ok, fine. I took off my face."

"But you were all, all—" Irvin mimicked the gulping motion that Moses' puffer fish face had done, completely with bulging eyes and puckered lips.

"This was a bad idea."

"No, no. It's just—you're a fish!"

"Now hold on, just because in your mind I resemble something that you've seen doesn't make me that thing. The evolutionary progression isn't the same on every planet. You don't think you all looked strange to me when I first got here?"

"How you boys doing? More coffee?" the waitress startled them both.

"Yeah, top me off," Moses said as he slid his cup towards her. "Irvin?"

Irvin looked dazed and didn't say a word, but kept unconsciously making the puffer fish face.

"Um, I think he's had enough. We'll just take the check when you've got a moment."

"Of course, dear," she smiled at Moses. As she left she gave Irvin a sideways glance.

"Listen, it's not that big of a deal. There's no invasion force out there looking to conquer the planet. We were barely able to find it and, frankly, it's kind of a dump. You've been left alone because there's really nothing here anybody wants. I'm not here to fuck anything up for you. You were a decent guy and I thought I'd tell you about it. I'm not trying to upset the apple cart or anything."

"But, this, all this, it's brilliant!" Irvin burst out. Other patrons and the waitress looked at him. Moses gave them a conciliatory wave to assure them everything was fine.

"Listen, you need to settle down. Forget I said anything."

"Forget? I can't forget this! Why would I want to? There's so much you can teach me!"

"Alright, fine. But somewhere else, ok? I actually kind like this place. Don't get us kicked out."

After they paid the bill (and Irvin got a couple more weird looks from the waitress) they headed out and reconvened at the reservoir near Moses' place.

"They say there are herons around here."

"Herons?"

"Yeah, big tall birds with long necks. They're pretty impressive. You have birds where you come from?"

"There are things like birds. Day to day life is pretty similar in a lot of respects. Or at least it's getting closer now. When I got here in the 70's I felt like I'd fallen through a wormhole, went back in time and fell on my keys in a giant pile of shit in the biggest backwater, godforsaken cesspool in the universe. No offense. But you guys have at least started getting some of the basics down technologically and I've gotten used to some of it. It's kind of quaint for the most part."

"You said earlier that some of the stuff I mentioned reminded you of things you heard growing up. What did you mean by that?"

"The stuff about heaven and perfection and all of that. My father was working on this project—it's part of what got me here. He was theorizing about Narratives. It's complicated, but the quick version is that there are other universes but they all follow more or less the same script. Some are better, some are worse. The theory is that there is a perfect version of reality and that each Narrative is trying to become perfect in its own way. When you were talking about heaven it sounded a lot like the perfect Narrative to me." Anyway, before I left he said he'd managed to confirm that they existed.

"So did they have Jesus on your planet?"

Moses shifted uneasily on the park bench. "I wasn't much into religion. I mean there were belief systems that had similarities to the ones here, but there wasn't a Jesus-type character."

Irvin gave a triumphant little shout and clapped his hands. Moses looked at him surprised.

"Don't you see? This is wonderful! Your name was well chosen, Moses!"

"Uh, I don't understand."

"Oh, but it's so simple! Moses, you know stories of Moses right? 'The Ten Commandments' and all that? You see, the story isn't just liberating the Israelites. It starts way back before that—Moses was an Israelite baby but the Egyptian rulers at the time ordered all the babies to be murdered. He was set afloat down the river and was found and adopted by a daughter of the Pharaoh.

"Now this is where the parallels are amazing—he was raised as a member of the royal family, but one day he saw a slave driver beating a Hebrew slave and Moses killed the slave driver. He had to go on the run because of his crime and disappeared into the wilderness. But after 40 years God appeared to him and told him that he was to return to Egypt and deliver a message to the Pharaoh and liberate the Israelites. Do you see now?"

Moses looked at Irvin with pure befuddlement. Irvin sighed.

"*You* are Moses! I mean, you are *Moses*, but you're *also* Moses, you see? You're the one God has chosen to return to Pancake —"

"Waffle."

"Whatever. You've been chosen to return to Waffle to tell your people about Jesus!"

"Uh."

"Don't worry, there's plenty of time to figure that out. Besides we've got enough work to do here."

"You know you can't tell anybody about any of this, right?"

"Of course. No, I was talking about the program. You have no idea how much this has inspired me. I'm going to go home and start working on an entire sermon series. You going to be ready tonight?"

"...Uh, sure."

Irvin slapped his shoulder with a hearty chuckle. "Good man. See you then. We got the Lord's work to do!"

*****

"Now tell me again—how do you know me?"

214

Nicola smiled and clasped her hands on the couch. Everything he said seemed to make her smile, but it wasn't a fake smile—that would have creeped him out. She seemed genuinely happy to be there with him.

"I've always known you. You've seen movies where two characters were always supposed to be together but they just didn't know it? It's like that except I've known it, we've just been a universe apart."

"And when you say 'universe'…"

"I mean Narrative. Or 'alternate reality'. That's a term you use here, isn't it?"

"So you're my alternate reality girlfriend?"

Nicola laughed. "No, I'm your real girlfriend from an alternate reality. We were supposed to be together—if you look at the other Narratives it's always you and me. These are just the circumstances where we make it happen here."

"You realize I probably should go to a hospital right now, don't you? First there's a little ghost girl who watches me jerk off and then I see a girl who says she's from an alternate reality and is supposed to be my girlfriend. Psychiatrists buy lake homes because of guys like me saying stuff like this."

"You tell me: do you think you're crazy?"

"…a little."

"Why's that?"

Lyle fidgeted. "Well, you know, all the stuff I said… and, you know…"

"Good things don't happen to you?"

"Well, sorta. I mean, even girls in this dimension don't go throwing themselves at me."

Nicola looked him in the eyes. She didn't move until Lyle returned her gaze. Lyle felt himself skip a breath as their eyes met. The intensity of her look seemed to bore a hole straight through him.

"I'm not a girl. I came all this way because you are important to me. I'm not throwing myself at you. I'm telling you what you already know—that this is the best thing that's going to happen to either of us. This isn't an act of desperation, it's an act of faith and hope and endless enthusiasm for the beauty I see in store for both of us. I mean, I can't wait to get started, but I'm happy to wait until you're ready to come with me. Do you understand?"

Lyle swallowed even though his mouth was dry and nodded. He'd had relationships before—flings, semi-serious encounters, the gamut—but she was right: there was something about her that he instinctively seemed to know and trust. Or at least something about her that made him want to trust her.

"So what do we do now?"

"Well, we still can't touch. I'm getting better at some of that, so maybe someday. But for now, I know all about you and you know next to nothing about me so we'll have to do things the old-fashioned way."

"What do you mean?"

"We have to talk, silly man," Nicola laughed. "I know you have questions. I'll tell you anything you want to know."

A silence dropped over them. Nicola sat back, legs crossed with a patient smile. Talking really had never been Lyle's thing, but in this case he really was interested in Nicola; he just couldn't think of anything to say. Finally he asked, "Well, what did we talk about?"

He shook his head after saying it out loud, thinking the question itself was silly.

"That's actually a good question. I mean we did a lot of things together but the parts that always stood out to me were when we were alone and would just talk. I remember the time we probably had the best sex we'd ever had but not because of the sex. It was afterward where we just talked to each other until the sun came up. That was probably the most fulfilling, intense night of my life."

"What did we talk about?"

Nicola laughed, "What *didn't* we talk about? It was in our first apartment and I remember I was lying next to you with my head on your shoulder and I was kind of freaking out. I mean we really rocked it that night. Not to brag, but it was very good. But as we were lying there I realized that I really wanted us to work and that I felt very vulnerable because it was something I wanted more than anything else I could think of. I wasn't sure what you were thinking or if you felt the same or what the future had in store for us—my mind was just racing a million miles an hour. I mean, I was really starting to get anxious about it and then you looked at me, and I'll always remember this, you did your little sly grin and said, 'Don't think that this means you get to hold the remote now or something.'

"You always were able to do that—all the worry and anxiety I had about things, you were somehow able to make them not matter. Whenever I was with you it felt like what I thought home should feel like. I know that's corny, but it's really true. It just felt like the place I could be safe and be me and everything would be alright.

"So we talked about classes and friends and things we'd done and things we wanted to do. Rufus came and curled up between us and fell asleep so we spent most of the night with a snoring dog between us but even that was great. It was one of those moments where everything seemed to be just right. You know that weird grey color everything gets before dawn? I remember that and it felt like there was a little universe just for us and Rufus and that moment was the one thing repeated in it. But it ended and we both fell asleep.

"I remember waking up a few hours later feeling tired and almost rubbery—you know how when you didn't sleep and you can feel exhausted and giddy and wobbly like you your bones have been replaced with precariously balanced globs of jelly? I totally felt like that.

"I looked over and saw you sleeping and Rufus snuggled up next you sleeping on his back, his legs sticking up in the air like he was roadkill. I thought to myself: If this is all there is, if this is as good as my life gets, then it was worth it.

"I don't know if I answered your question; I just kind of kept going. Sorry."

"It's ok. You sorta did."

Neither spoke for a moment.

"So why did you come here if everything was so good? Did something happen to me, or 'alternate reality me'?"

Nicola bowed her head for a moment. "We got lost. The two of us, we lost our way. It was all my fault. I realized I'd made a huge mistake and then…" her voice trailed off.

"It's ok, I don't need to—"

"No, you deserve to know. There was an accident and I lost you. You were alone and I should have been there. I couldn't have stopped it, but you shouldn't have been alone at the end. So I found you. I found you here and I promised that you wouldn't be alone again…"

"Oh…" Lyle couldn't think of anything to say. They both sat there, not saying a word for a few minutes.

"…This is so hard," Nicola murmured.

"What?"

"This. This awkward silence and not knowing what to say. We never had this problem before. It's just weird not knowing the right thing to do. I thought we'd just *know* when we were together. It's not going like I thought it might."

"I'm sorry."

"What? No, it's not your fault. I mean you have this strange woman showing up and telling you about a life that you've never lived and might never have even wanted for all I know. I just had it all pictured in my mind and it would just happen. It was silly."

Her voice waivered a little as she spoke. Nicola's ever-present smile had disappeared and she sat, clasping her hands, wringing them nervously as she spoke. She looked at Lyle. Before she'd always came across as quietly confident but at that moment she looked scared and vulnerable. Her expression seemed to be pleading for some sort of reassurance that what she wanted was possible. Lyle wanted to let her know that it would be fine, but he really had no sense that it would be, or even what "it" really was.

Lyle felt bad for her because she really looked as if she was laying her soul bare in hopes of some sort of meaningful, emotional return. Lyle didn't want her to feel bad and even hoped that he might be able to give her what she wanted, but even if he were successful, any gesture, for good or ill, would have meant more to her than to him.

"Before Rufus died he was the greatest dog," Lyle began tentatively. "I'd come back from work and he'd come out of the bedroom because he'd been napping on the bed. I'd take him outside and he'd do his thing and then we'd come back and sit on the couch. I'd watch TV and he'd sit on the cushion next to me. If I was having a bad day he'd lay his head on my leg until I scratched his ears. If I was stressed he'd bring his ball over and I'd throw it in the bedroom and he'd run and fetch it.

"He knew me really well. He just seemed to know what kind of things to do that would make me feel better depending on what kind of day I'd had. In the same way when I got home one day and he stayed on the bed, I knew he wasn't feeling well. That's when I took him in to the vet and found out he had cancer. It was because he knew me and I knew him and when something was off we could tell right away.

"That's how I remember him. That's what I miss when I think of him. He was such a great dog. But when I think a little harder I remember when I got him: he chewed everything, he'd piss on the bed, he barked and yelped early in the morning when I was trying to sleep, he drank out of the toilet, you name it. And it wasn't all bad. He was super cute and cuddly even then. I remember one day I came back from work and there was toilet paper everywhere. I'd bought one of those big packs and left it in the bag by the bathroom door. I didn't even think that he might do something with it. It was a pain in the ass to clean it all up, but it was kind of funny in retrospect. I mean there wasn't an inch of floor that didn't have toilet paper on it. I couldn't have done it more comprehensively if I'd tried.

"So, I guess that's what I'm trying to say. Rufus was great and I miss having him all laid back and cool when I get home, but in order to get there I had to deal with a puppy and all the chaos and poop that comes with that. Do you understand what I'm saying?"

Nicola's brow was furrowed and a hint of a frown tugged at the corners of her mouth. "You're saying that I'm your dog?"

"What? No! Well, not exactly. It's just a metaphor…"

Nicola gave a half-hearted smile. "I know, I was joking… Listen, maybe this was a bad idea. I should go—"

"No, you don't have to go. I'm sorry if it wasn't what you wanted to hear. It's nothing against you or anything."

Nicola shook her head. "No, what you said was fine. And you're right. You were always able to tell me things in a way that made sense. Everything you said was fine. I just need to… I just need some time to get my own head on straight. I wasn't being realistic and now I'm just being silly by feeling this bad," she wiped a tear that had started down from the corner of her eye. "It's not you. I just need some time to process all of *this*. Whatever 'this' is, you know?"

"You don't have to go."

Nicola laughed as she wiped another tear away. "I think I really do. Look at me; I'm a mess. Great way to impress the man I love that I'm a healthy, loving partner, right? Break down and cry like a baby when you're being kind and reasonable about everything."

Lyle felt his heart sink as Nicola kept trying to maintain her composure even though she was clearly feeling disappointed. Normally he would have felt just awkward, but he really did want Nicola to be happy. "Please stay," he said quietly. Nicola wiped her eyes and looked at him. She gave a sad smile. "See? Always watching out for me. Some things don't change no matter where we are."

"I want you to stay. We can talk some more."

"You're very sweet, but I do need to go. I'll be back. I promise. I just can't do this right now, ok?"

"Are you sure?"

"I'm sure. I'll be ok. I'll see you soon." And with that she was gone.

A sense of dread crept into the pit of Lyle's stomach. As improbable as the situation was, it felt like he may have somehow messed something up. He couldn't deny that there was an attraction and for all its contrivances she really did seem to be someone that he'd like. His mom used to say that he had the uncanny knack for finding angst in good things. He thought that might be truer than he wanted to admit.

*****

Nicola appeared out of the vast fields of gray, but said nothing. She seemed to be weeping quietly, although she kept her back half-turned as if to avoid letting Hope see anything.

"You lied to him."

"What?"

"You lied to him."

Nicola looked at Hope, confused. "I lied to him about what? Were you watching us? Grown-ups talk to each other in different ways. It's all normal."

"But you never lived with him before and you said you did."

Nicola sat down at the base of the tree and gestured for Hope to come to her. She had Hope sit next to her and had her rest her head against her chest. "What's the matter, dear?"

Hope wasn't sure what she was feeling. Part of her was bothered by Nicola's dishonesty, not because she thought Lyle was being wronged, but the principle of the thing. It felt as if she and Nicola were doing something exciting—like they were explorers or pioneers and it seemed disingenuous to have to lie while doing it.

The other part of her was annoyed. She had someone with her for the first time in a thousand different lifetimes and now Nicola was trying to spend time with Lyle. There really wasn't anything special about him other than Nicola said she loved him. And now, instead of having a companion, Hope was left to spectate as Nicola tried to convince him that they were supposed to be together.

The slow remembering of emotions within Hope had stopped being a new and novel experience as she found herself remembering boredom, irritation and hints of jealousy. She didn't like how they felt and she didn't like what they reminded her of. It was as if each emotion she felt was tied to what was currently occurring as well as a point when she was alive. She found herself dealing with pangs of loneliness and regret. The worst part was remembering moments of happiness. The joy from the memory created an inverse sense of sadness and hopelessness in her as she realized that she would be unable to have moments like them again. At the same time, there was something that felt very much like being alive in those moments.

"I don't feel good," Hope answered.

"Is it because of everything that's going on with me and Lyle?"

Hope didn't want to think about it and just shrugged as a response.

"Like I told you when you let me come with you, I feel like you're a part of my future here. I won't leave you behind. But in order to move forward I need to figure out things with Lyle."

"He didn't seem very interested."

Nicola sighed, "No. Well, he did and he didn't. I know him and he's trying to figure things out. It's tough because he's right—we can't be together, not really. I wonder if I just got all wrapped up in the idea and I've ended up going after something that's never going to work. I'm afraid all I can do is hurt everyone involved…"

Neither of them spoke for a while.

"I need to clear my head," Nicola finally said. "I'll be back, but I don't know when. I just need to figure things out."

"Can I come?"

Nicola ran her hand through Hope's hair and gave her a little squeeze. "I have to do this by myself. I'll be back though, ok?"

Hope felt sadness and indignation building up in her stomach, although she had a hard time understanding why.

"You should get to know Lyle a little better. You could do that while I'm gone. It might be good for you two to get to know each other, anyway."

Hope didn't reply. They sat together for a little longer and then Nicola carefully got up and headed towards a Memory that was skipping by. She gave Hope a little wave and then vanished with the Memory. Hope remembered what it was like to want to cry.

*****

Lyle felt conflicted.

Jeannine, the girl from the gym he'd been fantasizing about off and on for the last year had actually texted him asking if he wanted to go out for drinks with her and some of her friends. It didn't feel like a date—he had originally asked if she wanted to get together and she'd declined. They continued chatting as they did their time on the Stairmaster. She said she and her friends were planning on going out Friday night for a while. In a rare move of boldness Lyle said he was going out, too, and that maybe they'd run into each other. Jeannine said that might be fun. They swapped their cell phone information and Jeannine said that if they were out and going to be somewhere for a while she might text him.

Of course Lyle had no plans to go out and spent the night rebuking himself for his lack of balls. That had been two weeks ago—before Nicola or the little ghost girl. He'd seen Jeannine at the gym a couple times since then and she hadn't mentioned anything about it. He filed it away in his mental cabinet of little failures and moved on.

He headed straight home by way of a burger joint Friday after work. His home-time ritual had been interrupted by Nicola and Hope's arrival. Instead of settling in in front of the television or checking out the internet, he first did a sweep of his apartment to make sure Hope wasn't standing somewhere staring at him. She had gotten a little better and was starting to show human-like expressions sometimes, but there were still days when he sat down to take a dump in the bathroom and would glance over to see her staring, blank-faced and hollow-eyed from the bathtub. The worst one was the previous day when he'd gotten back from the gym and decided to make a sandwich. He opened the fridge, grabbed the jug of milk and as he removed it, he saw Hope staring at him from inside the refrigerator.

"Goddammit! Really? Really!?! That's the fuckin' creepiest thing EVER."

Hope didn't usually say anything, just stood and watched him. After he'd gotten used to the idea of Nicola, Hope seemed less scary or threatening, but her appearances could still be very unsettling.

He hadn't seen Nicola since she'd left upset and that had been nearly a week before. He wasn't sure if she was coming back. Part of him knew that if she didn't it would probably be a good thing—ghost-like girlfriends from other dimensions seemed likely to cause a bunch of complications that he probably didn't need. But he also felt bad for her and really wanted to talk to her again. Their conversation had been kind of surreal, but the more he thought about it, the less her familiarity with him seemed unnatural or stalker-ish and instead felt nice. Not "nice" in a generic, minorly positive way, either, but in a legitimate, pleasant, comforting kind of way.

He looked at the text and weighed the pros and cons.

Pros:
-Jeannine could not be readily explained as a schizophrenic delusion.
-Jeannine had a nice face.
-If she was out drinking there was at least a chance of at least a one-time hookup. A blowjob at least was possible.
-Even if things with Jeannine didn't work out, maybe one of her girlfriends was hot. Or at least game.

Cons:
-Didn't seem that into Lyle.
-A little heavier than he'd prefer.
-Had a kid—not that Lyle didn't like kids, but there was always extra baggage when kids were involved.
-Conversations were ok, but not often where it felt like they really "connected".
-Probably wouldn't like him if she knew him better.

Lyle thought over his list. It probably said more that he had to compile a pros and cons list. His mother used to make pros and cons lists. He never really understood it. For him it always seemed like if you had to make a list you didn't really care very much to begin with. In this case it seemed like he was trying to weigh the possible and uninspiring against the improbable and intriguing.

When he was in college, Lyle had a girlfriend who told him that given the choice between something immediate and possible and something fanciful and idealized, he would always choose the latter. He scoffed at the idea, but in the back of his mind he was always a little afraid that it might be true. As soon as it seemed like something might be attainable with Jeannine every possible fault of hers became glaring—she tended to snort when she laughed, her stretch marks weren't very appealing to Lyle, she liked the worst kind of mass-produced pop music, she talked shit about people behind their backs, and on and on. Of course all of that was true back before she had given him her cell phone number or texted him and it hadn't bothered him then.

On the other hand, Lyle reasoned, it was a lot like buying a car: it was one thing to say you'd love to have a Ferrari, but if given the opportunity it was much wiser to stop and realize that, as a primary vehicle, it probably wouldn't be the most practical choice. Somehow arguing that Jeannine wasn't the most practical option available made him feel less like a wuss.

Lyle sat at his kitchen table listlessly. For all his rationalizations at the core he felt like his options boiled down to either being disappointed by Jeannine or being an idiot for waiting on an ethereal potential hallucination in Nicola. His cell phone buzzed and hiccupped a few tones. He flipped it face up and saw a text from Jeannine:

U comin out? We'll have fun, promise!

And the decision was made.

*****

"Now my friends, I had revelation today. A good friend of mine shared his story with me and once again I was struck by the beauty of God's creation and the goodness of His plan for all of us. There's a thing in science they call 'Chaos Theory'. It basically says little, no-account details can, in time, turn into one big thing. It's more science-y than that and I don't mean to offend any of our more literate listeners. One illustration is a thought experiment of sorts that asks whether the flap of a butterfly's wings in Bolivia can set off a chain of events that will eventually turn into a tornado in Kansas.

"Now scientists will debate numbers and probabilities and any number of things that are way too big for my head. I don't know if a butterfly can create a tornado, but after reading about it, I can assure you, my friends, that I've been very careful not to offend any butterflies. I'm joking, of course, but what I'm trying to get at is that if there's a random chance that one very small thing can lead to a very big thing, how much more amazing is it when God lets one little thing happen? One little chance encounter. One little daily miracle. One kind word to someone who is suffering in silence. One little act of forgiveness that can heal a heart or a family. Those are all butterfly flaps, but unlike the theory where we have to sit and ponder after a tornado has laid waste to a town about what may have caused it, we can watch these little actions blossom and turn into a mighty thing before our very eyes.

"Look at the Apostle Paul who said one day, 'Let's take a little trip to Damascus,' or Abraham who said, 'There are three strangers outside, let me welcome them as honored guests into my home,' or even old King Ahasuerus when he said, 'I'm going to have a beauty pageant to choose a wife.' Things that seemed so simple, so inconsequential were all guided by God into something extraordinary—things that changed the world for the better.

"'So what does that mean for us, Pastor Dave?' you ask. Well, the thing is we don't know what the future holds. But we have faith that in Christ, anything is possible. It's not about knowing what will happen when we act rightly; it's about acting rightly and trusting that our efforts are not in vain. We are not called to unleash the tornado. The Lord just asks that we keep flapping our little butterfly wings and let him do mighty things.

"I can tell you, my friends, that in the past week my eyes have been opened to so many things. And for as grateful and awestruck I am at the world I find myself in now, I am also left trying to find answers for questions I never knew existed. I have to admit when I was confronted with this new view of the world my first response wasn't joy or excitement. No, I confess I was frustrated and upset. Things I had always believed were now called into question. I was resentful because God had the nerve—the sheer audacity—to make faith *hard*.

"I have long known the life of faith is fraught with challenges and difficulties. Living by faith means sacrifice. It means saying 'no' when everyone else is saying 'yes'. It means humility when the world says 'be proud,' and it means being thankful for enough when what you want is more.

"I'm no saint, brothers and sisters. I'm not saying that I've accomplished these things. But I had become complacent because I had overcome these challenges in the past and I was confident that I could do so again. So the Lord showed me that I still had much to learn.

"The Apostle Paul says, 'work out your salvation with fear and trembling.' While it's very poetic, he didn't write that as a literary flourish. When do you fear? When do you tremble? I don't fear monsters under the bed anymore. We think of the things that frightened us as children, but as it says: When I was a child, I spoke as a child, I understood as a child, I thought as a child: but when I became a man, I put away childish things.

"As a man I'm afraid of failure. I'm afraid of being wrong. I'm afraid that the little things I've built up throughout a lifetime—be it a house, a car, friends, family and yes, even beliefs—will be taken from me. And that's what I mean when I say the Lord made faith hard. I always had a core set of beliefs and then built my worldview around them. I had a way of reading the Bible that reinforced those beliefs. I had a way of living my life so that I could honor those principles. I had a way of viewing the universe as a whole—both the experience of the universe and the scientific definition of the universe—that complimented my faith.

"The Lord told me in His wonderful, terrible way that I was wrong. He told me that there were truths beyond the easy words I'd chosen for myself and that I would have to choose between the reality of the universe and comfort of my faith. And that, my friends, was truly terrifying.

"I was unable to sleep. I was despairing in my heart. I was praying and praying and calling out to God asking him to save me from this doubt and uncertainty. And the more I prayed, the louder it seemed His silence was getting. Silence from God is the loudest thing you can imagine. It rattles you to your very core. The Bible says God will always love you, but what it doesn't say is that God will always answer you. He always hears our prayers but He sometimes forces us to learn and understand His divine nature by feeling it out.

"It reminds me of when I was a boy—and you parents out there, I'm sure you'll know exactly what I'm talking about—I hated math. I used to get so frustrated when I didn't just know an answer. I ran to my uncle, who was a kind, wise man, and asked 'What's the answer?' At first he looked at it and would walk me through it and then would give me the answer. The next time I didn't immediately know what the answer was, I'd run to him again and ask, 'What's the answer?' And on and on it went until he said nothing. I asked him again, 'What's the answer?' and he didn't say a word. I got angry and I yelled at him, 'Tell me the answer!'

"Now my uncle was a man of great patience and great compassion—he mostly raised me so that should be proof of that. He looked me square in the eyes and said, 'No more answers. The method is more important than the result. I have shown you how to find the answers; it's up to you to do it.' I tell you what, I was fit to be tied I was so mad at him. How dare he keep the answer from me? That's what adults' job was—help kids learn and do things. I sat and pouted and stared at the paper all afternoon.

"Now, I'm not proud of this, but I can tell you that math was never my strong suit. I remember that I got a D in it that year, and I earned every bit of it for good and bad. It wasn't until many years later—many lessons and heartbreaks, successes and failures—that I really understood what he meant that day. If you're told answers you don't have to struggle with what the answers mean. My uncle was also a veteran of the Second World War. When he died he had the full military funeral honors and at the end my aunt was given the flag.

"When she passed away I was given the flag. I got one of those triangular wood displays for it. I'd look at it some days and think about all the sacrifices my uncle had gone through during the war. I thought about the many fine men and women I'd met who had been scarred physically and mentally by conflict. I thought about how most days it didn't even occur to me to be thankful that I had running water, or roads or the right to vote or any of the many, many blessings that I enjoy every day as an American—blessings that were secured and protected by men and women in the armed forces. That's when my uncle's lesson about math truly made sense to me. His flag was an answer, but it was just a flag. I could probably go to Wal-Mart and pick up one just like it for twenty dollars. The answer itself was just a simple thing, but what it meant— the history, the conflict, the struggle—that's what gave it substance. That's what made it important.

"So that's where I am now. I'm fighting to understand the method. I think I may have been wrong about some things, but the one thing that's good about God is that He'll use it to make the things that were right all the more meaningful. Flap my little butterflies! Flap your wings to heaven and watch the sky fall!"

Moses had stopped playing and was staring at Irvin. Irvin didn't even announce when they were done broadcasting, he just flipped the mic off and turned off the desk light next to the board.

"Are you alright?"

Irvin looked at Moses and smiled weakly. "Had a lot on my mind, my friend. No need to worry."

"You seemed fine before when we talked. You seemed downright giddy."

"Well, can't choose when or why the Lord impresses things on your heart. It's fine. I'm learning. Everything will be as it was meant to be."

"You sure?"

Irvin gathered his things as if he hadn't heard Moses. As he turned to leave he walked up to him and put his hand firmly on his shoulder. "You're the best friend I could've asked for. You just keep on doing what you're doing. I'll catch up. I'll catch up." With that he turned and left. Moses had never seen Irvin act like that before. He finished putting the gear away and then headed out. He didn't see Irvin anywhere in sight when he got outside. It all made him uneasy.

Moses didn't see anyone around so he slipstreamed home. There hadn't been anybody around and, after the day he'd had, instantly stepping through a miniature wormhole into his apartment was a welcome little indulgence.

Part VII: A Year of Graves

In any normal circumstance it would've been a great night for Lyle. By the time he arrived Jeannine was already kind of drunk. She bounced from table to table, flirting and laughing too loud but didn't seem to have any takers. When she was at his table she was draped over his arms, or sitting on his lap or trying to whisper gossip about her girlfriends into his ear. Even as an introverted and relatively inexperienced guy, Lyle knew that something could happen if he wanted it to. He really wanted to want it, too. He thought it through and believed it would be good for him to give a real, flesh and blood girl a chance. If afterwards he still was thinking of Nicola, he would have his answer. It wasn't as if it was cheating. If she existed at all, she wasn't even in the same dimension—it was the ultimate expression of the Zip Code Rule.

But instead he sat with a dejected look at his table, pushing the ice from his drink around mindlessly with a bright pink plastic drink stirrer.

"You should be nicer to me," Jeannine said as she came up behind Lyle and hugged him.

"I'm sorry."

Jeannine came sliding in next to him, bumping with her hips until there was enough of a space for her to halfway sit on the chair's edge. "You know what?"

"Hm?"

"I didn't think you would come out. I almost didn't even text you because I figured you'd just find a reason not to come."

Lyle tried to sound interested. "No, I wanted to come out. I'm glad you got a hold of me."

"You don't look very glad. You look all like Mr. Sulky McSulkerston with your little sad drink."

"No, not at all. It's a happy drink. Look, the stirrer is bright pink. That's happy."

"No, you totally are, you're all being," she made a pouty face and scrunched her brow and began talking in a low voice "Oh I'm Lyle. I don't know how to have fun. I don't like talking to anybody. I'll just sit here playing with my empty glass because I don't even drink that much. Grump grump grump grump grump."

"I don't sound like that."

"I don't sound like that. Grump grump grump grump grump. Watch me play with my pretty pink stirrer thingy."

"You think it's pretty?"

Jeannine punched him in the leg—distressingly close to his testicles. He jumped defensively to the side and Jeannine slid into the seat but she managed to hook Lyle with her arm that kept him from standing up. "Why are you so grumpy? I'm a fun girl, right?"

"You seem to be."

"Seem to be? Oh I'm fun. You have no idea how much fun I can be. No. Idea."

"I'm sure you're right. I've just been fighting off a headache all day—"

Lyle didn't even get a chance to finish because Jeannine was off like a flash and bounding into the arms of a college-age guy with a barbed wire tattoo around his bicep.

Lyle was pretty sure she wouldn't remember their conversation tomorrow, just as he was sure that he'd been about as close to getting laid as he had been in months. At the same time, he was as indifferent to the fact as was possible for an otherwise healthy male of his age could be. He felt so sexually apathetic that it depressed him. Jeannine had been right; he had barely had anything to drink. Lyle felt obliged to remedy that.

Other than drinking, the rest of the evening was devoid of highlights. Jeannine flirted with a few different guys. She may have gone home with one of them. Then again, maybe not. Lyle assumed she probably had, but in retrospect he may have thought that because he didn't want anything to do with her while simultaneously believing everyone was better at getting laid than he was. He wasn't sure how many drinks he'd downed but realized that Jeannine and her friends had left. He checked the time. It was only 11:45. It wasn't even late by his diminished standards, but he was plenty drunk and wanted nothing more than to go to sleep and wake up in a different life.

He'd made that wish most nights. That was one of the things that was most puzzling about Nicola. As he was drifting off to sleep he'd lie staring at the ceiling and wish for the life he wished he'd lived. The scenarios he imagined didn't seem too improbable: He'd stayed with an ex and things had worked out or he'd gotten a promotion and was travelling the world on the company's dime, etc. The banality of his dreams depressed him if he thought too much about it.

The Nicola thing wasn't just about maybe having a new girlfriend. There was a weird history thing—he wasn't just getting a girlfriend, he was getting an entire life that Nicola remembered sharing with him. He had started remembering more of the dreams. While it wasn't quite the same for him as it was for Nicola, there was a degree of familiarity, a sense of a shared past, that Lyle had always longed for but never seemed to be able to establish with anyone else. There was something that he envied about that feeling and now it was being given to him. But he couldn't shake the feeling he didn't deserve it.

Lyle wasn't sure how he got home that night. From the parking job he did, it was probably more by luck than by any measure of skill or competence. He rolled over in bed, shielding his eyes from the sun which pierced his brain and made his stomach turn. He pulled the covers over his head trying to block the light out as much as he could. There was a dull ache behind his eyes. He opened one just enough to try and see the clock on the nightstand. When he was able to focus he couldn't see the clock because there was a dirt-stained white dress in front of it. He squinted up and saw Hope standing in front of him, motionless and staring directly at him.

"Fuckin' creepy," he muttered. Hope didn't move. "You're just going to stand there regardless, aren't you?"

Hope tilted her head and bent down to look at him eye to eye. Her look was detached, but curious.

"Gaaaaaaaah," Lyle groaned as he gave up. He sat up and was startled by Nicola standing at the foot of his bed. She smiled and gave a tense little wave. If Lyle had felt better he may have felt more nervous about seeing Nicola again. He was a little confused as to what she was doing there, but he was glad to see her. He gave a nod in acknowledgement as he swung around to get out of bed. Instead of the carpet under his feet he felt something softer. He looked down and every inch of the floor, wall to wall, was covered in toilet paper.

He looked at Hope who stared back him with disinterest. It seemed unlikely she had done it. He looked at Nicola and she blushed and lowered her eyes in response.

"I'm willing to go through the puppy stage again if it means being with you," she said quietly. "If you want to, that is."

"You did this?" Lyle asked he kicked up a little arc of toilet paper.

"Well, Hope helped. It was my idea, don't be mad at her. I mean, I listened to what you said about Rufus and you're right. I thought this would be a way to show you I understood what you meant."

"...Toilet paper?"

"I said we should drape it over everything so it would look like a tent, but Nicola said no," Hope blurted out.

"No, it's fine. It works. I get it..." Lyle drifted off. "Um, I'm glad you came back."

Nicola's look of apprehension eased and a smile teased the corners of her lips. Lyle got up uneasily. "Can we talk in a bit? I'm still... you know, from last night."

"Of course. We'll be here whenever you're ready. Just say the word."

Lyle weaved into the bathroom. He left the light off in an attempt to spare his aching head. He sat down on the toilet and his stomach and intestines unloaded what they'd been begrudgingly hanging on to overnight. Lyle wished he could just sleep the rest of the day, but the part of his brain that wasn't in pain was very happy to see Nicola again. Seeing her smile made him happy in a way he couldn't really describe. He reached over to grab some toilet paper and the roll was empty. He reached under the sink for a new roll and found nothing. Then he remembered the floor of his bedroom.

"Sonuvabitch," he muttered to himself.

*****

"So how is this going to work?"

"How do you want it to work?"

"Well, I don't know. I've never dated someone immaterial before. I suppose I could call a couple ex's and get some pointers."

"Are you trying to be clever?"

"Well, a little. I thought it was kind of funny."

Nicola tsk'd at him. "We need to do something about that. I know you think being self-effacing is charming, but it isn't."

"Not even a little? I'm just joking."

"But you're not. I know you, Lyle. I know when you're being silly and I know when you're fishing for reassurance. You don't have to."

"Um."

"We'll work on it. Just don't think it went unnoticed," Nicola said with a wink.

"Ok, but my mannerisms notwithstanding, how is this going to go?"

"We spend time together and go through the steps as much as normal couples would. At least as nearly as we can."

"You say that, but where are you going to live?"

"Well I can stay in the Windy Place with Hope until it's time for us to meet."

"But that's not how it works, is it? You'll be all invisible and watching me and then will appear. And if you are in that other place it's not as if I can just dial you up, can I?"

"Well, no… Do you want me to stay somewhere else?"

"I didn't say that. I just need to wrap my head around this. It just doesn't seem fair that you can see me any time you want without me knowing and I don't really have a say in it."

"Ok, I understand. That's fair. So should we just set times? I can promise to stay away except when we decide to meet."

"That seems pretty rigid. I mean, I don't mind if you stay here, you just have to be visible when you're here."

"Well, I want to respect your boundaries. I can find somewhere to be."

"No. I mean, I think I want you here. I just don't want to feel like you're watching me all the time. I like having you around…" Lyle's words trailed off and he felt himself get self-conscious. When he said that Nicola smiled widely.

"I like being here."

Lyle felt himself smile and blush at the same time. He felt like an awkward high school kid again. The feeling both annoyed him and was thoroughly exhilarating.

"Are there things you want to do or go see or anything?"

"Well, I am kind of limited when it comes to doing things. I don't know, it always seemed to me that it wasn't about where you went or what you did but—"

"Who you did it with," Lyle interrupted. Nicola looked up and their eyes met. Lyle's look had an intensity she hadn't seen before. Neither of them spoke but they kept staring. It felt very aggressive, as if they were testing each other to see who would blink first, but instead of the shyness that Lyle usually slipped into he kept looking into her eyes with a fierceness. She smiled and bit her lower lip with a look of excitement and anticipation. It all felt oddly dangerous and intoxicating. Lyle cracked a small smirk in response, but his eyes never wavered. The silence seemed deafening but neither spoke for what seemed to be an eternity.

Nicola finally broke the silence. "I want to spend my days with you. Maybe that's a needy, clingy thing to say, but you are the best part of my day. I covet time with you when you're away. I don't disappear because I want to be away from you; I disappear because I think that it's natural that you want time away from me and I don't want to make you say it."

Lyle lowered his eyes for a moment in thought and then locked eyes with Nicola again. "Well, I don't want time away from you now. If I need a breather I promise I'll say something. And if you need some time away you promise you'll tell me, right?"

Nicola nodded. Lyle sat back in the chair and studied Nicola with a hint of a smile. "Are we really doing this?" he asked, smile widening.

Nicola grinned and nodded. "I think we are."

Lyle's look of intensity melted away and the awkward school boy look came back. "Can I ask you something?"

"Of course."

"If anybody were to walk by and saw this, I'd be talking to an empty chair, wouldn't I?"

Nicola laughed. "I suppose that's how it would look. I guess that means dates are probably going to be tricky."

"If we aim for closing time at the bar, no one would probably even notice."

"Maybe so. I think I could probably try and be visible, but with so many different people it would be hard."

"Why's that?"

"I can be seen by you because we're in sync. I can try and sync up with other people—it's harder because I don't have the same connection with anyone else. But I don't know if I could do a group of people. Two might be a challenge at the same time."

Lyle had a thoughtful look on his face. "So no one can see you unless you want them to."

"Yes, well, mostly yes. You can see me either way it seems. I can hide out of sight from you, but it's more like being in a place you can't see. When we're in the same room you always seem to see me. It's the connection we have. The only way I'm truly away is when I go back to the Windy Place."

"So... you could come to work with me then?"

"Well, I suppose I could. I don't want to be a distraction."

"Oh God, I would give my left nut for a distraction most days. Besides the guy in the cube next to mine is always texting or calling his girlfriend. We'll be fine."

"It would be hard to talk, wouldn't it? I mean it would just be staring at you all day, wouldn't it?"

"No. I just couldn't talk back, or at least not in a normal way. I could pretend I was making a call, or I could write out responses as if I were texting."

"I suppose you could. I don't want to get you in any trouble or anything."

"It'll be fun. Besides, it'll be nice to have something fun to do at work."

*****

To the rest of the world Lyle would spend his days working studiously in his cubicle, occasionally chatting or texting a mystery girl, and then going home and spending quiet nights in. In fact to the casual observer very little seemed different in Lyle's day-to-day activities. The one thing that was noticeably different was that he'd taken to reading entertainment and gossip magazines. There would always be one sitting open on his desk.

What they couldn't see was Nicola sitting across from him. When she wanted to talk she'd hold up her hand in a phone gesture and Lyle would pretend he was calling her and they'd just chat away in his cubicle. Nicola actually enjoyed the magazines—a guilty pleasure she confessed to on her first day at the office—and so Lyle would grab one on his way in from the lobby. He'd leave it open and turn the pages for her every few minutes.

Most days Lyle wasn't terribly busy so he and Nicola would have extended conversations where she'd talk about whatever occurred to her. For the most part Lyle didn't have to say much, he would just be able to nod in acknowledgement. Nicola joked that they'd skipped any courtship period and had moved straight into "old married couple" territory with that.

Nicola also enjoyed trying to get a rise out of Lyle at inappropriate moments. When his boss came by to speak with him she'd come up being him and make funny faces, or mimic everything he said in a raspy, breathy voice. Occasionally she'd use her incorporeal form to her benefit by suddenly peeking out from somebody's chest. She took particular glee in pretending to be Glenn's (a guy from accounts receivable whose ingratiating nature neither Lyle nor Nicola liked) penis. The first time she did it Lyle choked on his own spit. Nicola's head popped out from Glenn's crotch and she looked around in awe and said in a high squeaky English accent, "Please help me, I'm just a little fellow. He beats me. He beats me and berates me. I just want to find a forever home." They nicknamed it "Oliver" after a "please sir, may I have some more" joke. References to "Glenn and Oliver" would inevitably lead to giggling fits by both of them.

Nicola became more daring as she and Lyle grew accustomed to each other. There were times when they locked eyes like that night in the kitchen, but Nicola would raise the stakes. She started by leaning forward slightly, and running her hand along the neckline of her dress. Her eyes never left his, and she tried to make it look as if she was just adjusting it slightly, but she allowed her fingertips to stray over the upper part of her chest. She'd smile when she caught Lyle's eyes wandering over her. It escalated to her unbuttoning the top two buttons and then leaning forward, allowing Lyle a view down her top, teasing him with a tantalizing glimpse of her breasts. When she caught him trying to steal a look further down her top she'd sit up with a coy look on her face. "What?" she'd ask in an innocent voice.

There was something about teasing the boundaries of acceptable behavior that made it exciting for both of them. Their sex life was best described as "improvisational". Most often it was Lyle masturbating while Nicola lay next to him, whispering encouragement and pleasuring herself. It was a kind of forced voyeurism and while neither of them would have said they found pleasure in watching or being watched previously, it was playing off their mutual desires that kept them exploring and experimenting as much as they could with unexpectedly pleasurable results.

For example, Lyle for his part had never been very demonstrative in the act, but was learning how to add little performance elements in his actions that seemed to please Nicola. Nicola learned how to pace herself and, by extension,

Lyle, to draw out their sessions to the point of near torture. Secretly Nicola had been working at manipulating objects in hopes that at some point she could be able to touch things as easily as Hope seemed to. While she realized she would probably never be able to feel Lyle, she hoped that with enough practice she could at least offer some sort of touch to him.

Hope ruefully found herself trying to give Nicola lessons. Nicola had done her best to keep Hope included in day-to-day events with her or collectively with her and Lyle, but Hope's reticence combined with the intensely personal nature of Lyle and Nicola's relationship didn't make for an easy time of it. Hope would return to the Windy Place for days at a time until Nicola would appear looking for her. Nicola would always be apologetic and promise to do better. Hope wasn't angry with either of them, but she was remembering loneliness when they were around.

"I'm sorry, Hope. I feel like I'm not doing a very good job of things right now."

"It's fine. I like it here, anyway."

Nicola frowned and wrapped her arms around Hope's shoulders from behind, clasping her hands over her chest. "I like having you around. I really do. I know it's hard with me and Lyle together so often, but we want you to be with us. Both of us do. Lyle even said he misses seeing you around."

What Lyle had actually said was, "Well, maybe we'll see her around. She's always poking around somewhere. I'm almost used to her staring at me at random times during the day…" which wasn't exactly what Nicola implied, but she wanted

Hope to feel included. And it wasn't that far off—Nicola knew Lyle well enough that if he'd noticed she was gone that it was a sign that he'd grown accustomed to her presence. Lyle was a creature of habit and routine and accepting Hope into his routine was on par with giving her her own set of keys to the apartment.

"I'm so happy right now, I can barely stand it," Nicola whispered. "I never thought I could be this happy. Even when I imagined how it could be I couldn't have guessed how much better it really is. I think when things didn't go well right off that was the best thing that could happen, you know? Sometimes you have to have your preconceptions and dreams crushed to be able to see the bigger picture."

Hope and Nicola swayed back and forth slowly as Nicola kept talking to Hope. Hope didn't really pay attention to the words. She just closed her eyes and rested her cheek against Nicola's arm. Her mother had held her like that. That memory felt comforting.

After a few moments Nicola stopped swaying and gave Hope a squeeze. "I don't know what I'm going to do," she whispered. Her voice had lost the optimistic verve from a moment before and become introspective and mournful. "These are the waning days of this Narrative. It's all going away and I don't want to lose any of it: Not you. Not Lyle. Not all of us together. I'm scared. I thought I'd be fine with just being able to have happiness for a little while, but now... now it's not enough.

"I'm probably looking at it all the wrong way. I look at a calendar and instead of seeing days that are better than the last starting from the day we met, I see a little grave—another day gone that before was a buffer between us and the end. I mean, I know it's silly. And it's not even entirely true; when we're together I can't even imagine that there's another instant other than the one we're at right then. But afterwards, that's when I realize how quickly it's all going."

"What's going to happen?"

Nicola didn't say anything at first; she just kissed the top of Hope's head. After she gave her a little squeeze she sighed. "You can jump from person to person and see what's happened and what's going to happen, right? What do you call them, Memories?"

Hope nodded.

"Have you ever seen anything after September 14th, 2008?"

"…I don't know. I don't look at the numbers."

"I know. It's easier just to follow people or stories. But I haven't been able to find anything after that date. This Narrative ends. I don't know how or why, but this world is in its death throes. That's why no one cares that I'm here, because even if I could find someone who saw me and could understand what I know, there's nothing anyone can do."

"…What will happen to me if the world goes away?"

"Nothing, sweetie. You'll always be safe and sound. You shouldn't worry. Don't listen to me, I just talk to hear my own voice sometimes; you know that."

Hope liked that Nicola cared enough to at least try to lie.

*****

Irvin's behavior continued to grow increasingly erratic. He'd broken down crying for several minutes during a broadcast the previous week and there had been nearly twenty minutes of nothing airing except Moses' playing and sound of Irvin softly weeping. At the end of the show when Moses tried to ask him about it Irvin acted as if nothing had happened. If the outbursts had been limited to the broadcasts Moses may have even believed him, but he'd been unusually withdrawn outside of the radio station as well.

Previously, Irvin's attempts to get Moses to do things outside of their time in the broadcast booth had bordered on pestering. But over the course of the last two weeks Moses hadn't received so much as a phone call from him. When he'd asked Irvin if he wanted to grab breakfast Irvin said nothing, only grasped his hand and squeezed it hard. His eyes were red as if he were about to cry. He grabbed Moses' shoulder with his free hand and then gave him a pat on the arm. Irvin then turned around and left the building without saying a word. Moses had never seen Irvin act like that before. It coincided with Moses' confession, but anytime Moses tried to ask if they were related Irvin dismissed it. "You've done nothing but bring me happiness, my friend," he'd say with a weary smile.

Moses couldn't dwell on it too long, it was a drop day. Before he'd left Waffle, B had given him a small device that would randomly generate a time and location. B had one as well and every 38 days (the interval made more sense on Waffle where it was the equivalent of a week) they would sync up and confirm the rendezvous. Moses would wait at the spot for an hour. A transmission would be initiated from Moses' side. He would send his messages and if there was a response a bundle with supplies and return messages would appear in their place. If nothing came through then he'd have to wait another 38 days.

His father had explained that because of the vast distance and experimental nature of the slipstream technology that the only way to be certain things made it through was if both sides were simultaneously active. He explained it as "forcing a wrinkle in the universe and then creating a little neutral bubble in between the folds for things to pass through." Unless Moses received something back he had no way of being sure that the other connection had been initiated. It was possible that his notes were appearing in the middle of deep space somewhere or were spun off into an alternate dimension or something. The latter idea amused him. He envisioned his deeply personal notes and requests for supplies appearing on some far off shore like a Kubrickian monolith. He might have been the impetus for the all sorts of monkey-on-monkey violence and not even known it.

He hadn't heard from anyone in a few years. He sent new notes each time, usually to his father or B and always something for D. He had never heard anything back from anyone other than B although B would pass on messages from his father from time to time. He had been fortunate that he hadn't needed anything lately. The lack of response for so long made him suspect that something had happened and there wasn't anyone on the other end to receive or send messages anymore. B had been loyal, but since he'd heard nothing from anyone else he suspected that B may have been the only person who cared about him. The extended silence made him worry that something had happened to B.

Unfortunately his adaptive-protective environmental suit needed some patching and maintenance. He'd sent the request two cycles before and was losing hope that he'd be receiving anything anytime soon. The technology on Earth was primitive and largely useless for his needs, but Moses had been trying to cobble together a Plan B in case there was no way to repair the suit. So far the only option that seemed workable was moving to a small isolated farmstead outside of Amidon, North Dakota and avoiding human contact as much as possible.

Moses' thoughts were interrupted by a little crack and flash of light. Where his notes had been was a tightly bound package with a letter attached. He opened the package first and there were some repair supplies and a small, nearly palm-sized cube. The cube was a bit of mystery since it didn't look like anything he recognized and certainly wasn't anything he'd requested.

He wrapped them all back up to keep things as inconspicuous as possible, although in the middle of an open field somewhere in either Nebraska or Colorado there wasn't much chance of being seen, anyway. He opened the letter and was disappointed that it wasn't from D, but B, not that he really expected otherwise. It read:

M,
I'm sorry for the delay in response. I'm afraid I'm the bearer of bad news and worse news. I've refrained from telling you the former, but the situation the latter has created has made it necessary for me to tell you everything in order to keep a clear conscience. Law enforcement has been tailing me for years and nearly caught me several times. I've managed to

stay clear of them for the most part and they've never caught me with anything that incriminates either of us.

I've done my best to honor your requests, but unfortunately I am no longer able to act as a courier for your messages. Your father died in state custody a few months ago. I just learned of it yesterday, but I will speak to that momentarily.

I learned that the reason that I was under near-constant surveillance was that D has been in contact with the Special Police. The information I've uncovered indicates he's been cooperating almost from the start and likely sought them out to inform on you. I'm sorry. I didn't read your letters but since there was one to D each time I assumed you still had great affection for him. I'm sure this all comes as a shock and I will refrain from other details of my investigation as they will only cause you additional pain and distress. Suffice to say that his betrayal undid any progress there may have been towards your exoneration or any chance of future return. Again, I'm sorry, but they have kept the fires stoked against you very effectively and were, until recently, actively trying to locate you.

All that is secondary now. Your father continued his work and managed to validate some of his Narrative theory. Details are sketchy—I've been unable to confirm whether he actually was able to view other Narratives or was able to use his slipstream work to open a portal to a separate Narrative. My sources indicate that at the very least there was communication between us and another Narrative because the information and technology made a series of explosive quantum leaps in data and sophistication. These leaps in development occurred during the time your father was being held by the security forces. Again, I've been unable to get any solid information. Some sources say he was being held as part of an investigation into you. Others say he was being "sequestered" due to revelations involving his work.

What I do know is that he was taken by the Special Police and died while in their (or some other arm of the security branches') custody. I was able to secure a package he set aside specifically for you. The item I sent along with your maintenance kit isn't a standard issue data cube. According to your father it is an integrated slipstream portal manipulator with full interface. It's keyed to your genetic signature so only you can operate it.

There is an impending cataclysm that will consume the whole universe. I don't know if your father's work caused it or if that was how they learned of it. With your father's death, however, it seems that they have given up any hope of survival. I imagine his slipstream work and his Narrative experiments may have been the last desperate shot they had at a solution. I don't have much else other than it's expected to strike here in the coming weeks. The government has kept it under wraps but I don't know how much longer they can keep it a secret.

The information in the data cube will probably tell you more. Your father seemed to think you had more time than we did. I'll keep checking back as scheduled as long as I can. I'm sorry I can't do more.

It doesn't seem as if a reunion is in the stars. It's been a pleasure working with you and I'm glad I could call you "friend".

-B

Moses reread the letter. He couldn't believe it. He couldn't comprehend something so massive that both his home and his place of exile would be wiped out. But it was the revelation of D's betrayal that made it feel as if his world was ending. For so long he had carried on for no other reason than the memory of home and the hope of love and redemption. Without D, it seemed fitting that the universe was ending.

The wind rustled through the high grass and the stalks clicked hollow against each other. He sat on a rock pile and removed his faceplate. It was so rare he got to feel the sun and breeze on his real face. He had spent so long hiding away and trying to blend in that even when he had the opportunity in the past it often wouldn't even occur to him.

No use hiding now, he thought to himself. No one was looking for him anymore and even if they were, it wasn't as if there was anything waiting for him. He felt the sun drying out the soft tissue around his face. It wouldn't kill him, but if he didn't put the mask back on it would burn and itch for days.

The mask clicked into place and he felt the unit pressurize. The mask somehow made everything seem distant, as if the world he viewed through it was less real than when he had it off. Moses thought if there was ever a time for the world to be less real, that was it. As the mask recalibrated itself he felt the tears being siphoned away as the moisturizer recirculator kicked in.

Moses picked up the package and the cube. He examined it for a moment and considered leaving it. It didn't seem like whatever secrets it may contain could make things any better.

It felt heavier than he thought it would. He weighed it physically and mentally and decided it wasn't worth discarding just yet. He slid it into his pocket and with a crackle slipstreamed back home.

It was July 14th, 2008.

*****

"Are you close?"

Lyle grunted in reply.

"Mmm, that's it. You know I wish I could do this to you. I loved feeling you inside me. Do you think of doing that to me?" Nicola whispered, when Lyle didn't respond fast enough she repeated herself more plaintively. "Do you think about it, Lyle? Do you imagine us together?"

"Yeah, yes I do," Lyle replied breathlessly.

"What about the girl from the gym?"

Lyle grunted back again, but turned his head slightly away from her.

"Hmm," she purred. "She is pretty. It's ok if you do."

Lyle frowned slightly but said nothing.

"Do you imagine taking her from behind? Or maybe you'd like her to go down on you?"

"No."

"Maybe the two of us together? It's ok. It's just fantasy. Maybe both of us going down on you at once. I'd like to try that—" she was interrupted by a groan from Lyle as he ejaculated forcefully.

"Hmmm, that's it. Imagine that's all going into my mouth," she whispered as he came.

Lyle didn't say anything for a moment, but he kept his head turned away from her.

"Did I do good?"

"Goddammit, why do you do that?" Lyle sighed.

"Do what? You seemed to enjoy yourself."

"Talk about other girls. And I came because I was ready, not because of Jeannine."

"Is that her name? Jeannine?"

"…Yes."

"I don't mind. You don't have to be embarrassed. I don't care if you fantasize about her sometimes, or about situations with me and her. I know where your heart is. It's just for fun, something to stimulate your mind a little."

"I don't like thinking about her with you, ok?"

"Ok. I don't want to fight about it. I just wanted to do something I thought you'd like. I mean, I didn't mind that you went on that date with her or anything."

Lyle rolled onto his side away from Nicola.

"Ahhh, I wasn't supposed to know about that, was I? ... Surprise?" Lyle didn't move. "Why is this a thing?"

"It's not. I just don't want to talk about it."

"Baby, I really don't mind. You barely knew me then. Besides, I like knowing the things that turn you on. It's natural. It's not as if I expect you not to look at anyone ever again."

"It's not the same. I don't want to talk about it, because I don't feel like thinking about it, ok?" Lyle rolled over and faced her. "Anytime I think about things that happened before we met they seem like I was just passing time until the right thing came along—until you came along. I don't like thinking about it because it was all such a waste. I didn't start living—real life, not stupid college kid bullshit—until I saw you. Jeannine was a distraction for me when I didn't have the imagination to believe in something better."

Nicola watched Lyle for a moment. He was staring at the ceiling. He was lost in thought and those thoughts left him with a stony frown.

"I love you. I love you so much right now," Nicola whispered. Lyle turned and looked at her with a look of melancholy. Nicola smiled and slid next to him. "Hope's been helping me with something. I think you'll like it."

Nicola moved her hand over Lyle's crotch. She started to move over the area as if she were coaxing him.

"Do you feel that?"

Lyle looked down and shifted in a bit. "You're doing that? It feels…"

"Does it feel nice?"

"Yeah. It just feels weird." Nicola smiled as she saw him harden. As he became fully erect she started making a stroking motion with her hand. Lyle let out a little groan.

"It's not that same as the real thing, but it's a start, right?" she said as she began to move her hand more emphatically and with exaggerated motions.

"Mmm, yeah. That's good. That's nice."

"Look at me," Nicola said quietly. Lyle turned his head and found himself lost in her deep, warm, brown eyes. "I learned this for you. All of this is for you. Everything I've done is because of you."

Lyle couldn't describe the feeling. It wasn't touch so much as the suggestion of touch. Sensation-wise by itself it probably wouldn't have been able to accomplish much, but with Nicola's face inches from his, the sound of her voice, the way she made sure he could see every curve, all of it together it was very arousing.

She bit her lower lip in the coy little way that Lyle loved and she moved even more suggestively. The sensation he felt grew and he thought he would actually be able to cum from their interplay.

"Do you love me?" Nicola purred. Lyle nodded between little gasps and sighs. "I want to hear you say it."

"Uh… I love you… I do."

Lyle couldn't tell if she was feeling anything, but from her expression she seemed to be getting more excited as they continued. "You're the most beautiful girl I've ever known," he blurted out. It seemed to catch Nicola off guard and she smiled and turned her head to the side a little as her cheeks turned red.

"Don't look away," Lyle pleaded.

She looked him square in the eyes, still blushing a little. "I've never loved anyone as much as I love you," she answered. "You are the best person I've ever met. I've never been this happy." She kept moving her body and the sensation continued to build. Her expression changed as she saw that he was approaching his orgasm. She moaned softly as if she was also nearing climax, moving in time with Lyle so it almost seemed like they were truly physically together. Lyle suddenly felt it hit him and he bucked his hips suddenly. The sensation stopped suddenly and all there was was the faint scent of electricity.

"Goddammit!" Nicola yelled. Hope had been in the Windy Place while Nicola and Lyle had their "alone time" as they called it and suddenly Nicola appeared. "No, no, no! It's just... GODDAMMIT!"

Hope walked over and sat next to Nicola who was flailing angrily. Hope rested her head against Nicola's shoulder, but Nicola brushed it off. "Not now!" she barked. Nicola got up leaving Hope sitting by herself.

Nicola started pacing, muttering to herself. She was animated and clearly agitated. Hope only overheard bits and pieces: "Can't even have one goddamn moment of happiness... Get involved with a guy you can't even touch—great plan Nicola. Great fucking plan."

Watching her, Hope began to remember resentment and indignation. She thought about leaving Nicola, or saying something. Instead she stood quietly feeling the emotions burn through her stomach. She realized she was clenching her fists so hard they ached. Nicola didn't seem to notice that she was upset.

A blue orb appeared over Nicola. It grew in intensity and size until it was around the size of a basketball. Hope had never seen anything like it before. When it became bright enough to cast shadows, Nicola realized it was there. She looked up at it and as soon as she did it grew suddenly. There was a crack and bright blue bolt of lightning shot through it, hitting Nicola square in the chest. The act of striking Nicola seemed to sap its energy and the orb disappeared at the same time.

Nicola looked at Hope, wide-eyed and in shock. She looked felt her large orange body as if checking to see if anything was missing. Hope was just as surprised as Nicola. They looked at each other in disbelief before Nicola said, "Well, that was new…"

*****

It hadn't been easy, but Moses had gotten Irvin to go out for dinner. Irvin barely spoke and when he did it was in one word answers or grunts.

"What is wrong with you?" Moses asked pointedly after they'd been seated.

"It's nothing. Just being tested at the moment."

"Bullshit. Bullshit it's nothing. I've known you a good while and you can't tell me that this is ok. Look at you. You used to be the guy who always saw the good in something and when you couldn't you were happy to go looking for it. Now, man… I don't know. You act like you're completely falling apart."

Irvin hung his head, but said nothing.

"I'm not criticizing you. I'm not mad, but I'm worried," Moses continued. "You've helped me out. You've been a friend to me and I ain't gonna just stand by and let you be miserable. That's not what you would do and it's not how I treat friends, either. You got that?"

Irvin nodded.

"Now I'm gonna ask you again: What is wrong with you?"

Irvin sighed. "It's all so broken…"

"What do you mean?"

"I've put my life into my ministry. I've sacrificed time and energy and I haven't minded because if there's just one person out there I can help, one person that's saved, it'll have been worth it. I don't have spare time, I sleep, I go to work, I work on sermons all the time in my head, I try to be kind to everyone. I'm always 'on', you understand? I never take a break from trying to do good—from trying to be better.

"When you told me about your story and where you came from and all the wonders that the universe has to offer, my heart overflowed. It really did. I went home and started working on a series of sermons. The parables of Jesus take on all sorts of new levels and meanings when you consider that there are others out there. It was exhilarating.

"I should have known better. Whenever I get that excited I start to get prideful in my heart and the Lord seeks to teach me humility. I have an aunt. I know I don't talk much about my family, but I have one aunt out east. I'm the only family she's got and I try to keep in touch with her as best I can.

"A few years ago I helped move her out of her house into this little apartment. She couldn't afford her house anymore and it was too big for her anyway, especially after my uncle died. She refused to go to a home, so the apartment seemed like a happy medium. The place was owned by a couple from her church. Nice, sweet people—an older couple. They said they'd check in on her to see how she was doing from time to time.

"Things were great for a while. She loved having her own place and the owners were good about helping her run errands or with help around the apartment if she needed them. They really kind of adopted her.

"Well, he had a heart attack a couple years ago. They ended up retiring to Phoenix because he just wasn't up to maintaining things anymore. They sold the property to one of their sons. He told them he'd take care of everything.

"Once they were gone the first thing the guy does is jack up her rent. Now I know the couple there had kept the rent low, so I didn't say anything when it first went up. I figured they may have been renting it out at cost, maybe even a bit of a loss—they were just those kind of people—so an adjustment back to normal once they left was to be expected.

"Then my aunt would call me because she'd ask for help changing a light bulb or moving a chair and he wouldn't come over. I explained to her that she'd probably have to wait more now there was a new owner. I tried to calm her down and convince her it would be alright. You know, try and get her over the hump to adjust to the new situation.

"She kept calling every couple weeks saying how bad things were and I tried to comfort her. She had always been a bit of a fusser so I didn't always take it very seriously. She'd say how she didn't like the new landlord and that she didn't have any friends. I told her we could always look at going to a home if she wasn't happy—and I meant that in a nice way, not in a threatening way. She always said she didn't want to go to a home and that she'd stay at her apartment.

"Then she called just crying saying she was almost out of food and hadn't been able to do her laundry for three weeks. I thought she was probably exaggerating but I said I'd help her out. I called the landlord. He was a bit brusque but didn't seem unreasonable. He said she was stretching things a bit. He told me he'd picked her up a few things earlier in the week and she hadn't mentioned anything about laundry. He said he'd check in later when he got home and make sure everything was ok.

"I called her the next day to see what had happened and she sounded a little embarrassed. She kept saying everything was fine, she had everything she needed, the landlord had been very helpful, and so on and so forth. She said next time I came down maybe we could take a look at different homes in the area. I suppose that should have tipped me off, but I thought maybe she was coming to grips with the fact she was getting older and wouldn't be able to take care of herself forever.

"I didn't think much about it. I thought maybe I'd try and get there over the holidays and then after our conversation I didn't think any more of it. Next thing I know I get a call from the police. They say my aunt is in the hospital— apparently she'd fallen in her apartment and had been lying there for two or three days. They said she was dehydrated and had a hip fracture and a bruised pelvis. She'd been lying in her own filth until emergency services arrived. The doctors had said she'd be ok, but she'd have to go to a care facility of some sort.

"Then they started asking me about the eviction notice. I said I didn't know anything about any eviction. The officer said they'd discovered her when they'd come to serve an eviction notice on her. I said that I'd spoken to the landlord a month or so before and he hadn't mentioned anything. That's when it got worse.

"They said my aunt had been making some accusations against the landlord saying he kept raising the rent and then was stealing her things as 'collateral.' I couldn't believe what I was hearing and I asked what she said he'd taken and the cop says, 'Everything.'

"I asked, 'What do you mean by everything?' He tells me that when they found her there was one chair, a small card table, an old, dirty mattress in the bedroom and a pile of dirty clothes in the closet, and that was it. Her TV was gone. All her collectibles, gone. Any silverware or china she had were gone. Anything of value was gone. My aunt, she wasn't a rich woman, but she had a lifetime of knick-knacks and things she'd accumulated, some of it was worth something to the right people. He said the place was bare.

"And there it was. I felt so guilty for not checking on her— for not doing the Christian thing and make her burdens mine. But more than that, I wanted to kill that sonofabitch. I mean actually kill him. And I would have been fine with it. I still would. I know that's not the spirit of love and forgiveness that I'm supposed to have. If God wants vengeance, that's fine, but I'll be happy to collect a down payment for Him.

"I had this rage in my stomach and this incredible grief for my aunt's suffering and my own guilt and the entire time I'm talking to the officer, he didn't sound like he really gave a shit. I remember what he said, 'We're seeing more of this kind of thing lately. You might want to contact a lawyer; he might be able to help get some of your aunt's stuff back.' I asked him why the guy wasn't in jail and he said, 'It's a civil matter. We don't handle contract disputes or anything like that. Whatever your aunt and him had worked out for rent and what he did to get it is beyond anything we do. Social services has been called. Maybe there's something they can do.'

"I strive to be an empathetic person. I believe that's really what Christ calls us to be—empathetic to others. But I couldn't understand anyone who bore witness to all of that and was indifferent. And then I wondered why I did any of this. Why do I try and empathize and preach the message of love and redemption to people who don't care, or worse, people who seek out goodness and try to rape and pillage it for their own ends?

"All the suffering, all the evil, it's just... tragic. Tragic that the good is always beaten down by the dark and that no one seems to care. That's the part that makes me the saddest— when I keep crying out and showing that there are people out there who need love and compassion and the response is a shrug."

Moses waited a moment before saying anything. He wasn't sure if Irvin was done or not; he had a look like he was caught between thoughts a thousand miles away.

"Well, life seems a lot less tragic once you stop expecting people to care. At least that's how it seems to me."

"But what kind of life is that? That's not the way it should be. If there is a perfect plan or even a semi-interested deity out there then our hope for ourselves and other human beings should be more than that they fail us in only predictable ways.

"I've been praying that He comes and burns the whole of creation in fire. Because if there's truly a God of love watching over this, then He has to see all this and must realize that it's all gone too far. Justice must be brought to bear and that means it all has to burn."

"…Well, I guess this might be your lucky day then."

Moses told Irvin about the message from B and the impending cataclysm. Or as much as he could.

"What do you mean, you never found out what was in the cube?"

"I haven't had time. Besides, what does it matter?"

"What do you mean? Of course it matters. They wouldn't have sent it if it didn't matter, would they?"

Moses was getting irritated. He knew he'd brought it upon himself by finding Irvin and taking him out when he really didn't want to talk about any of it. In retrospect, it wasn't his best plan.

"Let's say there is something there. So what? Five minutes ago you wanted it to all burn because the world was so corrupt it couldn't be saved. Well, everything I was working towards—everything I had ever hoped for—is gone now. I've lived a long time and I don't have the energy to lie to myself in order to find a reason to keep trying. It's convenient timing. I can just wait and it'll take care of itself. It's a self-cleaning life."

"Then what do you have to lose? We can check it out together. It's not often I actually get what I ask for. It would be nice to get the details. Maybe the cynic in me thinks it might be too good to be true."

"The end of the universe qualifies as possibly being too good to be true?"

"It's been one of those kind of days."

"Can't argue with that."

*****

With a crackle and a little flash of blue Irvin and Moses appeared into the middle of a desert.

"You've been able to do that the entire time?"

Moses shrugged.

"I bet you've seen all sorts of stuff using this."

"Not really. Nothing raises suspicion more than random guys showing up out of nowhere. Keeping the energy signature to a minimum helps avoid detection from back home, for that matter. And frankly, there isn't much that's happened here that's been all that interesting."

"Nothing?"

"I remember liking 'Diff'rent Strokes'. That Arnold, he cracked me up."

"Are you serious?"

"What? You think I'd be impressed by the internet? Are you impressed by cave paintings as a means of communication?"

"...Fine. What are we doing here?"

"You wanted to see the cube, well the best place to do that is somewhere without any artificial lights or technology or... well, anything, really."

"Are you afraid of it being seen?"

"What? Not really. You all just have no sense of efficiency. The power leakage from your equipment—I'm surprised you haven't all grown a second head yet. Seriously, you'd all use a nuclear reactor to make a piece of toast if it were up to you. It's madness. If I tried to use this cube anywhere in a city the interference and distortion would make it damn near useless. It's a wonder you haven't burned this entire planet out already."

As Moses complained he held the cube out on the palm of his hand, squinting as if trying to put it in perspective with the surrounding area. When he seemed satisfied he lightly brushed his middle and index finger across the top of it. That activated it and started to rotate slowly in his hand. After a couple seconds Moses seemed to be satisfied with what was happening he stepped away and the cube stayed hovering in the same spot.

"Just give it a second. I've never actually used this kind before. It might take a minute," he said to Irvin. The cube began to spin faster and Irvin found himself creeping behind

Moses as if Moses would be able to shield him if things went wrong. The edges of the cube began to glow a dark violet color as it spun. As Irvin stared at it, it appeared as if the violet glowing edges were spinning away from the cube itself, as if the cube were spinning inside a glowing stick diagram. Suddenly the edges glowed very brightly and the stick box grew explosively, blowing past both Irvin and Moses, leaving them in a giant black box with violet seams. Irvin was startled by being swallowed up in the black box and he unconsciously grabbed Moses' arm and ducked behind him.

"It's just a neuro-spatial holographic containment field. Nothing's different, you're still in the same place you were; the walls aren't real. Think of it as a three dimensional computer screen projected into your brain. You might feel the need to sneeze. Don't ask me why. It just has that effect on some people."

The black box stopped spinning and it slowly dropped to waist level. Above the box appeared a waist-up figure of a puffer fish. It gurgled solemnly.

Moses removed his face plate and walked up to the virtual puffer fish man and gurgled back. The virtual puffer fish nodded and then a model of planets and stars surrounded them. The space seemed infinitely vast as if they were in the largest planetarium imaginable instead the middle of a desert.

A bright, emerald-like green planet swooped overhead and directly in front of them. The look on Moses' face was one of great sadness, at least that's what Irvin thought a puffer fish would look like if it had a look of great sadness.

The virtual puffer fish pointed behind them. They both turned and in the distance there was a little flash of light at a distant star, but instead of fading it seemed to get brighter and brighter and then disappeared. As they watched there was what appeared to be a giant wave coming towards them. The view zoomed to the wave and they saw it burning out planets in its wake, engulfing whole solar systems. As it kept moving, however, it seemed to lose steam.

The puffer fish then pointed back at the planet and gurgled and zoomed into a point on the planet. They swooped into a continent, a city, a building and into a laboratory where the virtual puffer fish stood in full figure, doing some adjustments to a giant machine with a number of other uniformed, very grumpy looking puffer fish standing around him. The machine came to life and the air in front of the puffer fish men started to get wavy until ripples of light seemed to emanate from them like light flashing through a blind caught in a breeze. There was a flash and it looked like a giant gust of wind suddenly blew through the room, sending equipment flying and forcing the puffer fish to hold up their arms to shield themselves. The scientist puffer fish quickly hit some buttons and the waving stopped.

Suddenly they were whisked back above the planet where the "gust" was shooting into space. As it went, it created ripples behind it. At first it didn't seem like much but some of them kept waving and then it appeared like little cracks began to appear in the waves. The cracks were bleeding light and seemed to slowly creep out longer and longer. It reminded Irvin of watching a crack in a windshield slowly grow.

The gust moved at an incredible speed and suddenly they were whisked through space to the crest of the gust. The giant wave they'd seen first rolled towards it and when they collided, the first wave swallowed it up. The gust just vanished. It seemed a little anti-climactic at first but then the wave hit the first crack the gust had left behind and suddenly the wave started growing. It began to glow and pulse and in its wake where the cracks had been, huge swaths of reality appeared to have been torn apart. What was left were rapidly rising and falling misshapen planets and imploding stars that burned cold. They zoomed in on one of the planets and creatures were created, ripped apart, reassembled and ripped apart over and over again. There was nothing but chaos and misery. It was the most horrifying thing either Irvin or Moses had ever seen.

All of the images faded away leaving only the virtual puffer fish gurgling stoically. The image then changed to Earth. Irvin couldn't tell how far they had travelled from the oncoming wave but it seemed to be a vast distance. There were little orange points that bubbled up over the globe, rising and popping before doing the same somewhere else. The virtual puffer fish pointed at them and then some graph-looking things popped up that the puffer fish gurgled about in a very animated manner.

The virtual puffer fish held up a virtual version of the black cube. There were different annotations and diagrams pointing here and there over it. The puffer fish ran his hand over top of it and the cube's top popped open and a small arc of blue light shot from it. The puffer fish pointed towards one of the graphs and then an orange bubble appeared. The blue light mixed with it and then a gateway appeared. The puffer fish gestured as it gurgled excitedly. A model of the gateway appeared and showed it joining two different giant orbs. A little puffer fish animation ran through the gateway and it closed just as the first side was engulfed in fire.

The puffer fish gurgled a few more things and then vanished. The cube slowed its spinning and Moses came and took it from midair. As he did the black area surrounding them collapsed and they were standing in the desert again.

Moses put his faceplate back on, stretched his back and sighed. "Well... there goes the neighborhood."

"What? What's going on?"

"The quick version is the universe is being ripped to shreds by an energy surge caused from a mini-big bang kind of implosion that got mixed with some sort of alien alternate-reality feedback energy."

"Is it coming here?"

"It's coming everywhere. You wanted fire and judgment? Well, you got it... in spades. I didn't believe in a Hell until I saw that planet that was caught up in it. That's coming here. That's coming everywhere."

"What was that bit about the Earth? The orange bubbles?"

Moses sighed. "There's a theoretical chance that if some of the slipstream technology combined with some the Narrative-crossing equipment my father developed can be safely used if combined with a sympathetic energy signature from another Narrative. He thinks a gateway could be opened that could theoretically allow someone to theoretically escape the great universal undoing by slipping into another Narrative where they theoretically wouldn't be instantly vaporized, unmade or otherwise molested... Theoretically.

"The orange bubbles were possible sympathetic signatures that my father detected from Waffle. Or it could be a little cloud of methane from a cow's ass because he was trying to observe this from the other side of the known universe. It's kind of like trying to read Swedish furniture assembly instructions with a pair of binoculars if you were on the moon and the instructions were on Earth... on the horizon... under water. So, you know, the odds get better and better.

"Thing is, the energy may not even exist here, and even if it did, it would have to be occurring somewhere right now. The little blips you saw popping up in the simulation were over a span of decades, even centuries. So it could be just about anywhere, at any time, or not even real."

"How would you find it?"

"In theory? Activate the cube and if there's an anomaly it would tag it and send the coordinates back. Like this—" Moses ran his hand across the top of the cube and it opened up, the blue of arc of light appeared, like it had in the simulation. "So now it's scanning. It'll run some tests and if we're lucky it'll process for a moment and tell us the last time an anomaly—"

An arc of lighting shot through the blue light and for a brief moment there appeared to be a hole. There was a large orange figure being wrapped in the lightning and behind her a little girl peering at them curiously. There was a crack and then hole sealed itself back up and the box closed. A little light flashed from the surface of the cube.

"...Well, huh," Moses said.

Part VIII: Songs from the Dead Earth

"What just happened?" Irvin asked.

"Uh… that super rare theoretical near-impossibility I was talking about apparently just happened."

"So what does that mean?"

"…I don't know. One of two astronomically improbable things that would have had to have happened, just happened. I didn't really pay attention to the second part since the first didn't even seem possible."

"Can we stop it? The big, destructive wave-thing?"

"What? No. That was never an option. But now it's slightly more plausible that we might be able to open an incredibly dangerous and unstable portal into another Narrative to escape to."

"Are you going to try it?"

"Um, maybe? Although that might end up being worse."

"But you could have a chance to escape what's coming. I saw the same thing you did on that planet. How can it be worse than that?"

"Well, that's the problem. It might be the same as that. And why would I run? I'm alone here; D betrayed me and my home has been, or is just about to be, consumed by some huge galactic tsunami of terror. There are worse options than just waiting it out here and enjoying what bit of normalcy the universe has left."

"But what if it's better there? You said Heaven sounded a lot like a theory about the Narratives, right? What if this is your chance for that? Couldn't there be a place for you there where you and D can be together—a place with no suffering or death? This might be the literal gate to Heaven, Moses."

Moses thought for a moment. From what his father had told him of the Narratives, it was possible there was a "Prime Narrative". It was a longshot, but the thought of getting a second chance with D, the idea of some sort of reward for his work or redemption for righting the wrongs of his youth was an attractive one.

*****

Lyle cleaned himself off with a shirt from the hamper. As soon as he'd opened his eyes he realized what had happened. He had been so close though that it hadn't taken much to finish the job. It had been frustrating, but he felt worse for Nicola. He knew that it would bother her a lot more that it had him. He wanted to be with her, but he was ok with the limitations of their relationship; he was just happy to have her with him. She tended to obsess more about trying to make things perfect. It was one of the many things he found endearing.

Even though she'd become stronger over the past months, it was likely going to be several hours before Nicola could return. Hope might pop in and out, but usually if Nicola was gone Hope was with her. It was the first time in a couple months that Lyle could remember actually being completely on his own.

He wasn't sure what to do with himself. He watched TV for a while, but the manic programming only made him more restless and bored. He got his duffle bag together and headed to the gym. The thought of activity seemed almost novel after spending so much time at home with Nicola.

He was settled in and on an elliptical machine when he felt a hand on his shoulder. "Hey stranger."

Lyle turned, startled by the touch and saw Jeannine. "Oh, hey. How are you?"

"I'm good. Haven't seen you around in a while. I thought I might have to find a new workout buddy if I didn't see you again soon."

"Ah, well, I've been busy, I guess. You know how it is."

"Yeah, gym is always the first thing to go, right? I texted you a few times, but never heard from you. I figured you were probably busy."

"Oh, yeah... Sorry. I saw them and I was just wrapped up when I got them and then didn't think to send something later. Sorry. How have you been?"

"Fine. Good. Good and fine. Just the usual day-to-day stuff. Nothing special," she said with a wry grin. Lyle thought she seemed a bit more engaging then he remembered. She moved towards him and gave him a little bump to the side of his leg with her hip. "What about you? You look like things are going well. Whatchya been up to?"

"Well, work's been ok. I've been kinda seeing someone for a while. That's been good."

"Ah, a man of secrets, I see. So is that why I never heard back from you?"

"No. I mean, I *have* been busy. I haven't been able to keep up with nearly anyone. It's not because she's—"

"Of course not. I mean it's not as if we were—"

"Exactly. I mean, we're workout buddies, like you said."

"Just friendly."

"Right. I mean that time we went out wasn't a date or anything."

"No, no. Just friends meeting friends. Just hangin' out and doin' our thing."

"Not that, you know, you're not great and all."

"I know," she answered with a smirk. "I am sorta great."

"Anyway, it was good seeing you again. If you're ever free, maybe we could hang out again."

"Yeah, that would be nice. I'm busy for the foreseeable future, but, yeah, that would be cool. You could meet Nicola. I bet you two would totally get along."

"I'm sure… Or maybe, you know, you could just come on your own. Whichever."

Lyle chuckled, a little self-conscious, "Well, anyway, it was nice to see you again."

"You take care of yourself, buddy," Jeannine said with a little wink as she headed towards the weights.

Lyle watched her go. A year before she barely seemed to notice him—he had felt like he had to insinuate himself into situations to even talk to her. Now she was acting as if he were catnip.

"She likes you," said Hope quietly right by his ear.

"Jesus Christ!" Lyle jumped. "Seriously, do you even have any idea how terrifying you can be sometimes?"

Hope got a weird little smile on her face, "Yeah."

It was the first time Lyle remembered her being funny and he blurted out two loud laughs that were nearly sneeze-like. He quickly glanced around to see if anyone saw him talking to empty air. He grabbed his towel and started wiping down the machine as he spoke quietly.

"What are you doing here? Is Nicola ok?"

"She had to go somewhere."

"No, I know. It was my mistake that sent her there."

"No, she had to go somewhere else."

"What do you mean?"

"There was lightning."

Lyle looked at her, puzzled. "What? What are you talking about?" Lyle knew a little about the Windy Place. Nicola didn't explain much about it other than it was a place where she and Hope would go when they weren't with him. Lyle assumed that wind was involved, but aside from that, he didn't know much. Presumably from what Hope had said, lightning was not typically involved.

"She got hit by lightning. Then she said she had to find something and left."

"Like actual lightning? And she's ok? What do you mean by 'left'?"

"She's ok. It didn't hurt her. She went to the Memories. I lost track of her after a while, she was jumping around so much."

"'Memories'? I don't know what you're talking about."

Hope shrugged. "If you'd seen it, you'd understand."

"You know what?" Lyle asked, exasperated. "...Fine. Thank you for telling me."

"Who's the other girl?"

"What?"

"The one who likes you." she pointed at Jeannine.

"She's... she's no one. Just someone I know from here. And she doesn't like me. She barely talks to me."

"She talked to you today."

"Yeah, well, I don't know what that was about. She's not interested."

"Yeah she is. She keeps looking over here."

"It's probably because she sees me talking to air like a crazy person. I'm surprised everyone isn't staring."

"I know why she likes you."

"What? How can you know that? I mean, it's not even true."

"You're a nice person."

"Well, I was a nice person before and she didn't give a shit. I'm not nicer than I was then."

"You're a nice person and you look happy."

The last bit struck Lyle. He had been happier since Nicola had come to him. There were challenges to be sure, but the world didn't seem like a giant tar pit of disappointment and inevitable despair. Maybe that did have some bearing on how people viewed him, but the revelation didn't seem particularly interesting. In his days prior to Nicola he probably would have killed to have that bit of swagger, but now it just seemed to be a happy accident of sorts.

"C'mon, let's go."

Hope was a bit surprised. Lyle had never said much to her other than to explain to her how her behavior was unnerving, annoying or otherwise beyond social norms. In fact other than to occasionally ferry messages back and forth between him and Nicola when she was in the Windy Place she didn't recall having any kind of conversations with him. She wasn't sure to make of it, but since Nicola was gone it wasn't as if she had anything else better to do.

*****

"Friends, you have heard the predictions before; you've heard the warnings: the End is nigh! And surely that day is quick upon us, but that's like saying 'A thief is about and will steal from you.' If you could stop it by simply knowing about it or trying to prepare for it then it would be your fault if it happened. It would be within your ability to control the thief. So it is with the end of days—even if you were to know the exact day and hour there would still be unbelief because we only believe in things we can control. That's why we like to blame victims. That's why natural disasters seem so terrifying and why they make us question God and ourselves. If something happens and there's nothing that could have been done to correct it or protect ourselves or our families then it surely can't be just. There can be no balance in the universe if things just simply happen, right?

"We like to believe bad things happen because they are deserved or because they are signs of something far worse that is also deserved. When tragedy does strike close to home we cry out to God saying 'Lord! How is it that you allowed this to happen?' or even 'Why have you done this to me, O Lord?' I suppose it's the law of averages. Day in and day out we get up, go to work, come home, eat, drink, sleep, dream and nothing much really happens so we feel like it's unnatural for catastrophe to strike.

"Then we see in the book of Job how Job's afflictions were part of a great test. But we misunderstand the test. Everyone says Job was being tested to show his faithfulness. But let's look at it closely, here's what the Devil says: 'Does Job fear God for nothing? Have you not put a hedge around him and his household and everything he has? You have blessed the work of his hands, so that his flocks and herds are spread throughout the land. But now stretch out your hand and strike everything he has, and he will surely curse you to your face.'

"Now I can hear you saying 'Pastor Dave, that sounds exactly like Job is being tested.' Maybe you're right. But the one thing we've learned is that the Devil is subtle in his ways and his lies sound like truths. Does Job need to prove his faithfulness to God? God already said that he was upright. It seems to me that the Devil is testing God. He's approaching God and saying, 'How can you claim to be just when those you say are blameless haven't undergone anything to challenge them? If you are truly all-powerful then why should this man's righteousness spare him the fate of all men?'

"He was challenging God to show that his love for humanity wasn't a weakness—that He would put both the righteous and unrighteous to fire the same. The Devil was daring God to be impartial because whatever God would withhold meant that God was afraid of losing—God couldn't allow his love to interfere with the business of being God.

"We see this again when Abraham is told to sacrifice his son Isaac and when God Himself allowed his only Son to be crucified. These are all connected. We are shown that obedience sometimes means bearing witness to painful and confusing things and that sometimes all reason is thrown aside when something of universal importance is at work.

"But don't despair. While horrible things will happen—lives will be lost, families broken, love will go unanswered—it also means that there's a plan. It means there's something so much bigger at work that the law of averages can't apply. If we think of things in that context, what could be better? Average isn't good. We can survive with average, but average doesn't make us happy. It's only by throwing out the status quo that we can truly be something better. By discarding all that we've settled for in life we can finally be the creatures that God envisions us to be and through great tribulation can we see the true vastness and awesomeness of God.

"The end is upon us. We won't know why or how or even when exactly, but it's soon. Like Paul wrote to the Thessalonians, God did not appoint us to suffer wrath but to receive salvation. We will be surrounded by great suffering and horror, but we know that that pain is part of our salvation. What is wrath to those who don't understand the love of God is salvation to those of us who know the truth.

"So even as the finale to this great story of love and grace begins, there is another end. This is the last time I will be broadcasting to all of you. I have been very blessed over the years that I've done this program through all of you. I've been fortunate to make friends who have been like family to me like Karl, the station manager here at KBQJ, my friend and brother Moses who you've heard playing the beautiful music night in night out over the past year or so and before him my dear, dear, departed brother in Christ, Jim Prado.

"It is time for me to say goodbye. I've run out of things to say and time to say them. For everything there is a season. I pray that the coming days you all learn to see the beauty and goodness that God has surrounded us with and take comfort that even as my time as a messenger to you has come to a close, that He will always be there to speak words of love and encouragement to each of you.

"God bless you all. Farewell and... um, farewell, I guess."

Irvin got up and gave one last look at his little makeshift console and the empty space where Moses and Jim had played. He hadn't planned on it being the last show, but Moses hadn't shown up and it seemed appropriate that that should be a sign. It was only an hour into his scheduled block, but there was nothing more to say. The last of his belief was spat out and dissipated into the atmosphere like the last burp of air flopping out of the open end of a balloon. Irvin took some satisfaction that he thought the last earnest words he would speak had been good.

Moses hadn't intended to stand Irvin up. If anything, he was concerned about Irvin. So much had gone on and it would be natural for Irvin to be conflicted, troubled or depressed, but the last time Moses had spoken to him he had been strangely monotone. Irvin's sermons had continued to become more abstract and rambling. Moses wasn't that familiar with theology or even a lot of the stories themselves, but it was beginning to sound like the conclusions Irvin had been reaching weren't even completely rational.

Moses had been tidying up his apartment. If the world weren't about to end he would have had to move. The neighborhood had gone from bohemian to über-trendy and increasingly expensive. The one advantage of knowing what was coming was the Moses wouldn't spend the last days of the universe packing, an activity which he detested.

Moses poured himself a bowl of cereal. He doused it in milk and left it on the counter. When it got soggy it was easier for him to process and, besides that, he actually thought it was tasty. For a primitive society, he had to credit them for developing Lucky Charms.

"Holy SHIT!" He turned to find a pale little girl in a dirty white dress had been standing right behind him.

"Nicola wants to talk to you."

"Child, where the hell did you come from?"

"Did you bring the lightning?"

"What? What are you talking about?" Moses tried to guide the girl towards the futon but his hand passed right through her. "Jesus Christ. What are you?"

"Nicola says you brought the lightning and that no one here should be able to do that."

"Are you from Waffle?"

"She says the people here don't have the portal technology or the knowledge of Narrative theory to make such a device. She wants to know where you came from."

"Listen, I don't know what you think you heard or saw, but I'm just house-sitting for a dude right now. I don't even live here."

The little girl gave him a thoroughly annoyed look and then turned and spoke as if there were someone else there. "You tell him," she grumbled. There was another pause as she crossed her arms and pouted. "He says he doesn't know." She gave an exasperated sigh and then turned back to Moses, "Nicola says that there's something coming and that you have a… what?!? A meta-spacetime transdementia—" she huffed out of frustration at the invisible correction she received. "A meta-spacetime transDI-MEN-TION-AL—" she said with added emphasis with a look of irritation at the invisible person, "portal bridging device."

"Listen kid, I don't know who or what you are, but you need to get the hell up outta here."

The girl tilted her head at him with a look of mild surprise. "Or what?"

"Or else you're gonna see some scary shit."

She giggled.

"Oh, you think I'm foolin' with ya? Now get. You won't like it if you stay."

The little girl looked back at the empty space and shrugged at it nonchalantly.

"I warned you," Moses reached up and, in one fluid motion, popped off his faceplate and lunged at the little girl and made the most ferocious gurgling sound he knew how.

"It's a fish!" the little girl clapped delightedly.

"...Dammit," Moses muttered. "Look, I got to go. I don't know who you are, but you're barking up the wrong tree."

The little girl didn't seem to be paying attention; her invisible friend seemed to be talking. Then it looked as if she grasped something in one hand and then she reached out and touched Moses. It was the strangest sensation, kind of like having to sneeze and burp at the same time while slightly drunk with a sudden chill running down his back and having déjà vu.

"Can you see her yet?" she asked. Moses didn't know what she was saying and then suddenly there was a seven foot tall orange Gumby-looking creature standing in front of him.

"Holy SHIT!" he yelled for a second time.

"I think he can see you," the little girl said.

"What the fuck is that thing?" Moses said to himself. The orange cocked its head slightly as if studying him.

"What do you see?" it said.

"A fuckin' giant orange Gumby-looking thing. Why? What am I supposed to see?"

The creature looked at the little girl. "Do you think you can make me appear like I do with Lyle?" The little girl shrugged. "I suppose it doesn't matter. It's not as if you haven't seen other life forms before, right?"

"I've never seen a giant orange Gumby before."

"What's this 'Gumby' thing? Oh nevermind, it doesn't matter. Let me start again. My name is Nicola and this is Hope. I'm from the Neo-Enlightened Golden Epoch of the Second Greater Universal Narrative. Perhaps you've heard of us?"

Moses stared at her blankly.

"Oh, well, it's a very, very nice Narrative. For reference this is the Fourteenth Lesser Narrative, so you can see that it's one of the best Narratives. You do know about the Narratives, right?"

"Science was my father's thing. I was never the academic type."

"Then how did you manage to find me?"

"That was the modified data cube. I just activated it. If you're looking for much more than that, I'm afraid you're on your own."

"But did he say it was looking for me?"

"Oh, geeze, I don't know. Something about finding external energy signatures to act as a stabilizer for a portal. Something like that."

"That sounds like a great way to melt your face off."

"How do you mean?"

"If you open a direct portal to another Narrative there's energy bleed that can de-stablize both Narratives, or, if you're lucky, just turn one of them into a spontaneous self-sustaining nuclear furnace through every instant of its spacetime. You need a neutral space—kind of like an airlock. Thank goodness your father never tested that theory. It would've been catastrophic."

"…Well, funny thing that…"

"What do you mean?"

"There's a giant energy wave thing that's on its way. It's going to destroy the entire universe."

"What? How?"

"Probably best I just show you," Moses sighed. "I apologize in advance for the distortion."

Moses activated dug the cube out of his things and re-played the simulation for Nicola and Hope. Nicola seemed especially interested in the cracks created by the initial gust and then the energy wave rolling up and absorbing them.

"In other Narratives those cracks just grow and grow until the Narrative collapses in on itself. This energy wave is something I've never even heard of before."

"So that's what's in store for us. If the portal thing won't work, then we're screwed. Well, I'm screwed, at least. I'm not sure about the little girl. If she's real she's probably screwed, too."

Hope didn't seem particularly interested in the conversation; she was captivated by Moses' puffer fish face. With each breath she beamed as his gills moved and fluttered.

"Not necessarily. I said opening a portal into another Narrative directly would be disaster, but if we set up a Bridge Narrative then, well, then there's a possibility."

Moses shrugged. "Look, I'm fine with going up with this universe, really. You aren't even actually here so you don't have anything to worry about. The little girl is picking her nose. She doesn't seem too worried," Hope looked up at the mention of her name, index finger still buried in her nose. "This is dangerous stuff. Look what it's already caused. We should just leave well enough alone."

"Don't you want the chance to live out your life happy and carefree?" Nicola asked. "Isn't there someone you wish you could see again or another chance at the life you always wanted? That's what this could mean. I can't do anything on my own, but with your device and my knowledge we can make it right. You can be happy. I believe that it's worth trying, but we can only do it with your help."

Moses' thoughts immediately went to D. The idea of being able to be with D in a world where none of the ugly things had happened was the kind of thing he hadn't dared to dream about. Perhaps all his time trying to do good hadn't gone unnoticed. It was as close to believing in Irvin's idea of God as he had come.

"Well, what do you need from me?" he asked.

Nicola looked pleased. "Two things. First, access to your data cube so I can try and work out what I need to supply from my side."

"And the second thing?"

"Your name," she smiled.

*****

Things were changing in the Windy Place. There was a black, inky spot that was slowly spreading across the sky. As the black spot grew, there was a chill in the air that hadn't been there before but the wind itself seemed to be diminishing. Hope went to the tree in hopes of finding a little warmth and comfort, but as she approached it she found the trunk was covered in the brown half-shell growths. She touched the tree. It felt oddly mushy and clammy. There was still some warmth radiating from it, but it felt wrong.

"Don't say anything to Lyle about anything we learned today. I need to tell him when the time is right."

Hope looked up at Nicola who was standing with her hands clasped behind her back, swaying slowly side to side.

"Did you lie to him like you lied to Lyle?"

"What do you mean?"

"You didn't tell him the truth about what you knew so he'd help you."

"It's more complicated than that, sweetie."

"Do you lie to me?"

"No, I couldn't even if I wanted to. You know me better than anyone, Hope. You're my conscience."

"Why can't I see beyond that day?"

Nicola shifted uncomfortably, weighing her answer. "It's because something is going to happen. Something big."

"Is it something bad?"

"You shouldn't worry. You'll be fine."

"The pictures showed that everything would be destroyed. That's what you told the fish man, too."

"I know. And that's something that could happen, but you don't need to worry."

"Why not?"

"Because I won't let anything happen to you. You, me and Lyle, just like I said before; we'll all be together and safe."

"Me, you, Lyle and the fish man, right?"

Nicola paused. "Of course. That's what I meant: me, you, Lyle and Moses."

Hope hugged Nicola around the waist as they walked. She closed her eyes and smiled. She liked the sound of Nicola's voice when she was lying.

"I'm going to have to be gone a lot in the next little while. I have to work things out with Lyle and get Moses' device working and then I have to go home to make sure everything is ok there. I don't want you to feel like I'm leaving you behind, ok? I just need to do these things so we can all be together. Do you understand?" Hope nodded into her side. Nicola petted her head lightly. "When this is over, we'll all be so happy. I can't wait for us to be together like a family.

"I have to go to speak to Lyle now. I'll see you soon, Hope."

With that, Nicola was gone. Hope stood unsure of what to do. The Windy Place felt empty without someone with her. The inky black sky had expanded further overhead. It still wasn't that large overall. When Hope held her hand up and made a fist and squinted down her arm with one eye the black space was just visible around the outside of her knuckles but it didn't seem long ago that it was a small spot the size of a pea. She went to her tree and started kicking at the mushrooms on it. They'd crumble away and turn to black mist before they hit the ground. It reminded her of how the Memories had looked when Nicola touched them. There were still some chunks stuck to the tree and the tree still felt clammy. There were less leaves then when she'd arrived, too. Her tree was beginning to look spinsterish and frail.

Hope could tell the Windy Place was coming to an end, or at least it would never be the place she belonged anymore. She didn't know what would happen to her when the big wave hit the world, but she could tell Nicola thought the Windy Place would be caught up in it somehow. She wanted to believe that Nicola would take her away with her, but Nicola was a dreamer at her core. So much of what she had promised Hope and Lyle were just wishes and flights of fancy from what she could tell.

Hope decided she needed to do what she had been dreading. She grasped a passing Memory and started hopping from Memory to Memory heading towards September 15th, 2008.

*****

When Irvin finally answered the door Moses was taken aback. While not the most fashion-minded person, Irvin had always maintained his appearance and hygiene. The Irvin that answered the door hadn't bathed in several days and apparently was still wearing the same clothes from the last time he had. His hair, usually carefully coiffed in a comb over was now tussled and sticking out the side of his head like a bird's wing. He looked very tired, but smiled a little when he saw Moses.

"Hey, I was worried about you," Irvin said.

"Sorry. Something came up last minute and I couldn't get away. I tried to call later but you weren't answering. I dropped by the station and they said you quit."

"Yeah… it was time, I guess. Newer and bigger things, right?"

Moses studied him for a moment. "Listen, let's go get something to eat. You haven't eaten yet, have you?"

"I don't know. I had some crackers earlier. I'm not really hungry."

"Well, then come watch me eat."

"…Naw …I'm not feeling the greatest, I was about to lie down."

"C'mon, man."

"It's ok. We can try again another time."

Moses tried to argue but Irvin slipped back inside the house and closed the door. Moses stood on the step for a minute, hoping maybe Irvin would change his mind. He didn't hear any moving around inside and it seemed like Irvin had fully retreated back into his hole.

Moses wasn't sure what to do. If there was a chance to get away he felt obligated to bring Irvin along. Moses didn't have many friends and B and Irvin were the two people who had been loyal. After considering his obligation to them he decided he had to try Nicola's scheme. He would tell B of the plan and try and convince Irvin to come along, too. He didn't know if Nicola or Hope were entirely trustworthy, but under the circumstances, if they weren't it didn't much matter. He realized that there might be a limit to the number of people who could go, but he had leverage—it was his cube after all —if she gave too much resistance he could always insist that they had to come or there was no deal.

It all left him with an uneasy feeling, but at least there was a possible alternative to being unmade, reassembled at random just to be torn apart again on the atomic level. That didn't sound like much fun, Moses decided.

*****

"I have something I need to tell you," Nicola whispered to Lyle. They were both nude, lying facing each other. It had been raining throughout the night and it was still overcast and foggy, muting the morning light with a dreamlike pall. Lyle nodded and grunted still half asleep.

"No, this is important. I need you to listen to me."

"Mmmph, I'm up. I'm listening."

Nicola smiled, "No, you're not. I need you to really listen, ok?"

"No, I am. I really am."

"You know how we talk about how we'd like to be together if things were different?"

"Mm-hm."

"Well, something's coming. Something is going to happen and everything is going to change."

Lyle blinked and squinted at Nicola, unclear about what she was trying to say.

"I'm going to have to go away for a while."

"You're leaving?"

"For a while."

"When will you be back?"

"…I don't know. I don't know if I can come back."

"What? What do you mean?"

"It's complicated. I don't want to go—"

"Then don't."

Nicola gave a half smile as her eyes welled up with tears. "I don't want to," she whispered.

"You can't just do that. You can't be here and be amazing and turn my life upside down and then say you're leaving," Lyle's voice cracked.

"Shhh, shhhh," Nicola tried to soothe him. "It's not all bad news. I'm leaving but it's because of something I have to do."

"I don't want you to go. I don't care what you have to do. I want you here with me."

A rogue tear escaped the corner of her eye and slalomed down her cheek. "I know, baby. I want to be here with you, too. I know this is sudden, but this could be good for us…" her voice trailed off. Neither of them spoke for a moment. Nicola reached over to him; she wished she could touch him, to offer a little bit of comfort.

"Life is always finding new ways to make you say goodbye. Sometimes you just need to find a way to say hello. This is me trying to find us our hello."

"What do you mean?"

"What I'm going to do it could make it so we're together forever."

"So you'll be back."

"I hope so. And if it works we'll be together for real. We'll be able to touch each other. We'll be together like a real couple. We will be a real couple."

"But you're not sure?"

"…No. It's not like anything that's ever been done before."

"Then stay."

"What?"

"If this is all we can be, that's ok by me. It's not ideal, but I'd rather have this than nothing. If this is as close as we can get, then my life is still pretty damn good. I don't need more. I just need you. I love you."

Nicola wiped away the tears from her eyes and tried to smile. "Thank you. I love you, too, I really do. If it could be any other way I would stay with here with you. There's no one else I've ever met that I've wanted to be with more than you. But I have to do this. I can't explain now. You have to just trust me—I'm doing this for both of us. I want us to be together. You have to trust me, there is no other way."

"When are you leaving?"

"As soon as we're done here."

"You can't just drop this on me and disappear."

Nicola sat up and her clothes reappear over her frame. She stood, back to Lyle. "Come back to bed," he pleaded.

"I can't. I'll be back when I can.," she turned her head and so she could see him out of the corner of her eye. He was sitting up staring at her with a look of profound sadness, lip trembling as tears ran down his cheeks. "Goodbye," she whispered as she vanished.

*****

Moses and Nicola had watched the simulations over and over again. It had been weeks in isolation for the both of them in the middle of Kansas and while they had made limited progress, a solution was proving elusive. Nicola had wanted to move their research closer to her base of operations. Moses didn't have much of a preference and had slipstreamed to meet her there.

Things had been going so poorly that Moses hadn't even mentioned his desire to bring B or Irvin along. The way things were going it didn't seem likely that they'd be able to get it to work at all. Their latest attempt at least had the appearance of some headway, but after the first burst of data came through, Nicola had already started shaking her head.

"The Bridge Narrative never fully stabilizes," Nicola pointed out in the simulation replay as the gateway broke apart seconds after being established between the two Narratives. "There's just not enough energy to maintain the sync from this end. You see there?" she pointed at a wavering line between the Narrative and the bridge. "It can't even fully connect with this Narrative."

"Well, it stays open for a few seconds, is that enough time?" Moses asked.

"It's not even open. It's formed, but if you tried to push through without the link established you'd be turned into hamburger by the void energy. Without that sealed completely you're basically walking into a giant swirling blender of invisible energy."

"Well, what if we create a bridge from this side and then cut it loose, connect with your Narrative and come through kind of like a ferry?"

"Two problems. First cutting a Bridge Narrative loose from inside the Bridge Narrative itself has never been done and I doubt that the energy you'd have would be enough to sustain it long enough to make the transition. Second, without the two stabilizing Narratives we're going to run into the same kind of problems we would with a straight Narrative-to-Narrative portal. Assuming you have enough energy to maintain the bridge initially, the differential between the Bridge and my Narrative would pretty much pull you inside out at the speed of light."

They both studied the simulation from within the data cube field. Moses got a slightly confused look on his face and turned to Nicola.

"Now wait, if the energy disparity is too great between the bridge and the individual Narratives, how is it that anyone is able to move from one Narrative to another? Wouldn't it require an extended period in the bridge with the forces equalizing kind of like a recompression chamber? Even then, that's assuming that the energy and matter is fully compatible between the two, right?"

"Oh, it's fine. We do it all the time. It's the Second Greater Narrative for a reason. There are all sorts of machines and filters that take care of all that kind of technical stuff. If we can establish the bridge then everything will be fine."

Moses gave her a skeptical look. She seemed very confident, but the sudden lack of detail made him wary. On some level it didn't really matter if she was being completely forthright since Moses realized he didn't have any other options. Still, he thought it would be wise to keep an eye on her. Besides, when came down to it he knew he'd do what he needed to do, even if it didn't exactly line up with what he had told her.

"So how much energy are we going to need?"

"A lot. But it has to be a specific kind of energy—it has to be Narrative energy. Have you ever seen a kid rub a balloon on their head and then stick it to a wall? In a very simplistic way, that's similar. Think of the balloon as your Narrative. You live inside the balloon with all the air and such, then there's the rubber that acts as a barrier between the inside and everything else. Well, Narrative energy is like the static energy —it's attached to the rubber or border. Bridges require that kind of energy. It exists everywhere, but where it's concentrated and easy to manipulate is along the outside of the Narrative.

"We've developed means of arranging and harvesting that energy and directing it to where we set up the portals to the bridges. It's that same kind of technology that allows me to be seen here. I'm not actually here, but energy and matter are being directed from my side to this one to maintain this projection. Same idea except on a much bigger scale.

"Unfortunately this Narrative has neither the technology, the knowledge nor the time to figure out how to do that. We can keep trying with whatever random pockets of it we can find, but it's just not going to be enough. The Bridge Narratives we use require steady stable power in order to work, but for our purposes here if we could even get a good surge it should be enough for an emergency link… But where can we find some?" Nicola studied the space map, scouring through galaxies and solar systems everywhere.

"When do we need it?"

"Hm? Well, the sooner the better, but I suppose as long as we have an hour or two lead that would be sufficient. But that also limits the amount of space we can try and locate it in."

Moses studied the diagrams for a moment. "What if we get too much?"

Nicola laughed. "Too much? I don't think that will be a problem."

"Seriously. What if we get too much?"

Nicola looked at him quizzically. "Well, I suppose we could set up a kind of venting system that would siphon off the power we need and vent the rest out into a second unsecured portal into void space. That could cause similar problems long-term as Narrative-to-Narrative portals, but it probably wouldn't matter that much since, well, this Narrative doesn't exactly have a long-term future. Why?"

Moses pulled up the record of his father's Narrative portal attempt. "You see that gust? It looks to me as if that energy was drawn to the portal, right?"

Nicola shrugged, "Possibly, but having an unsecured portal sucking in void energy doesn't help. That would just create another event here and hasten things degenerating. If we had enough time, resources and preparation it's possible we could open a portal and skim some energy off, but right now we don't have any safeguards, no way to store it and no way to regulate it."

"But that's the right kind of energy, right?"

"Well, yes. But again, opening a second portal outside of the Narrative isn't viable. It would be like creating a spark in a room full of gas in order to light a candle—even if you managed to light the candle everything else would be absolutely destroyed in the process. We need a source within the Narrative to tap. Finding that—that's what we need to be focusing on."

"But we've got one."

"Where?"

Moses zoomed in on the energy wave, "Right there. And it's coming right for us. We don't even have to go looking for it."

"It'll hit the planet and we'll be cinders—if we're lucky—before we have a chance to try and use it. Plus, there's the original energy. We can't use that and it we can't separate it."

"I think we can.," Moses said. "Look, if we use the portal as just a slipstream device only we can open a connection out to space. The Narrative energy is drawn to the portal. We could use it to siphon off some of the energy and direct it through the other end to the bridge."

"But we'd have to be constantly recalibrating the slipstream portal."

"Yes, but we know generally how fast it's moving. It doesn't have to be perfect; if we have a series of coordinates that open in succession we'll be able to draw energy out as it gets closer. It's not very efficient, but there's so much that even if we miss a few slipstream portals, we should have more than enough power."

"Your slipstream setup is fine for one-off transmissions, but if you need them in quick succession, it'll have to be close. We won't have much of a window between setting up the portals and the wave hitting with your method. And if it doesn't work, there's no plan B."

"Well, if you can think of a better plan, I'm happy to use it, but this one provides us with the necessary kind of energy, gives us—just barely—the time we need, and should give us more than enough raw power to get the job done."

Nicola didn't respond. She just stood staring at the projection like a giant orange statue. "Let me take this back and see what I can figure out on my end. It's getting tight time-wise anyway. I'll run it through some simulations. If it looks at all feasible I'll be back and we'll start getting set up."

"Sounds like as close to a plan as we're going to get."

"Yeah… it probably is," she turned to him. "Hopefully I'll see you soon, Moses."

Nicola vanished leaving Moses alone. He turned off the data cube projection and found himself once again standing in the middle of a field in Kansas. One thing was for certain: time was running out. It was August 20th and the next day would be the last transmission date, assuming that Waffle was still intact. Moses sat down and scribbled a note to B telling him that his only chance for survival would be to make the jump that day. Moses hoped B would come, although it was hard to say. B had a family and it was likely that he would stay behind rather than abandon them.

Then Moses wrote out a note to D.

B told me everything…

*****

Hope had never been to the ocean when she'd been alive. She'd seen it as she followed Memories. She'd seen people walk by it, play and swim in it, even sail over it, but that was it —she was only able to observe. She'd often wondered what the experience of the ocean would have been like. She wanted to feel the breeze, hear the ache of waves running to and fro against the shore. She wanted to smell it, to feel sand beneath her feet and how they all came together in one immersive moment.

Hope knew she'd never know the feel of the ocean, but September 15th was close in its own way. She'd followed Memories from everywhere—people, animals, buildings, vehicles, even a dandelion that grew up through a sidewalk in Madison, Wisconsin—and each one dropped her in the same place. It was the end of the Windy Place, or at least that was the best way to describe it. They'd get to a point and then Hope found herself standing in a soft white area. Behind her the Windy Place tapered back to its usual grey. The sky had little cracks running from it to the space before her. Before her was all of time and space for the world in a giant white glowing sea. It ebbed and flowed like waves at her feet and had a dull staticy roar. It was so big and it ran out of sight both to her right and her left—it just seemed to spread out forever. It felt oddly peaceful and she dipped her toes into it.

It made them tingle, even tickled a little while sending a cool shiver up her back.

When she looked into it she could see countless lives being made and unmade. It wasn't just them being destroyed, she could see their entire history by gazing into it from the beginning of time until September 15th when it all changed and then into the chaos afterwards until everything broke down and dissolved into nothingness. Hope slipped off her shoes and ran up and down the shore, splashing through the time and Memories playfully. She lifted her dress to keep the hem from getting "wet" although she didn't know if that was necessary or just habit from her time being alive.

There was an odd sense of balance to everything. She knew how it all ended and it seemed appropriate in its own way. The wind had become a breeze blowing in off the great white sea of time and energy. Hope closed her eyes and could almost remember the feeling of the sun on her face. She ended up just sitting, the waves licking up in between her toes, under the soles of her feet and licking her heels before scurrying back.

She remembered her tree and how it seemed to slowly swallow her up before. This was different. She didn't feel as if she were a part of the ocean of Memories, hopes, dreams, time, space, matter and potential, but she did feel as if it were something she was meant to appreciate for its vastness and finality. She felt very small sitting on the shore in a way she imagined an ant felt small: that there were things so much larger than her, but that she was just the right size anyway.

The shadowy Memories all seemed to stay a safe distance away from the sea. It was just her, sitting on an invisible beach basking in the light for the first time since the last day of her life. Time didn't mean anything in the Windy Place, but it felt as if she'd been lying back by the water for quite some time. She opened her eyes and looked across it. She knew that she couldn't stay there, that the sea was not the place meant for her, but she felt a strange sense of contentedness that she'd been there to see it.

As she slowly mustered the will to stand again she caught a glimpse of something out of the corner of her eye. A single Memory had made its way from the grey safety of the Windy Place and was slowly shuffling towards the shoreline. Hope watched it, expecting it suddenly veer off and fade away as Memories tended to do. Instead it kept on its heading, moving deliberately towards the sea. When it got within about twenty feet of it Hope decided to go study it. It wasn't difficult to catch up to it, it was moving forward in a kind of lurching shuffle like a very old man would.

The Memory got to the edge where the waves rose and receded. Hope moved closer and as she approached she could see the rough form of a man inside the constantly shifting edges of the Memory. It turned its head towards her and it became more defined than she'd ever seen a Memory become. She could make out the round face of a man; his hair was unkempt and he was balding. He was kind of stocky and stood with drooping shoulders in a tired slouch. Their eyes met and it was if he could see her. She cocked her head, confused. The man just gave a tired smile and a little nod and then suddenly the Memory crumbled, collapsing into dust and dissolving into thin air at her feet.

Moses couldn't bear to look at Irvin's body crumpled at his feet. The smell of gunpowder burned his nostrils and when he closed his eyes the only thing he could see was the tired smile and the nod to signal he was ready. The shot still rang in his ears and in his mind he watched Irvin drop, heavy and inert, to the ground over and over again.

*****

The transmission had come and gone. Moses had sent his messages but nothing came through from Waffle. Moses had stayed hours afterwards, partly hoping that B would appear somehow, but mostly trying to say his goodbyes in his head. Waffle was gone. Everyone he knew or ever cared about was gone, or would be soon. In the back of his mind there had always been a flicker of a hope that he'd return home someday. Even in the past month when he knew it was impossible he still would catch himself remembering and fleetingly dreaming of walking through the vast forests or by the great green oceans that he'd run along as a boy, of nights with D, or even working alongside B and seeing his father and mother again. But it had finally set in. All the things he remembered, all the things he had been working toward seeing again, were completely lost to him.

With Nicola still gone, Moses had taken to wandering. The sorry little Earth wasn't without a few charms and sights. Moses had slipstreamed from point to point as the mood suited him. No longer concerned about being discovered, he moved freely about the open spaces, the turgid slums and ghettos, the great meeting spaces and marketplaces and the isolated and hidden spots that he'd read about.

Beyond the great loneliness and sadness he felt, he'd actually enjoyed most of his little field trips. He'd spent the first part of his life trying to rise above the crowd and the second part trying to blend into it. Now he found comfort just being around it. He wasn't sure if that made him more invisible or less, but it did feel relaxing as if for the first time he was living within himself instead of trying to divine the observations, beliefs, suspicions and intentions of everyone around him.

However with that sense of liberation also came the gnawing realization that there was still one thing left unresolved. For a time he had given up trying to proactively help Irvin. He hadn't ignored him, but instead of going by his house every day and calling and doing anything to speak to him he had been content to leave an answering machine message once or twice a week. Part of him felt a bit guilty about going through the motions of concern, but the other part felt like worrying more wouldn't have had any different effect and would've been a waste of both of their time. Now there was news and a plan (albeit a shaky, untested, risky and possibly doomed plan) and that meant that Moses needed to speak with Irvin.

He didn't really want to speak with Irvin. If Irvin had continued on his downward trajectory from the last time they had spoken it would be difficult to stomach. At one time Moses would've thought himself beyond such sentimentality —East St. Louis had beaten it out of him for a long time. But, like it or not, he felt invested in Irvin and was concerned about his well-being.

He called a few times, leaving messages each time. The last message was simply, "I'm going to be there in twenty minutes." He was hoping that the directness of the message would've prompted Irvin to pick up, or at least call back for no other reason than to avoid having Moses come over. When he heard nothing he knew that he had to follow through. Moses had stood outside Irvin's front door knocking too many times to expect that would work so when the time came he slipstreamed inside.

The first thing he noticed was the smell. There was something rotting in there. As he entered the kitchen he saw the garbage can overflowing. The kitchen sink was full of dishes that still seemed to have most of their meals untouched on them. On the counter was a bucket of fried chicken that had been abandoned at least a week or two prior. The air was hazy and the smell of cigarette smoke and body odor clung to everything. The house was sealed up tight—an open window would have helped immensely. Moses came around the corner into the living room and saw Irvin sprawled out on the couch, eyes glazed-over slits, a burned-out cigarette dangling between his fingers. His hair was a greasy, wild mess and he had a splotchy beard growing. He was in boxers and an undershirt neither of which looked or smelled anywhere near fresh. There were empty bottles of beer and whiskey strewn across the coffee table. A Spanish-language soap opera was playing muted on the television.

Moses said "Irvin," a few times, but Irvin didn't so much as stir. He finally went over and shook him by the arm, but even then he didn't respond. Only between shaking him forcefully and shouting his name did Irvin start to come around.

"You with me?"

Irvin blinked and looked at Moses as if he barely recognized him. He groaned and reached out to Moses arm and grasped it. "You awake?"

Irvin noticed the cigarette in his hand and gingerly flipped the ash off into an ashtray that was on the arm of the couch.

Once the cigarette butt was disposed of he turned his attention to Moses. He gave him a scowl as he tried to get his eyes to focus. He gripped Moses' arm to stop him from shaking him and then pushed him back slightly to get him within the range his eyes would actually focus in on.

"Mmmph... Moses? Moses?" Irvin reached up and gave Moses' cheek a pat. "Moses. I didn't hear you come in... Sorry the place is a bit of a mess."

"It's fine... What's going on here?"

Irvin acted as if he didn't hear Moses. He awkwardly tried to stand, "Here, let me get you a place to sit. Just give me a second, I'll clean you a spot."

"That's ok, buddy. I can get it."

Irvin wobbled and fell back into the couch. He gave up trying to stand and pointed towards a nearby chair. "I'm sorry. Just clean off that chair there. Don't worry about the stuff on it, that can go anywhere. Just throw it on the floor. I'll take care of it later."

Moses scooped up a pile of unopened mail and an old pizza box and set it down next to the chair. He was wary of sitting in the chair given the overall state of things. After a moment of indecision he sat down cautiously although he didn't lean back in the chair.

"So, uh, how are you doing?"

Irvin blinked and squinted at Moses still trying to get his eyes to focus. "I've been sleeping a lot. Sleeping makes the time go by faster."

"...You're not looking so good."

Irvin let out a quick clap of laughter. "Well, if I had a nickel every time I heard that, although usually I get that from the ladies."

"I'm serious. You look like hell. What are you doing?? What's with all the sleeping?"

"Sleeping is easier. Especially with the pills, although they haven't been keeping up lately. A little nip of something seems to help with that."

"You know that's dangerous, right? You shouldn't be mixing those."

"Because I'll die if I do? C'mon Moses, you know as well as anyone that we're almost out of time. I'd prefer not to be conscious when it happens. You can't blame me for that."

"No, but there's something I've been working on. We can get out of here. There are a few of us but I told them you were coming along with me. We can get to a safe place—another Narrative. It might even be the perfect one, I don't know, but there's a way."

"Ah yes, you and your 'Narratives'—a scientific way to heaven. Doesn't really sound like my kinda place."

"You were the one who was trying to convince me to go there, remember? Why are you doing this? C'mon, let's get you cleaned up and ready to go. It'll be ok, I promise," Moses stood and grasped Irvin's arm and attempted to get him on his feet. Irvin flopped around like a rag doll for a few moments before Moses realized he was being intentionally difficult.

"Dammit, Irvin, do you know what I went through to get this for you?"

Irvin smiled apologetically. "I never asked you to."

"What's that supposed to mean? You're my friend, of course I'm going to try and help you."

"That's a funny word."

"What?"

"Help."

"I don't have time for these games, man."

"You know Jesus said that no man who put his hand to the plow and looked back was fit for the Kingdom of God. Did you know that?"

"What does that have to do with anything?"

"I've done a lot of looking back, Moses. I've seen a lot of ugly things. This world is full of ugly things. I was so mad at that man for what he did to my aunt, but I also understood him. He didn't actually want to hurt her; he just didn't give a shit.

"I've spent so many years trying to care, trying to love, trying to be the best person I could, but at the center of everything I really didn't care. I think that's one of the things that scared me most, that if I were left to my own devices I wouldn't do good, I'd just let things do what they did. I preached the Word of God. I spoke of love and redemption and forgiveness but at the end of the day, I was pretending that that was the person I was.

"At some point I hoped I'd become what I pretended to be. On some level maybe I did. I became Pastor Dave and when I was him, boy did it all feel like it was true. But in my heart I knew I wasn't him. I knew that I was a well-intentioned fraud. I hoped that maybe others would be able to find the faith that I believed was out there. I thought if one of them found it, maybe I could someday, too.

"A funny thing happened to me, though. When that guy screwed my aunt over, I wanted to hurt him and I liked wanting to hurt him. I realized I preached to the lost and the heartbroken because I was both of those and I liked being them.

"This is such a sad, broken world and it is so beautiful in its failure. I thought about your Narrative 'heaven'. I imagined being in a place where everything was the way it was meant to be and I hated it, because this world—this is the world the way I think it's meant to be. Jesus came to this world and it killed Him and He still loved it. I understand that. I might be happier in a perfect Earth, but I will never be better than when my heart is broken.

"I am afraid of what is coming. I saw what happened to those creatures that were left behind. The tribulation that John described is nothing compared to that horror, but that may be what he saw. I do believe that the most terrifying moment in human existence is about to take place—"

"Then what's the problem? Let's go. This is the easiest decision ever."

"I can't. I just can't. This is my world. This is where I belong. Is it possible to belong somewhere and still be so lonely? Only here… Only here.

"Listen, I've failed in everything. I still believe just enough to believe that if I stay here my soul may have a chance at redemption. But I'm not going to be able to hold on much longer. The closer it gets the more I start to believe that there is no purpose to any of this and we're just a mistake of physics and chance—and your perfect place seems to prove it. You said you wanted to help me…"

Moses nodded.

"You know in most religions suicide is one of the worst things you can do. I've come close a few times in the last week but then I'd drink some more and take some pills and fall asleep. But if I die that way, that's still a suicide. Maybe they'd write down 'accidental' but in my heart I know each time I do it that it will kill me eventually. Now being murdered, that can make you a martyr if you die because of your faith…"

"What are you asking me to do?"

Irvin smiled sadly, "I'm not asking anything. I'm just making some observations." He got up and wobbled and walked to a book shelf. He opened a small wooden box and produced a shiny silver revolver. He flipped open the cylinder holding it up so that Moses could see each chamber had a bullet in it, before rotating it back into place. Irvin walked back unsteadily, setting the revolver on the coffee table before standing by the window, looking out on the boulevard.

"You know Jim, the guy who played organ before you?"

Moses nodded.

"I was with him in the end. He had a massive heart attack and was hooked up to all these machines. The doctor said he had a 50/50 chance of making it if he made it through the night. Well, I was sitting with him and after all the doctors and nurses left I said to him, 'Jim, I know you can hear me. You've been a friend and a brother. If you want to come back I'll be here waiting for you and will help you every step of the way. But if you can see our Savior's smiling face and can hear Him calling to you, then you go. You don't stay. You run as fast as you can because you've got your faith and if they see fit to reward it now, then you go home. I'll be fine. I will miss you, but I will be happy because you left this Earth with your faith.'

"No sooner than I said that then he got this really peaceful look on his face and I could tell he was leaving. He died the next day, but after that I could tell it was just his body—that the real Jim was gone. When I look back at everything I've done, all the good I've tried to do, that was the one time I knew that I really did something positive. I could tell he was in such pain and was confused and I was able to help him let it all go and find some peace."

Irvin paused as he heard the click of the hammer on the revolver behind him. He turned his head slightly. He could see it all—all of time and space and the end of everything. It was so peaceful and bright and just as it was meant to be. It was like all of creation was serenading itself a goodbye. A little girl was watching him. He smiled slightly and nodded to her as the colors swirled and surrounded him. It felt like falling, he thought.

*****

She hadn't visited him in his dreams since he was a boy, but there she was.

"You're back?"

She blushed. "Mostly. I needed to talk to you privately," he said as she wrapped her arms around him from behind, rest her chin on his shoulder. "…And maybe I liked the idea of touching you."

Lyle clasped her hands in his instead of letting her run them up and down his chest. "I can't do this if you're just going to go again."

"Shhhh," she hushed gently. "It's almost over. We'll be together—like really, really together. I figured out a way to make it happen."

"Then why are you in my dream?"

"I'm on the other side of a great divide. I've met someone who can help us bridge it, but I won't be able to come back before then. I'll be able to meet you there. Think of it like I've been on a trip and you're meeting me at the airport," she nibbled on his earlobe playfully. "The only person I can talk to directly is Hope. She'll relay any messages I have for you until then."

"When can I see you?"

"Soon. It won't be long now. I actually need to discuss it with you. I need to tell you some things that you can't tell Hope. She wouldn't understand."

"Understand what?"

"So much. She's not like us. She's a child in her heart and has a mind that's seen eternity. She's seen so much but she doesn't understand how the world works. She doesn't understand that sacrifice is required sometimes if you really love someone." Lyle tensed as she hit a sensitive spot below his ear. She giggled at his reaction.

"Now I need you to settle down and listen," she said as she quit teasing him. "There's a scientist who's helping us. His name is Moses. He's actually an alien, but that part doesn't matter—"

"He's a what?"

"Alien. Kind of a big fish. It doesn't matter. He's able to help us. I need to explain what will happen, ok?

"I'm bringing you and Hope with me. You can't be where I'm from. There's nothing left there for me. And, of course, I can't join you there because it's all about to go very wrong there."

"Wrong how?"

"It doesn't matter."

"Should I warn anyone?"

Nicola smiled, "That's why I love you, always thinking about others. It won't matter. There's nothing that can be done."

"Well maybe if we tell them, some can get to safety."

Nicola sighed, "Lyle, sweetie, there is no safety. Your universe is ending. It's about to vanish and anything that has the bad fortune of lingering will be... Well, let's just leave it at 'bad fortune.'

"But the point is, where we'll meet will be a place just for us. It will be you, me and Hope and all the memories you can carry."

"What do you mean memories?"

"It's how these things work. You bring memories with you and they'll populate our world. They'll fill the void. Memories are powerful things, Lyle. It's like transplanting plants but instead of tomatoes you'll have bits of reality sprouting up around you. I know it sounds strange, but really it will be like nothing happened. If you remember it, then it will have happened there."

"But what if I remember it incorrectly?"

"There is no incorrect. What you remember will be what happened. That's why I came to you in your dreams as a child. When you remember that, it will have happened. You see? That's what I meant when I said it was all for you. You will have the life you always wished you lived. It will be you and me together from the beginning, the way it was meant to be."

"What about Hope?"

"She'll be along. She's different. She'll be as she is but her memories won't affect anything. She's an observer not an actor."

"You're forgetting someone."

"Hm?"

"The alien scientist."

Nicola didn't say anything for a moment. "Well, that's why I needed to talk to you alone. He won't be coming with us."

"Why? Where's he going?"

"I don't know. Once we've established our bubble I can't do anything more."

"What's going to happen to him?"

"Well once I jettison our space he can create a portal to wherever he wants to go."

Lyle wanted to believe her, but it seemed too convenient. "If that's the case why doesn't he just leave now?"

Nicola tussled his hair, "Silly boy, we had an agreement. I helped him with his tech and some calculations and in exchange we get first dibs."

"Why can't I say anything to Hope then?"

"Well, she's gotten attached to him. She needs to come with us. She'll have a home with us. Moses has his own path to find and a little extra-dimensional phantom girl would cramp his style."

"I don't know. I'd watch that show."

Nicola laughed and then gave him a playful bite on his back. "Enough talking. You'll wake up eventually. I'd prefer it if you woke up messy."

*****

"Heads up!" Moses barked as he tossed a pair of socks at Hope, who flailed in attempt to catch or deflect them as they passed harmlessly right through her. "Ahhh, that never gets old," Moses chuckled.

Moses reminded Hope of her older brother who would pull little tricks on her and then laugh. Unlike her brother, though, when she got tired of it Moses would stop and would be nice to her. Her brother would've just kept going on until she started to cry and their mother would yell at them for creating a ruckus.

Moses was trying to organize his pack. He had the cube ready to go, or as ready as it could be and he was trying to distill the rest of his belongings into a single pack for the journey. "Never thought I'd have to be packing like this twice in my life," he said.

"Why are you still wearing your face?" Hope asked.

"Mm? This old thing? I dunno. Force of habit, mostly. That and I haven't met your other friend yet. Don't want to scare him too much right away. Besides, I don't know where we're going, I may need the suit there, too. Always better to be prepared, I s'pose.

"So you're coming along too, right? How does that work? I mean how will you translate into another Narrative? Do other Narratives have ghosts?"

Hope looked at him quizzically. Moses tried to explain, "You know, the place we're going, where Nicola is from, will you be a person there or like you are now? Has she told you anything?"

"We're not going to Nicola's home."

Moses chuckled, "Well, maybe not her *house*, but her planet, or Narrative or something like that."

Hope shook her head. "We're going to a special place that's just us: you, me, Nicola and Lyle and we'll be together forever."

Moses looked at her skeptically, "I've been working on it with Nicola. Maybe you misunderstood."

"Nuh-uh. It's a special place that's just us. We can't go to her place."

"Is that so? What else did Nicola tell you?"

"Nothing much. She's been talking to Lyle in his dreams but they don't tell me what about."

Moses nodded as if he were thinking about something. He took out the cube again and activated it. "You run along, now. I'll be there presently, I just need to double check some things."

"What should I tell Nicola?"

"You just tell her I had some last minute packing to do. It'll just be a few minutes, ok?"

Hope nodded vanished. Moses accessed the simulations he'd been running and then checked the log against the data thresholds Nicola had requested from him. Nothing seemed to jibe. He started a new batch of simulations with the parameters changed slightly.

In the Windy Place Hope saw Nicola standing by the tree. The tree itself now was mostly barren. One of the branches had broken off and lay by the base. Overhead the sky was almost completely black. The wind was cold and had a faint odor of smoke. Both had become more intense over the past weeks.

"It's all coming down," Nicola said as she ran her fingertips against the bark of the tree.

Hope said nothing, but walked around the tree, wrapping her arms around the trunk. It didn't feel warm anymore. It just felt rough and cold and lifeless. She tried to remember how it felt to have its bark slowly embracing her and bringing her together with it, but all she was able to feel was sadness that everything she had felt and loved about it was gone. All that was left was its hulking, dried-out skeleton with the mushrooms, like little cancers, growing back around it.

Nicola came up next to her and wrapped her arms around her. "I have to tell you something," she whispered.

Hope looked up at her expectantly, but Nicola didn't return her gaze. She kept her head turned to the side. "Where I'm from, I have a child—about your age, in fact. I…" her voice trailed off. Hope squeezed her hand reassuringly. Nicola cleared her throat and started again. "I don't know if I can leave him alone. I know I promised we'd all be together and I love you both but you're both… how do I put this? You're not real. I mean you are real and I know you're real, but we've never really touched, you and I, we just have this impression of touch. I've never touched Lyle. I've never had to make hard decisions with him, it's all been… it's just a wonderful fantasy.

"I'll make sure you're both safe. I've got the plan set up with Moses and I'll do what I can here I just… This is so hard. I just don't know if I can be with you. I have to do the right thing and I thought I wanted that to be with the two of you, but I don't know anymore…"

330

Hope turned around to face Nicola but Nicola turned to leave at the same time.

"You can't go," Hope said softly. "I don't have my tree…"

"Tell Lyle… Just tell him I've left…"and with that Nicola vanished.

Hope remembered what it was like to be heartbroken.

*****

Hope didn't know how long she'd stayed in the Windy Place or what time it was in the real world. She appeared in the apartment and saw Lyle sitting at the kitchen table.

"Is it time?" she asked.

"No, not yet. I'm sure Nicola knows better than I would, though. You should ask her."

"She's gone."

"She'll be back soon."

"No. She's *gone.*"

"What do you mean by that?"

Hope shook her head and looked away.

"Well, where would she be then?"

"She went back. She said that there was something more for her there."

"More? She said everything was gone."

Hope shrugged. "Maybe she's like me now. Maybe there was something she wanted to see."

Lyle's brow furrowed as he tried to sort out what Nicola being gone meant. "Did she say if she was coming back?"

Hope shook her head.

"'No' as in she didn't say, or 'no' as in she's not coming back?"

"Words don't mean the same there as they do here," Hope didn't want to think about what Nicola had said. Besides, she thought, Nicola had said she might come back.

It was cool for a day in mid-September, maybe about 70. It was almost serene outside. In contrast, there was a ball of nervous energy in Lyle's stomach. He was excited to be with Nicola, although the message from Hope was confusing and all the while the prospect of global destruction lurked in the back of his mind. Nicola had assured him that it would all be fine, but it was hard to ignore the consequences of what was about to happen.

"Am I interrupting anything?" came a voice from behind him. Lyle jumped and gave a little girly yelp. Hope clapped her hands happily. Lyle found himself eyeball to eyeball with a giant puffer fish.

"Fish man!" Hope squealed. The fish man gurgled happily and waved at her. He then extended his hand to Lyle. "Name's Moses. I was told you'd be expecting me."

Lyle swallowed even though his mouth was bone dry. "When Nicola said a 'big fish' I thought she meant a VIP."

Moses cocked his head at Lyle and then gave a giant bubbling chortle. Hope giggled too. Lyle thought she seemed much more attached to Moses than she'd ever been to him.

"Sorry about the surprise, I had some issues with my faceplate and I was running short on time."

"Oh, no, it's fine. Just didn't expect you to just appear is all."

Moses looked Lyle over. He wasn't anything special—just a guy. Moses wasn't sure how Lyle had gotten mixed up in everything, but he supposed that if he was cool with being in love with a giant orange Gumby woman, it was probably more of a niche thing.

"So is Nicola about?"

Lyle looked at Hope who was hiding behind Moses' legs. "Uh, no. I don't know. I haven't seen her lately."

"It's fine. She really didn't need to be here for this part. She needs to establish the bridge on her end, anyway. No worries."

"…So, uh, is it time?" Lyle asked, his legs suddenly feeling rubbery as he realized what was about to happen.

"Yeah, just about. I need to get some things set up here. When it happens, it'll happen fast so be ready to move."

Lyle reached his hand out to Moses and spoke in a hushed tone, "Listen, Nicola told me what you're doing. It means a lot. I'm sure it's risky letting us do our thing but we're really happy. This will be a fresh start for all of us."

Moses nodded. "Of course, of course. It's my pleasure. I'm just glad to be able to make it work for everyone. Listen, I've got some last-minute things to do here to get ready. The thing is, when you get the signal, you just go, ok? You keep that little girl close—she'll tell you when it's time. And when you go, you don't stop until one of us says it's ok, you got me?"

Lyle nodded.

"Now you go grab a seat, or get your stuff together or do whatever stuff you need to do. I need to stay in here to operate everything. You got to keep this door closed—radiation, alright?"

"Ok… uh, do you want a drink or anything?"

Moses, chuckled, "I'm fine. Thanks, though."

Moses watched him carefully as he left the room. Everything would have to go just perfectly or this would blow up in all of their faces—quite possibly in the literal sense. He caught a glimpse of Hope looking at his pack which was sitting partially open. She had both hands over her mouth covering a shocked smile. Moses put his finger to his lips, they had a secret now. Moses waved her over. He spoke very softly to her with a smile. "Now listen, this is my little surprise, ok? You don't go tellin' anyone," Hope nodded excitedly.

"Now you do exactly as I say, understand?"

*****

Lyle sat in the living room, fidgeting. He had to pee, but not really. He'd already been back to pee twice in the last half hour and each time next to nothing came out. Now it was getting closer and closer and the only thing Lyle could think about was how much he wanted to pee.

There was a rumble that came from the bedroom and the smell of electricity. Lyle looked around, but didn't see Hope anywhere. He hoped that she would be ready. He began pacing as he felt the floor vibrating. He looked out the window and everything seemed normal. He looked at his watch; it was 5:58pm. Suddenly the air in front of him began to warp like the air above a road on a hot day.

Lyle initially recoiled as the distortion grew bigger and more distinct. Through the waves light started to bleed out in uneven flashes. Soon the light became bigger and more pronounced until it was just a giant oval of light, nearly blinding in intensity.

"Go! We need to go now!" he heard Hope cry. He saw her dart into the portal and disappear. Lyle took one big gulp of air and then followed behind her.

It felt like blacking out, but he was sure he was always conscious. Lyle weaved unsteadily on his feet. There was no ground and no sky. Everything was bright white, but when he walked it felt solid beneath him. He nearly fell forward trying to gain a sense of direction and maintain his balance. As his eyes seemed to adjust to the lack of any perceptible depth or height he looked to his side and saw Hope standing there. She was looking away from him. He craned his neck and saw two figures standing beyond them.

The first was Nicola. A wave of relief washed over him and he stumbled towards her. "Nicola," he called out. The second figure turned to look at him and it was... Lyle. Nicola looked at Lyle and then the Lyle standing by her with alarm. The other Lyle grabbed her by the arm. She struggled and swung at him, catching him in the side of his head. She recoiled in surprise as his face popped off.

"Fish man!" Hope laughed and ran towards them.

Another portal of light started to appear. Nicola began screaming, "No! No! You can't do it!"

Lyle didn't know what was going on. He stumbled forward to try and reach Nicola. The closer he got the more she looked strange. Giant cracks were running up and down her body and a bright orange substance appeared beneath.

"Stay back, Lyle!" she yelled out to him. "Just stay back!"

Hope kept running towards them. The second portal stabilized and Moses wrestled Nicola off to the side. As he ran through Hope reached him, wrapping her arms around his waist with a triumphant cheer.

"No!" Nicola screamed as she grabbed Hope's leg. She began frantically trying to pull Hope back out of the portal. The light seemed to become wavy again. Lyle didn't care what Nicola had told him and he ran to help them.

Nicola looked up at him, her face cracked and flat orange pulsating stuff started to bulge out, "I'm sorry. I'm so sorry." Hope was struggling to crawl backwards, but not moving. Nicola kept pulling, but nothing seemed to be happening. She gave Lyle one last look and said, "It was always you."

With that she stepped into the portal. There was a giant crackle, louder than any thunder clap Lyle had ever heard. There was an explosion and body parts flew everywhere. It wasn't gore, but parts of a body as if someone had blown up a mannequin. There was an arm flailing erratically as if it were alive. He saw part of Hope's face staring at him. All of the pieces seemed to still be alive. He saw the bottom part of Hope's head a few feet away. He tumbled towards it. As he picked it up and turned it over the mouth opened and screamed.

Epilogue: Leaving Hebron

"You say you saw the little girl explode?"

"Yes."

"But she also speaks to you, correct?"

"Yes."

"Just her mouth? I mean, is that what you see, that part of her head talking to you?"

The hospital had the same odd scent that recalled both antiseptic and urine at the same time, just as he'd remembered. "No. Well, sometimes. Usually it's just her."

"And do you see her now?"

Lyle looked over and Hope sat on floor cross-legged, leaning back on her hands. "Yes."

"Is she saying anything?"

"No. She doesn't talk when you're here."

"And why's that?"

"Because it's rude."

"I see. And she told you this?"

"No, I told her that, but she listens. She's a nice little kid, really."

"And has she been showing up more, less or about the same since we started the new medication?"

"The same. It's not a medication thing. I've told you that."

"I know, I know, but we agreed that we'd try some medical things didn't we, Lyle? We're all here trying to help you. We want you to be as happy and healthy as you can be, right? That's the goal we're working towards."

Lyle sighed and wiped his eyes. "I know. It's just not going to work."

"Why do you think that?"

"Because she's real. It takes a lot to make real things go away."

"So the screaming half head is real?"

"No, as I've explained: That's just a remnant. That's an error that's imprinted on this reality."

"Can we talk about that?"

"About… reality?"

"Yes."

"You don't like my answers."

"I wouldn't say I don't like them, Lyle. I would say that they seem a little far-fetched and that they seem to make you very unhappy. Is that fair to say?"

"I suppose."

"So explain it to me again and maybe we can discuss a few specific things, ok?"

"If that's what you want…"

*****

Moses closed the door and listened for a moment to make sure he didn't hear Lyle mulling around.

"I've told Lyle to follow you. You see that little timer over there?" he pointed at a small display sitting next to the black cube, "I need you to stay in here. When it gets to zero you do your little teleport thing to the other room with Lyle and you get him to run into the big light as fast and as hard as you can, ok?"

Hope nodded, grinning.

"This'll be our little secret. I just need enough time to get there a little ahead of you to talk to Nicola, ok? That timer will tell you when it's time for you and Lyle to come through. Do you think you can handle that?"

Hope nodded resolutely.

"Good girl," Moses said, smiling. "Now let's get this rolling, shall we?"

The cube called up a little display. Moses gestured around it and then made a couple quick flips with his hand. "Alright, here we go. I'll be gone, but don't worry. You'll be safe. Just watch that timer, ok?"

The air became wavy and light started to ripple through. Moses reached into his pack and pulled out his new face plate. He attached it and Hope giggled. "I look just like him, don't I?" Moses said with a grin, or more accurately, with Lyle's grin.

The light stabilized and turned into a bright shining hole. "See you on the other side, Hope," Moses said as he ran through the light. Hope waved goodbye to him and then stared intently at the counter. Sixty seconds. Fifty-nine seconds. Fifty-eight. Fifty-seven...

Moses found himself dizzy in blinding white struggling to find balance.

"I'm here."

A hand reached down and he grasped it. He looked up and saw a pretty-ish brunette girl smiling widely. She helped pull him up.

"I'm sorry. I didn't mean to scare you. I just had one more thing to do. I wasn't sure if I could come back, but… sometimes you just know the right thing in your heart.

"You're the right thing for me. I remembered that first date we had and how I felt when it didn't go as I'd hoped and then how much more amazing it all was afterwards. I knew I couldn't give up on us. I knew you were the right one for me," the girl paused and gave him a look. "Where's Hope?"

"She's coming. I keep *my* promises," Moses replied. "Going to leave me behind, eh? Listen I don't have any desire to crash your little party here. You can stay in this Bridge Narrative to your heart's content. But you promised me safe passage and you're going to give it to me."

There was a crackling and a rumble behind them as Hope and Lyle tumbled through the portal. Nicola didn't seem to realize what had happened until she saw the real Lyle with Hope. She tried to pull away from Moses, but he grabbed her arm.

"Open up that portal to your world and let me through. You don't owe me any help or favors over there, I'll take my chances, but a deal's a deal."

She struggled and as she the skin began to break apart showing her orange body beneath. "I've killed people for doing less to me," Moses hissed. "I'm a better person than I used to be, otherwise this would all be going very differently right now. You were going to leave me there to burn. You get me through and our business is done, but you don't, well this whole Bridge Narrative thing isn't designed to handle all of us, is it?"

She caught Moses with a surprise shot, knocking his face plate off. "No! No! You can't do it!"

"We're running out of time. Besides, you're looking a little orange. I take it Lyle doesn't know about you."

Nicola looked up at him, tears running down her cheeks. "Please, don't ruin this. Just go," she whispered.

The portal began to form next to them. Nicola called out, "Stay back, Lyle! Just stay back!"

"I hope it works out for you. I really do," Moses said before he pushed Nicola off to the side. He closed his eyes and thought of D one last time before hurtling through the portal. But just as he had passed through he felt a grip around his waist.

"Fish man!" Hope grinned. Moses felt the portal beginning to destabilize. He grabbed her hands and unhooked her. She was halfway between the portal. "Listen, you need to get back right now. Where I'm going, you can't go. You listen to Lyle and Nicola, ok?"

Hope frowned as Moses gently tried to push her back. The waves were coming back and the light was disappearing. "You gotta get back!" Moses yelled at her. Hope tried to scramble backwards but seemed stuck. She looked frantic and then suddenly she was pulled backwards up to her chest. Her body was jerking as if something was pulling on it. Hope looked around and then suddenly a leg shot through the portal and then half a torso. Nicola came partially through and grabbed Hope by the shoulders.

Moses knew the portal was collapsing. "Be safe," he yelled to Hope and he gave Nicola a nod before running towards the light.

There was a crackle of electricity and the smell of burning air. Hope felt whatever was holding her in place get tighter. She started to claw desperately backwards to get free. She felt Nicola's hands on her shoulders.

"You'll always be my family," Nicola whispered to Hope as she peeled her back through the portal. The portal snapped closed while Hope was falling through and there was a blinding light and everything blurred and then went dark.

When Hope gained her bearings again she realized she didn't feel anything. She saw Lyle scooping up chunks of something in a panic. She tried to pick up one of the pieces at her feet but her hand passed right through it. She'd barely had time to adjust to the sense of touch and being able to interact with physical objects. She didn't even realize she had been able to until she'd hugged Moses.

She had a great hollow feeling inside of her. All her emotions were gone, but it felt like they'd left impressions inside her like little footprints. There had been something there at one time, but now there was nothing. Just memories of what feelings were.

*****

Nicola had been right about the memories. Slowly the bright white world began to fill in with color and objects. Lyle's old life was methodically rebuilt around him. He awoke in his bed in his apartment. The places he went the most were the first to appear and were the most vivid: the apartment, the grocery store, the drive-thru, work, the gym.

Oftentimes Lyle would nearly sleepwalk through his routine. He'd wake up, go to work, stop at the gym or the drive thru (but most often the drive thru) and come back home, turn on the television and watch random flashing images until he was tired enough to go to bed. The more time passed the more things resembled his old life: the shows on television became actual programs instead of random snippets and clips, people would walk around work appearing busy, there would actually be people at the drive thru or others using the equipment at the gym.

In time he could actually talk to some of them. It was always small talk, never anything of importance. Jeannine would appear at the gym sometimes. They'd share pleasantries and then go their separate ways. After a month it hardly seemed different than his life had been. Hope had been able to explore the world and, at a certain point, it seemed to fill itself out. People began carrying on lives beyond what Lyle had remembered. Buildings and cities appeared as did great open spaces, farms and mountains. Lyle had started it with his memories and then a whole reality seemed to blossom from them.

The only thing that wasn't quite right were the body parts. Parts of Hope would randomly appear to Lyle. Aside from Hope, he was the only one who could see them. The other people would walk right through them as if they weren't there. There were days when Lyle couldn't see any of them, but the scream from the part of Hope's head that he found would go on for hours on end.

"It's not real," Hope said.

"I know. None of this is real."

"Most of it is real. Just not the parts or the screams."

He gave Hope a tired smile. "How do I know you're real?"

Hope shrugged. "It doesn't really matter if I'm real."

"Have you seen Nicola or Moses?"

Hope shook her head.

"Well, what do you think? Are they out there somewhere?"

"...Somewhere."

*****

"Do you believe I exist?" the doctor asked.

"Kind of."

"How can something 'kind of' exist, Lyle?"

"I believe you're in this room with me now."

"Ok, and what about before then?"

346

"It depends."

"Depends on what?"

"Do you remember your first kiss?"

"Yes."

"No you don't."

"No, I do. I was in fifth grade—"

"—And Sherry Peris, a girl with super curly black hair whose brother was in your class snuck around the corner of the building at recess and kissed. She tasted like Juicy Fruit gum. You didn't care for it much."

"…Uh, well her name wasn't Sherry—"

"Fine, her name wasn't Sherry, but the rest of it, that's how it happened, right?"

"Um."

"Because it didn't happen. It's an experience that you got because of a memory I had of my life. You didn't kiss a girl in the fifth grade because you've only existed for a few weeks, maybe less. I didn't meet you until last week so you might only be a week old."

"So you're saying that because we didn't meet personally until a week ago, I didn't exist until then?"

"Probably. I am the Big Bang. All matter and everything—matter, consciousness, all of it—originated from me and bits of me are in everything here."

"That's a very grandiose claim."

"It's just the truth."

"Can you prove it?"

"I just showed you."

"Well, I know other people who didn't kiss a girl in fifth grade."

"No, but they have other memories that were stolen from me. You're all products of the world as I remember it."

"Except Hope."

"…Yeah, probably."

"Probably?"

"Well, I'm not exactly sure what Hope was before. Was she a ghost? Some random memories floating around? I have no clue. I'm pretty sure she didn't come from me."

"And the body parts you talk about?"

"Those… I don't know how those happened. Something with the portal collapsing. I don't know."

"Do you see any of them now?"

By the doctor's foot was Hope's left temple. An intact eye was fluttering and darting around blindly.

"It doesn't matter."

"Lyle, I think it does matter. You came to us seeking treatment for symptoms including depression, auditory and visual hallucinations, delusions, paranoia—a whole range of very serious conditions. You're aware that the diagnosis for these is very serious."

"Yes, it's the full range of schizophrenia symptoms. I know. That's why you think it's schizophrenia, because that's what I remember it to be. If I'd remembered these symptoms as being associated with erectile dysfunction you'd be prescribing me Viagra now instead of talking to me."

The doctor was fidgeting with his pen, looking frustrated. "Ok, let's try another approach, what happens to me when you fall asleep? Do I go away?"

"I don't know. I don't think so. I'm pretty sure you do whatever it is you do. I was just the model for the rules for this Narrative. Once the ball got rolling you all kept going on your own inertia.

"Or maybe you all disappear or materialize naked in high school if that's what I'm dreaming. I don't know. How does anyone really know what happens for sure when they're asleep?"

"Wouldn't that be horrible," the doctor chuckled. "There are a few dreams in particular I wouldn't want to put anyone through."

"Like the ones where your teeth fall apart or come out?"

"Yeah, those, falling dreams—"

"Ones where you're being chased."

"I wouldn't mind that so much. I hate going to the gym, if I just ran because some unknown person or creature were chasing me it might make it easier. That and I wouldn't have to work it into my schedule; I just wake up when I'm done. That would actually be kind of brilliant…"

There was an awkward pause. Lyle went back to looking disinterested and the doctor flipped his pen through his fingers.

"So, in this new reality that you believe yourself to be the origin of, why would you admit yourself into a psychiatric care facility?"

The eye was bulging, darting around wildly as if it were afraid or spasming. Lyle closed his eyes to avoid seeing it. "The only real person I see is a dead girl. There are body parts that appear and sometimes scream at me out of nowhere. My home was destroyed by some sort of interdimensional death storm and I'm surrounded by physical embodiments of my memories. Where else should I be? This is not the life I wanted. There's no hope here for me. That's why I came here.

"If I can't find something that can make me happy, I should at least go somewhere where they can numb the pain— somewhere sheltered from all the rest of it. That's why I'm here. I'm not here because I believe I'm going to get better. I'm here because at least here there's a chance to shut out some of the noise."

"Are you saying you don't want treatment anymore, Lyle?"

Lyle sighed, "I'll do whatever you want. You're a doctor, I'm a patient. We can jump through whatever hoops you come up with. It doesn't matter to me. It's all the same in the end."

"But you don't think it's going to be effective?"

Lyle didn't answer. He just stared out his window while twirling a thread that was hanging loose from a seam in his gown.

The doctor looked at the clock. "We're about out of time, Lyle. I wanted to let you know that she called me again today."

"And?"

"Are you going to see her?"

"Probably not."

The doctor folded his hands in his lap. A flash of frustration crossed his face. "You keep saying how there's nothing for you here, but then a girl—who is absolutely crazy about you, if you'll forgive the phrase—keeps trying to see you and you refuse to see her. It seems self-defeating."

"I can't."

"Forgive me, but that's bullshit and you know it. Just go down and see her. Give her a hug. Ask her how she's doing. Listen to her. Do the things that people do with other people they care about."

"It's not her."

"It is. I know. I've spoken to her. She's very much a real, physical true-to-life person."

"It's not Nicola."

"Well, why don't you go talk to her and prove it to me then?"

"Did you shake her hand?"

"Excuse me?"

"When you met her, did you shake her hand?"

"I believe so," the doctor answered, confused.

"What did it feel like?"

"Shaking her hand?"

"Yes."

"Like shaking a hand?"

"Was her grip firm or gentle? Was her skin smooth? Did she have sweaty palms? Did she smell like perfume, or shampoo or maybe just a little sweat and deodorant?"

"Oh, I don't recall—"

"You don't recall because I don't know. You remember doing the action, but none of the sensation because I never got to touch her. I don't know any of those things. All those senses beyond sight that you come to know somebody by just aren't there."

"Lyle, I just don't remember. I meet a lot of people. She was lovely. I spoke to her."

"But you didn't really touch her…"

"She's going to keep coming until you see her."

"…I know."

"Why not tonight?"

"I already have a real ghost and random invisible body parts following me. How haunted do I need to be?"

The doctor sighed as he stood up and gathered his notepad. "I can't make you do anything, Lyle. But just think about it. I think you'll be glad you did it."

"Is it Salisbury steak again tonight?"

"…I think so."

"I wish I could've remembered better hospital food," Lyle muttered.

That evening he sat by the window looking out at the grounds below. Hope stood looking over his shoulder. Below Nicola was standing across the street looking up at him. When she saw him she smiled widely and waved. Lyle didn't respond. Nicola kept smiling, but her eyes had traces of confusion and sadness. She blew a kiss to him and stood awaiting some sort of reply. When none came she gave an exaggerated shrug as if to say "I don't know what to do". She kept watching him and kept smiling although the she briefly broke into a frown when she wiped her eyes.

"You could talk to her," Hope said.

"I know."

"She'd be happy to see you."

"...She's just a memory."

"Maybe. But isn't remembering her a good thing?"

Lyle gave one last look down at Nicola before turning away, his own eyes burning with barely restrained tears.

"Remembering is the worst part," he said.

Also by the Author:

All Things Right and Beautiful

All the Stupid Little Children

All the Lights That Have Shone

www.ingramcontent.com/pod-product-compliance
Lightning Source LLC
Chambersburg PA
CBHW031944260626
47157CB00017B/2318